GLORY DAYS
& OTHER STORIES

John Mack

Glory Days
& Other Stories

2017 © John Mack   www.johnmack.co.nz

ISBN 978-0-473-41888-5

**The Little Red Hen
Community Press
Po Box13-533
Tauranga Central 3141
New Zealand**

Cover Painting and Illustrations by Mary McTavish
Editor: Jenny Argante

Glory Days
&Other Stories

Again for thee, Mary,
and Dirk too.

Glory Days

When we were born the sky was the limit
Our horizons beyond the curve of the earth.
We went around the world
Boxed the compass from south to north, west to east
We stepped on the planet's highest and lowest places
And gazed in wonder at what might be beyond.

We saw innocents starve, dispossessed and flee
We saw the gullible fight, maim and kill innocents.
Why?
To satisfy the egos of squabbling madmen, that's why.
We knew better people who did right and good.
.
Our horizon comes ever closer
Until it is close enough to peer over
And we learn the Earth is as flat
As the walls of our room and the ceiling, our sky.

Then understanding and regret dawn in equal measure
To diminish our glorious journey.
We lament the passing of our glory days
That turned out to be not so glorious after all.

Except to me and thee.

Contents

GLORY
DAYS

Ross

It's better when we're busy. No time then to wish the clock hands would rotate faster. Time passes quickly enough checking car after car: brakes, bearings and steering.

On a day like today when the wind-blown drizzle funnels through the laneways not many punters turn up to get their cars tested. Bloody good thing too, even if time drags and smoko never seems to get any nearer. No punters means no getting dripped on. Although I usually take care to pass on the pit job to Maureen on days like this so she gets the drips.

God knows what the hell girls are doing in this job. In my day, girl mechanics were unheard of. Testing stations, garages and race crews were no places for females. Except in pictures, the more scantily clad the better, tacked or duct-taped to the walls.

No way I'd want to see Maureen's picture on the wall, scantily clad or not. She's a big girl, shapeless before she puts on her mechanic's overalls, more so afterwards. Foul-mouthed, too; swears like a trooper. At my age, though I'm not easily shocked, she makes me cringe when she lets fly with a stream of obscenities.

I'd just checked the clock again and was relieved I only had to wait another half hour before heading off to the pub. Then a rusty Holden ute splashed up to the laneway. The rain had made mud of the dirt and dust coating its sides. The mud fell in wet lumps, like cow's turds, around the vehicle.

Maureen, the bitch, must have twigged my trick of sneaking off to the bog whenever a cruddy job came in. She was nowhere to be seen. I suppressed my irritation, but couldn't help wondering how I'd ended up in this dead-end job. To think I once travelled the world working for McLarens.

The fact I knew Bruce and Denny personally counts for nothing here.

Now I've got to check this layabout's heap. Fancy turning up without even washing his ute that's now dripping mud and oil on the workshop floor. Another bloody mess to clean up. I'll teach this useless prick to come in here with his dirty truck and expect to pass the warrant. In his dreams! I wouldn't mind betting he's the sort that's got tattoos and wears an earring. I'll find plenty to fail him on, no worries.

With a bit of luck I can string this job out to closing time and that'll cheese off the other silly punter just arrived with a trailer that looks like a recheck. Serves him right; should've got it right first time. Shouldn't come here in this weather anyway, and just on knock-off time.

▲

Maureen

I'd already spent most of the day in the pit checking underneath vehicles for defects that might fail them a WoF. I don't mind; all part of the job. Ross thought he was putting one over me, tricking me into copping the drips and the grime. You'd have thought he had loose guts he skived off to the crapper so often.

When the chance came late in the day to even the score I took it. I saw a dirty old ute pull up, one wiper dangling, mirror broken off its arm, headlights askew. Moments before, the laneway entrance had been empty and Ross had made the mistake of assuming that was it for the day. He had his back to the entrance and was busy wiping clean his spanners. I scarpered out of the pit and made for the staffroom where the ladies loo is. As I pushed the door open I snuck a glance back to the laneway. Ross stood there with his hands on his hips, glaring disapprovingly at the ute. Now behind it was a car and trailer that I recognised was back for a recheck.

How Ross came to be mucking about with muddy old utes in a back street city testing station is a mystery to me. I mean, I don't know him all that well, wouldn't want to, seems a bit of a sour old bugger. I was told a trade's a good thing to have; you could always fall back on it. Ross seems to have fallen well back.

Not that I'm complaining. This job means everything to me and I'm bloody stoked to have it. Ross couldn't care less though, and lets me know it at every opportunity. But then he's not a single mum with a couple of kids at primary school. I kind of feel like I'm on the way up passing him on the way down.

▲

Jack

I could tell Roger's old man was a bit on the caustic side when I jumped out of my ute and ran into the shelter of the laneway. I knew it was a bad look what with the rain and being close to shutting up shop time. That, plus my ute isn't the prettiest vehicle, or the cleanest.

Ross recognised me as soon as I shrugged off my wet weather gear and took off my sodden beanie. It was only a couple of weeks since I'd been with his son, my mate Roger, downing a few cold ones down the pub. Ross seemed to relax and even gave me a grin.

"Bloody hell, Jack!" he said, "I wish that son of mine would stop directing all you no-hopers here."

"Why's that, Mr Fleming?" I asked as innocently as I knew how.

"Ross, my name's Ross and you know damn well why. Roger and you lot think I'm soft on your crappy old vehicles."

"What are mates for?" I admitted cheerfully.

"Come on then," said Ross, "Wheel your heap in over the pit and I'll do my best for you. As long as your brakes and tyres are OK I'll pass your warrant of fitness conditional on you getting fixed whatever else I find wrong, before it falls due next time."

I jumped to comply and pushed my ute into the inspection bay.

"On your own, Mr F, ah, Ross?"

"Yeah, dunno where that lazy, foul-mouthed slag is. Probably drinking coffee in the staff room. Look, mate, I can handle this on my own. You go and grab yourself something hot, and I don't mean Maureen."

I didn't need telling twice. I found the staff room no trouble, mainly because it had a sign 'Staff Room' in large black letters across the door and a smaller more officious one underneath 'No Admittance to the Public.'

"Can't you read, mate?" said a shapeless woman dressed like a mechanic who, it wasn't hard to guess, was the slag Ross had mentioned.

"Course I can. Probably better than you," I retorted well aware that my appearance matched my dilapidated ute.

"Well, then; bugger off," she said.

"I don't think so. Ross is my mate Roger's father and he said to come in here and have a coffee while he sorts my truck out."

Then, just to rile her up, I added, "Black, no sugar, thanks."

"Help your bloody self. I'm not your fucking servant," she hissed. "I didn't know the old bugger had a son. I don't know anything about him and I'm not sure I want to."

"You shouldn't judge a book by its cover."

"What do you know about bloody books,' she scoffed. "I bet you've never read a flaming book in your life."

"I told you; you shouldn't let appearances fool you because that's just where you're wrong. Not many people know this, but I'm the Book Fair Bandit."

"What the hell is a book fair bandit?"

"One of my hobbies is turning up at book fairs and by use of cunning strategy collaring the inside track to get first go at the books," I said. "I'm off early tomorrow to a big one over at the Mount. That's why I need a WoF tonight and why I might look a little unkempt. All part of the plan to scare the punters off."

"Yeah?" she said, still sceptical." What about the old fart out there? I don't see anything special about him."

"Wrong again. Ross may be past his glory days, but once, not so long ago, he was up there with the best in the world as far as spannering goes."

"What! That old coot," she laughed. "Tell me about him, if there's anything to tell."

"I can only tell you from what little he's told me in the pub. Mostly his son Roger has filled in the blanks and shown us bits and pieces that prove it's true."

"Tell all, why don't you?" She helped herself to another coffee.

"I've seen his Trades Certificates so I do know he's qualified. Like, really qualified, from a time when it meant something. Proper time served, years in an apprenticeship, not much theory, all on the job stuff, working with older guys who had years of experience. Those were the days when New Zealand tradesmen could walk into a job anywhere in the world. They were the best. That's how he got the job with McLarens, I suppose. Those Formula One teams only took on the top guys."

I paused to see if she was listening or just humouring me.

"He couldn't have gone straight from being a fucking apprentice to working for the great fucking Bruce McLaren could he?"

She *was* listening.

"Of course not! Ross worked his way up like anybody else. Just like you are now. Except he was one of those gifted mechanics that worked their way up through racing teams in the different formulas. Like, I think he first spannered for a guy who won the British Formula Vee championship, then the next year Formula Ford and so on right up to the pinnacle. It took him a few years to make it to the top, and he was always going to get there sooner or later. If not for McLarens, then for another top team."

"Bugger me!" Now she was impressed. "I had no bloody idea. What the hell happened?"

"Well, he told me it was a great life travelling around the famous racing circuits. Hard work, long hours for not much pay in those days, but all the glamour and as many groupies as you could handle. Everything was so good sometimes when they got on the turps after a race he could hardly believe his luck."

"I bet." The smirk she gave was more like a grimace on her pudgy face.

"Until the day Bruce died. One of the crew hadn't tightened the wing nuts holding the spoiler onto the chassis of the Can-Am car that Bruce was testing at Goodwood. No-one was blamed and no-one owned up. Could have been any of them, so it became all of them."

"Was it him? Did he make the mistake?"

"Roger says Ross wasn't even working on the Can-Am cars at that particular time. Apparently the crew swapped and changed from Can-Am to Formula One for a whole lot of reasons. Be that as it may, from then on things turned sour for

14

Ross. He won't talk about it. Roger told me his father took on more of the guilt than the others in the crew and they were happy to load him up with it. Drinking became a panacea rather than a celebration until eventually he was let go and his glory days came to an end."

"That is so sad," Maureen said. "Is that how he ended up here?"

"Not entirely. There's a lot more to his story yet if you want to hear it."

I still wasn't entirely sure she was interested. But then, I reasoned, any true mechanic would at least be sympathetic and she seemed all that so I continued.

"Roger told me his father was broke and unable or rather, unwilling to return to New Zealand. Pride, I suppose. He got a job easily enough, in a small garage in Ruislip on the northern outskirts of London. His plan was to sober up and save enough to get back to New Zealand and start again where nobody would know about his part in the tragedy.

"Largely his plan worked. After madly traipsing around the world locked into the insular world of motor racing, he liked the village atmosphere of Ruislip. He came to enjoy his job in the garage off the High Street. His boss was a nice old chap who respected Ross's talent. Spannering was a doddle after his recent experience and he soon got a reputation as 'the Kiwi mechanic.'

"Then he met Margaret, his English rose. She was a nurse in one of the big London hospitals, commuting there from Ruislip. She brought her car in for a service and was intrigued by his accent. Not many Kiwis in Ruislip in those days. She didn't know anything about cars; couldn't even stand the smell of petrol. Despite that, one thing led to another and soon they were married. With no relatives close on either side that was a quick and easy thing to do."

"I'm guessing she is Roger's mother?"

"You guessed right," I said. "Roger is technically a Pom. He was born a year or so after his parents married. Glorious days again. Their own little semi near the centre of Ruislip and not far from the tube station. Even though they were well settled, when Roger was about two they decided New Zealand might be the better place to bring up children."

"Ross has never mentioned Margaret. Is he still married to her?"

"We'll get to that," I said. I checked the clock on the wall. "It's almost knock-off time. I'd better go and see if Ross has finished my ute."

"No, no," she said. "He'll come in here when he's finished. Carry on, please. This sounds like a happy ever after story."

I looked at her sideways. This wasn't the coarse slacker Ross had led me to believe she was. I noticed she had stopped swearing.

"OK." I decided she was genuinely interested. "Settling back into life in New Zealand was easy for Ross, and Margaret found it good, too. Ross got a job with the Mercedes agents in the city and quickly became their service manager with a clean, comfortable office. At weekends he was often in demand as a mechanic for club racers, although Margaret rarely went. Roger hadn't started school, so he could only have been about four.

"Then one time, convinced she would enjoy a day out, Ross persuaded Margaret to go out to the Pukekohe track with him. It was a test and practice day for the next day's clubman's meeting, so fairly low key. No resemblance to the drama of his glory days, but as enjoyable, if not more so.

"Margaret didn't much like the smell of petrol so she noticed immediately when it grew stronger. She'd been to check Roger was still asleep in the back of the Mercedes, which was parked at the rear of the pit garages in the shade, behind the solid concrete block wall they're made of. Coming back through to the front, where she'd been half-keeping an eye on the barbecue, she noticed a twenty litre can of high octane had toppled off a stack and spilled fuel on the garage floor. She must have rushed to stand it upright, as anybody would, and in the next instant the fumes hit the barbie and whoomph!"

"Oh, no!" Maureen's eyes were wide with horror.

"She was the only one in the garage. Ross and his mates were out on the pit wall across the pit lane. It was a test day so there were no fire-fighters nearby. Margaret was horribly burnt and died the next day."

Maureen covered her face with her hands as though to ward off the ugly image. She said nothing, and I waited a moment until she withdrew her hands and nodded slightly to my unasked question.

"Again he took the blame. Understandable, I suppose. You know, saying to himself, 'if only...' He reverted to the bottle. Job and son went at the same time; his son into foster care."

"But you said his son Roger is your mate?"

"Sure. And we're talking almost thirty years ago. Ross was well-known in motor racing circles and some of those who knew him took it upon themselves to help him out. He wasn't an alcoholic as such, and Roger came out of foster care when he started high school. He and Ross have got on like a house on fire ever since."

"Unfortunate choice of phrase in the circumstances," Maureen observed. "If Ross recovered how come he's working in a testing station?"

"While he was on the bottle he could only get crap jobs. Like this, with respect, relative to what he'd achieved."

"Might be crap to him, but not to me."

"I know," I said. "I only meant it's been a comedown for him. 'How the mighty have fallen,' if you know what I mean. He certainly didn't want anything to do with motor racing after losing Bruce and then Margaret and, in a manner of speaking, his son. Don't forget he's in his sixties now, on the super. Roger says his dad works here for something to do. He's happy enough."

"You could have fooled me," said Maureen, bitterly. "He's a grumpy old bastard."

"That's his cover. He isn't like that at all. I said before, you shouldn't jump to judge and he's a classic case of the misjudged."

▲

Ross

Jack's ute wasn't as bad as it looked. Don't know why he drives around in his old farm hack when he's got that smart Grand Cherokee he picks up Roger in for footy practice. Knowing him, he must have a reason. Anyway I passed his ute for its warrant and even gave one to the punter who'd been waiting with his trailer for a recheck on a faulty tail light.

I barged into the staffroom and tossed Jack his keys.

"Here you go, bro. Wash it next time, eh?"

"Thanks, Ross," Jack said. "I'll be off. See you, Maureen. And hey! You don't have to swear and carry on like a butch dyke to be accepted as a good mechanic. You just have to be a good mechanic. And don't forget what I said about judging books by their covers."

"Strange fellow is Jack." I laughed as his ute coughed into life. "Talk about the pot calling the kettle black. If there's any judging books by their covers to be done it should be about him. He thinks my son and his footy mates don't know he's into all that intellectual stuff."

"Calls himself the 'Book Fair Bandit,' " said Maureen. "Why he should want to keep something like that secret beats me."

"Guess we've all kept secrets or wish we had." I shot a look at Maureen.

Something different about her took me a moment to pin down. Then I got it. Every second word she uttered wasn't a swear word, and she seemed less confrontational than usual.

"Jack's been telling me a few things that everybody else probably already knew," she said. "I didn't."

"Hope he hasn't been talking out of turn."

"Oh," she said, "He was just telling me about glory days, yours mostly."

▲

Epilogue

About a year after Ross and Maureen began a more harmonious working relationship Roger took time out from his demanding I.T. career to help ease his father into ownership of a small service station with workshop attached. Even though it was still nominally within the city boundary, the business was surrounded by orchards and farms. Housing subdivisions were creeping ever closer.

Ross offered Maureen a stake and of course she jumped at the opportunity. The garage was closer to her house than the testing station and the regular hours made looking after her kids a little easier. Being her own boss helped too.

Their clientele were unaccustomed to dealing with a female mechanic and, like all country people, wary of extending friendship until they considered newcomers worthy of it. For a while Ross wondered if she might revert to the hard swearing butch persona she imagined made her 'one of the boys.' He was relieved when she didn't.

No one was surprised when Roger talked Ross into building a go-kart for his grandson. This broke the ice on his self-imposed ban on having anything to do with motor sport. As a natural progression, with Roger's support and Maureen's willingness to take over management of their business, he turned almost his entire attention to fabricating karts and later, race cars.

People forgot about his 'missing' years and to a certain extent so did he. Yet even if they wanted to no-one was allowed to forget Ross's glory days. How could they when the walls of the showroom and workshop were adorned not with the traditional pictures of scantily clad women, but those of the Bruce and Denny Show and the wonderful cars they raced.

MOVING ON

I looked around the room filled with my rellies as we waited for the lawyer. My two uncles and their flash wives, who for as long as I'd been living with Gran had, as far as I knew, never visited the farm. To be fair, a couple of my cousins had put in an occasional appearance. They needed somewhere to crash while they went surfing. I never noticed any of them helping out on the farm. The other six, I hardly knew their names.

They all had that flush of excited anticipation people get when they're convinced they're going to benefit from something. In this case, Gran's estate. There was the promise of money, lots of money. The farm had been overrun by the bloating city. Re-zoning to residential had been approved long before Gran breathed her last. There was never any doubt the rellies would opt for liquidating the lot by selling out to a developer. Consultation and discussion about my past role and future involvement had been carefully avoided.

"Cheer up, Jack," called out Uncle Simon. "Your Gran is sure to have left you zilch."

He cackled as though he'd made a joke. If he had it was at my expense. Truth was Gran had talked with me about her will soon after she'd learnt that she was definitely on the way out. After all, she was well into her eighties and even though she was a tough old bird capable of holding her own at any book fair, she had to go sometime.

Uncle Simon didn't know how truthful his jibe was. Gran explained to me that with Pop long gone she was duty bound to leave most of her assets to her sons, even if it did mean their soppy wives and kids would benefit. Apparently, she said, I was capable of looking after myself and to inherit too much money at my age would only lead to trouble and slothfulness. I wasn't sure if she was joking.

"Trouble and slothfulness," I said. "I should be so lucky."

My words were probably ill-advised.

"On the other hand I might leave you *a little something for yourself,*" she added, slyly ignoring my sarcasm as usual.

Even though I'd been working the farm for nearly a decade, ever since I'd come back from Massey, and had it ticking over like clockwork, Gran still seemed to think I might one day suddenly get into trouble or, worse, succumb to slothfulness. To be honest I didn't care about any inheritance. I loved the farm and I loved Gran and I knew she loved me. Even when we ended up rivals at book fairs and car boot sales.

The lawyer made his pompous entry as though an actor relishing his moment in the spotlight. Proceedings seemed to go according to script. The uncles got what they didn't deserve; Gran's estate split equally. Untrue to her word and to everyone else's badly concealed disgust and much to my surprise the 'little something' she promised me turned out to be not so little after all.

Suddenly I was richer by one hundred large. Not enough to do anything meaningful with except, say, the deposit on a house in Papamoa or some other outer suburb; on the other hand, a nice wedge of walking around money.

The cacophony of squabbling had already started as I tuned the rellies out.

"Thanks, dearest Gran. As always you have given me not too much and not too little, for which I will be eternally grateful."

I must have spoken out loud without realising it. The rellies had fallen silent and were looking at me astonished.

"Nice to see you all again," I lied. "Perhaps under happier circumstances next time."

Reminded of the circumstances they immediately removed from their faces the smug joy at their good fortune and belatedly replaced it with what they guiltily deemed appropriately sad expressions. I gave them a big grin and a wave as I left them to it with the lawyer.

I didn't care whether or not I saw any of them again. Neither of my uncles had shown the slightest interest in my future after Mum and Dad went down in that Air France disaster off the coast of Chile.

It was a strange feeling being at a loose end. Especially with a cheque for a hundred grand nestled in my back pocket that I compulsively checked was still there, reassuring myself it was real. I knew that I must have looked like some kind of pervert walking away from the lawyer's office fondling my bum, but I couldn't have cared less.

I still had a few weeks before I had to get out of the old farmhouse, though it upset me to be there when the surveyors and then the earthmovers took over. I suppose I should have been grateful and I suppose I was, for the money.

Before I moved on I thought I'd drop in on Ross and Maureen for a chat down at their garage. As I gunned the Cherokee down the motorway I mused that the urban sprawl that had seen Gran's farm become suburbia was the same process that had benefited Ross and Maureen. I remembered when Ross's son, my mate Roger, had colluded with his Dad to sign up Maureen to go into partnership in the garage that was then surrounded by orchards.

What a difference a decade makes. Strange how progress, so called, makes winners of some and losers of others. Mind you, I wasn't any type of loser with my newly-acquired wealth as compensation and I wouldn't have wished it any other way for Ross and Maureen. Maybe we were all winners.

"Watch out! It's the book-fair bandit," Maureen yelled in mock alarm as I pushed open the big glass door of the showroom into her office. One of the salesmen behind the parts counter took her seriously for a moment and ducked before turning back sheepishly to his customer.

"Yeah. G'day, mate." I yelled back.

It was a standing joke between us that I treated her as one of the boys; something she had aspired to be long ago, though she now perished the thought.

"Still not married eh?" I couldn't resist teasing her. "Would have thought you'd have snared some poor sucker by now seeing as how you're a successful businessman, er, person."

"Trouble is, Jack; marry me and you get two kids, teenagers, as well." She laughed. "I do believe you mentioned that as an impediment to your acceptance of my last proposal."

"I don't remember that," I hedged. "Sure you're not thinking about Roger? Ross would have been pleased, maybe."

"Wouldn't that have been a fairy tale ending? I've got to admit the thought did cross years ago, but Roger's such a tech wizard he was way out of my league. It all worked out for the best; look how happy he and Ruth are. Maybe I should ask you again seeing as you've come into money?"

I skipped her question.

"Maureen, I didn't drop in to talk about your non-existent love-life."

"You brought it up," she retorted.

"Yeah, well, is Ross around?"

"He's out the back workshop mucking about with a prototype racer. Go on out, he'll be pleased to see you."

As I shouldered my way through the workshop door I blew her a kiss, which she answered with the single digit salute and a big smile. Maureen was a bit of a character all right, but then you have to be to make it in a man's world. I strolled through the large workshop getting a wave and a shout from the busy mechanics.

Josh, the foreman, assumed correctly I was looking for Ross when he pointed me towards the far end of the building. When the race car side of the business had started to impinge on work space, they had added a purpose-built annex as big as the original workshop to the left of the folding doors.

Ross was hunched over an engine intent on some detail among the complexity that was all shiny pipes, wiring and ducting. He wasn't aware I was observing him. He had to be in his seventies; a man who still relished his work. His was a stroke of genius and, I suppose Roger's, to take Maureen on as a partner in the firm. Between the two of them, three if you count Roger's consulting input, they had made an amazing success of their enterprise.

Maureen, a fully qualified mechanic herself, 'technician' as they liked to be called these days, managed the front office and showroom forecourt and Ross supervised the workshop. In reality he spent most of his time building race cars, the demand for which seemed never-ending. Josh and Maureen ran everything, which suited everyone.

In the early days, before Ross again became involved with competition cars, Roger might still have been a partner. I never inquired, wasn't any of my business. I knew Ross liked to keep his son involved as a means of staying connected, so he probably was, and silent. He rarely put in an appearance except when he came home from one of the exotic locations his high-tech consulting jobs took him.

"Whaddya know, the rich man has found the time to drop in on old friends. Thought we weren't good enough for you now you've come into a fortune."

Ross unfolded himself from over the engine.

"Thought wrong then, didn't you, mate? Dunno where everybody got the idea I've come into a fortune. Must be my rellies spreading nasty rumours."

Ross laughed. "Whatever. Now what can I do for you?"

"I'm off on my OE so I thought I'd better come and say goodbye to you and Maureen."

"I'm not surprised. About time you spread your wings. Go and see some of those places you've wasted so much time reading about."

He laughed again, to take the sting out of his jibe.

"Thought I'd start in Oz and look up Roger and Ruth. That's where they are, isn't it?"

"Wish you would." Now he was serious, and sounding wistful. "Haven't heard from Rog for weeks. Isn't answering emails."

"Give me their address then and I'll check them out."

It wasn't like father and son to stay incommunicado for long, contrary to the situation between me and my uncles.

Ross walked back out with me to join Maureen in the office. He recovered his joie de vivre en route.

"The Bandit's finally giving up the farming lark." He clapped me on the shoulder. "Off on his OE; see if he can clean out Hay-on-Wye apparently."

"Does that mean our wedding plans are off?" Maureen laughed. "If so I'll have to look elsewhere."

"Afraid so, Maureen. Tell you what; if we're both still single when I come back in a few years I'll give your proposal serious consideration."

My turn to laugh.

"OK, children," Ross interjected, "I've got to have that car ready by the weekend so I'll say 'see you later' and leave you two to chat. Don't forget about Roger, please, pal."

He looked at me imploringly and gave a little wave as he exited Maureen's office.

"He told you, did he, about Roger?" asked Maureen becoming serious.

"Yeah, wants me to look him up. I was going to anyway because Oz is as good a place as any to start my odyssey."

"Odyssey," she said. "Sounds important. For anyone else it would be just a trip. I am going to miss your big words."

"I'm going to miss using them to impress you." I realised the truth of it as I spoke.

"I'll get Rog's last known for you."

She fiddled with her computer and wrote the address on a scrap of paper.

"Thanks, mate. I'll be going now so I'll just say; see you later."

"You're not getting away that easily, Bandit."

She came from behind her desk and enveloped me in a hug, burying her face in my shoulder.

"Take care, Jack," she whispered. "We'll miss you. Come back when you can."

I gently prised her off and held her at arm's length, surprised to see a tear trickle down her cheek. Hard-bitten Maureen never failed to surprise me.

"Don't worry, old girl. I'll be back and I'll see what Roger is up to as well."

With that I hurried from the building. I had the same feeling of loss as when Gran died. I realised Ross and Maureen had over the years become my de facto family as my uncles, their wives and my cousins had not.

When I'd decided on Oz as my start point I had intended Sydney and its hedonism as stark contrast to the farming grind I was used to. But here I was back out in the sticks on the far side of the continent as far from Sydney as you can get.

The chubby girl behind the rental car desk at Perth Airport had said I'd do better to try and get on one of the feeder flights to Newman. She said it was about 800 kilometres north, some of it on dirt roads. I did try, but seats were booked out by miners for two weeks ahead and I couldn't see what I would do in Perth to while away that sort of time.

I pulled in to Newman soon after midday of my third day on the road. The town looked similar to Te Puke without the greenery and traffic. Thinking about it, apart from the long main street, I don't know why it reminded me of Te Puke. I checked into the only motel I could find and after a quick wash I strolled over the road to a 24-hour convenience store. The store like the street was empty. I helped myself to a pie from the warmer.

After a while an old guy wearing a dirty white singlet and equally grubby shorts appeared from out the back.

"What can I do for you, mate?" He was rubbing his eyes as though he'd just woken up.

I showed him the pie I'd half-eaten. While he rang that up I fished out the crumpled bit of paper Maureen had written Roger and Ruth's last known on.

"Can you tell me where I can find this address, cobber?"

I tried a bit of Aussie vernacular. He glanced quickly at me to check if I was taking the mickey. I kept a straight face and showed him the address.

"Bloody miles away down the main street. Wouldn't want to be walking around town in this heat. Locals mostly only come out at night."

The location he'd described didn't sound miles away to me, but then, from the haven of an air-conditioned shop anywhere might seem distant to an old guy like him.

The dry heat wasn't too bad; bearable, in fact, though I did consider returning to the shop to buy a hat.

It didn't take long to find Roger's street because all the streets came off the main one like fish bones off a spine. The streets soon dwindled to nothing facing out to the emptiness of the desert. Their street was the third I came to and the houses seemed flasher than those I'd seen so far. Even with that deserted look about it Roger's must have been about the best in Newman.

No-one answered the door. I walked around to the back yard with no result, no washing on the line, the place clearly deserted. Then a grumpy looking bloke's head popped above the fence.

"Not home," he said, without preamble nor enquiry as to what I was doing.

I took his brevity as a cue.

"Know where they are?"

"You're not the only one looking for them, mate." The bloke ignored my question.

"Yeah, like who else?"

I was uneasy about this turn of events. Coupled with Ross and Maureen's misgivings at Roger and Ruth's silence my imagination was tending towards the bad. Comes from reading too many Robert B. Parker novels I suppose.

"How should I know who else? I'm just the bloody neighbour."

"Did they leave anything, a message or forwarding address?"

"Depends."

I waited without success for grumpy to elaborate.

"Depends on what?"

"Depends on your nickname."

This was a strange turn-up. Like, how did Roger know I was coming if the question was for me? Then I twigged he must have received his father's email telling me I was coming. With nothing to lose I said, "Bandit."

"Pleased to meet you, Jack," he said, his face transformed by a wide grin. "Show me your passport, just to be on the safe side."

When he'd checked that I looked almost like the photo, he opened a gate separating the two backyards and beckoned me through.

"Tom's the name. Roger and Ruth told me about you, asked me to keep a look-out for you. Come in the house; they left me something to give you."

I was intrigued by this turn of events. I had no idea I registered enough in their lives to be talked about to others. I worried what they had got themselves into that warranted this level of caution.

"What's with the cloak and dagger stuff?" I asked.

"Not so much cloak and dagger, just being careful. You knew Roger was consulting for BHP the big mining company?"

I nodded, though I rarely knew exactly what Roger was doing at any given time.

"Seems while he was organising their roll-out of new computer systems he was working on 'a little something for himself' – his words."

"Do you know what?"

"Not exactly. He explained a little to me, but I'm just a mechanical engineer at the mines so most of what Roger said was over my head. For all that he was a brain box, he and Ruth were kind to me while they rented next door. My missus said she couldn't stand Newman anymore and took off not long before they arrived. I knew Roger's contract was coming to an end and he and Ruth would be moving on. Sooner than I expected they came over one evening and said they were leaving that night. I was a bit surprised because they weren't the sort of people to run out on the rent and anyway Roger must have been pulling in a small fortune as a consultant."

I had to laugh at the thought of Roger and Ruth reneging on anything, let alone their rent.

"Apparently," Tom continued, "the mining company had got wind of his 'little something' and wanted a piece of it even though it was nothing to do with them, no part of the consulting job he'd been doing. Roger said his emails had been hacked and other companies were sniffing around as well. I'd seen some suits visiting next door a couple of times, which made me wonder. Especially the second time they turned up with muscle."

"Don't like the sound of that" I said.

"Oh, Roger said he wasn't too worried. He just wanted some time to perfect whatever it was he had invented and get it patented. He said it was best for me not to know too much about it at this stage, but he wanted someone else to know, which is why he gave me this for you and only you. Beats me how he knew you'd turn up."

Tom handed me an unmarked envelope containing a letter.

'Bandit,' Roger began, which made me smile. *'Ruth and I knew from Dad's emails you'd turn up sooner or later, which you must have done or you wouldn't have met Tom and be reading this. Tom is a good bloke, and we thought it best for him if I he didn't know too much at this stage.*

'My need to be onsite for the BHP contract has ended. In my spare time I've been working on a device that simply put (to match your IQ!) uses a form of deep penetration digitised optics to analyse all sorts of apparently solid objects including the earth's strata. Mining companies and others have got wind of the success of my trials and have hacked my computers and I suspect my cellphone too.

'Some see it as a threat to their current aeromagnetic and remote sensing exploration businesses, others as an opportunity. Either way we have attracted some unwelcome premature attention so by the time you read this hopefully we will be in Canberra with patents in hand. If so we will soon be coming out of the closet, so to speak.

'Can you let the Old Man know we are OK and will be coming home as soon as possible and might be needing a bit of workshop space.

'Nice to hear you've come into a little bit of cash and given up the farming game. Maybe you'll even read less and have a go at writing? Thanks for everything, take care. Roger and Ruth.'

I handed Tom the letter and when he'd finished reading I said, "Can I use your phone, mate?"

"Sure." He pointed towards an old dial-up. "I thought Roger was up to something like this. Didn't think he was in any real danger. Incidentally where does *'Bandit'* come from?"

"It's a long story."

I left it at that as I began to dial Ross's telephone numbers. I could imagine the phones pealing out in the far away showroom until someone realised that if they didn't pick up then no-one would. This usually resulted in more than one staff member answering simultaneously resulting in a few moments of confusion until either Maureen or Josh in the workshop took over. Beats me why they didn't hire a receptionist.

Eventually Maureen came on the line and when she heard my voice yelled, "Bandit, is everything OK? We haven't heard from you. Do you need help? Where are you?"

"Settle down," I broke in, inwardly touched that someone was concerned for me. "I'm OK and I've sorted out Roger and Ruth's mystery so can you tell Ross to be patient and expect to see the pair of them soon."

I read Roger's letter to her, leaving out the bit about my inheritance and how the hell did he even know about that?

"Thanks for everything, Bandit. Ross will be relieved and so am I." Maureen paused. "Now what about you. Are you set on continuing your foolish quest in search of book fair nirvana or are you coming home to take up my matrimonial offer?"

I had to laugh.

"All in good time, old girl, all in good time."

▲   ▲   ▲

THREE BROS

My two brothers and I grew up in Waihi. Some smartarses down the RSA would say we never grew up, anywhere. They reckon we carry on like kids. I wouldn't know about that, but I do know it's a hell'uva lot better having a bit of a laugh than caving in and giving up, like, letting the fat cats born with a silver spoon walk all over you.

We call ourselves the Three Musketeers although as far as I know none of us have read the book, which apparently came out before the film. We've seen the film a few times. Not at the movies though, because Waihi hasn't got a picture theatre. We have to rent movies from the video shop which mostly has rom-coms and chop-socky. Waihi movie aficionados aren't sophisticated. The Three Musketeers movie just about qualified as high culture.

My bros and I have never been called the Three Musketeers by anyone else. It's our own private name for how we think of ourselves. I wouldn't be surprised if the good citizens of the town had a few choicer names for us. Like the Three Stooges or Three Blind Mice. Especially that dozy cop Bill Walker. He's supposed to be stationed up the Coromandel Peninsular on a cushy number at the beach. Instead, the grumpy old bastard spends a fair bit of time helping out around Waihi, which is sort of part of the Peninsular, I suppose.

His latest name for us was Three Stupid No-Hopers when he caught us raffling prime meat cuts down the pub. The meat was stamped *For Export*, with the AFFCo logo plain to see. How were we to know Jackson, who we'd got raffle stuff from before at knock-down prices, had branched out into dodgy meat and small goods? The copper was right though, we were stupid; we should have stuck to the RSA. Those old codgers don't mind a dodgy flutter.

The RSA was our spiritual home. I'm the oldest and the only one of us who comes anywhere near to being a returned serviceman, which entitles me and my 'guests' to patronise the RSA. I didn't serve overseas; got my birth date pulled out of a hat and ended up doing National Service in Her Majesty's Army.

Some would say it was a complete waste of time pretending to defend the country by running around the foothills of Ruapehu. Fat chance the commies would target a bunch of amateurs slogging up the Desert Road when the nearest beach invasion point was at least two hundred miles in any direction you cared to point.

From my point of view, I thought it was good to get away from Waihi and mix in with about a thousand other boomers. I learned a few things. Some haven't been much use since, like how to shoot people and blow stuff to smithereens. I did learn that even though they've got birdshit on their shoulders and use long words officers were as clueless as everybody else. Just like the suits that run around Waihi's mine calling themselves executives.

I learned a few other things too. Like, how to have no respect for authority and that a little bit of bravado goes a long way, and most blokes are sheep, and an amazing number can't read or write and have never read a book in their brief lives. The thing I learned that surprised me the most and has been handy to recall whenever the shit hits the fan was that I wasn't afraid of anything. Before that I considered myself a bit of a wimp. Then I found out I wasn't, when other bigger, bolder and supposedly braver blokes were crying for mummy.

Hugh and James, my two younger brothers, came of conscription age after the Labour Government abolished National Service. In my opinion a bit of soldiering would have done them good. Hardened them up and made them stand on their own two feet instead of following along on my coat tails. Mind you, it might have wrecked their lives just as easily as it surely did for some of the poor bastards I rubbed shoulders with.

If they'd done National Service at least Hugh and James could've boozed in the RSA without being signed in as my guests every time. Didn't occur to the silly buggers to sign up with the Cosmopolitan Club or drink down at the Rob Roy. They liked the cheap grog and grub at the RSA and so did I.

Our parents lived in one of those old cottages across the road from the Martha Mine. The house must have been at least a hundred years old, which made it a miracle it still stood as it hadn't exactly been built to last. It might have looked cute, but it was cold as a miner's grave in winter and bloody small although, being the eldest, I had a bedroom to myself while poor old James and Hugh had to bunk in together.

The mine must be the biggest hole in the southern hemisphere. It is so deep that tourists flock to a viewing stand thoughtfully provided free of charge by the town council. Depending on their shifts, either Hugh or James does a collection from the punters for 'injured miners,' sometimes if the weather is fine two or three times a day.

Hugh, if he's feeling up to it, takes his walking stick to imply he's been in a mining accident. The take always goes up when he does that. Never mind his genuine limp dates back to the after-match function of a home win when he was playing club rugby. He was so pissed he tumbled into one of the big concrete drainage channels and broke his leg trying to get out.

I count the takings and the cash becomes our walking around money. I have to say we do get brassed off with the number of times mingy tourists chuck useless foreign currency into the bucket, especially since the recession hit.

A few years ago a big mining outfit from Denver, Colorado in the USA came and bought the mine for a knock-down price. The Kiwi company that owned it was desperate for somebody or something to come along and bail them out. All we were waiting for way back then was for some rich bugger or maybe those no-hoper politicians from Wellington to come along and save our bloody jobs. Then who turns up? The bloody Americans with all their flash and greenbacks.

I have to admit, the mine never looked back.

My brothers and I were knocking back a few cold ones with our mates down at the RSA the other day. We were moaning about the Yanks buying up everything good around the place and stealing all our gold when they already had more than they could ever use locked up in Fort Knox.

Yeah, we get paid a fortune to work in the damn thing. But we reckon the mine belongs to us Kiwis. No bloody foreign outfit has a right to come in here and plunder our country of its riches and cultural heritage. I was explaining all this to some of the Maori blokes who just about live down the RSA when they aren't working in the mine. I don't know how they qualify for membership, but where cheap grog and grub is on offer there they will be.

"Well, what are yous jokers gonna do about it then, eh boy?" spoke up Hemi, one of the Maori blokes. Everybody thinks he's named after his ancestors, but he nicknamed himself after his pride and joy, Chrysler Valiant's Hemi engine.

Hemi's question prompted me to reveal a scheme I'd been thinking about off and on for some time. Maybe a way to get a bit of our own back, show those thieving Yankee know-alls that you can't push Kiwis around.

"You blokes know the size of the trucks that haul the ore out of the hole?"

They nodded wisely.

"Well," I continued, "Every load like that contains about half an ounce of gold."

"Bugger all then," said James. "Not worth worrying about."

"Yeah, but," I said. "Do you know what gold is worth?"

They started guessing like we were having some kind of pub quiz until Hemi raised his voice above the chatter.

"More than a thousand bucks an ounce," he said.

Hemi was definitely a bit brighter than the rest, including my two brothers.

"Holy crap!" they chorused.

I explained. "All we have to do is divert a few tonnes a day of spoil off the conveyors and we can make a big score."

There was silence as they absorbed that.

"Yeah, but," Hemi began, doubt in his voice. "There is only a minute trace in the spoil. The half-ounce or most of it has already been extracted by the time the waste gets on the spoil conveyors." He paused before adding, "Bro."

"How you gonna get te gold outta te rock, bro?" piped up one of Hemi's cousins, equally doubtful.

"We can't, but it's not the trace gold I'm thinking about, it's the spoil, the metal itself." They looked askance at me as I continued. "The Yanks won't miss a few tonnes. They've already got what they want out of it."

"I was right then," James interrupted. "The gold isn't worth worrying about."

"If you blokes will let me finish, the point is that the spoil makes excellent base metal for roading. We'll be getting about fifteen tonne a day for free. James and Hugh can provide a truck. We'll stockpile it behind Hemi's place next to the marae. Impossible to say where it came from once we're away from the conveyor so no worries there."

"What about the cop?" Hemi asked.

"Bill? He may be tough, but he's fair. Unless the Yanks complain, and why would they because they'll never find out and we're almost doing them a favour getting rid of spoil, even if it is only a little bit."

"Who are we going to sell the stuff to?" piped up James.

"I do believe there isn't a farmer from here to Coromandel who wouldn't appreciate cheap roading metal and no questions asked," I replied.

"One of my cuzzies is council purchasing officer for roading and footpaths," said Hemi. "He says the council is always on the lookout to save a few dollars even though our rates go up all the bloody time. If we cut him in he'll be sweet. Might even get a promotion for saving the council money."

"That's it then, it's true." I lifted my tankard to make a toast. "To our streets, which will be paved with gold – sort of!"

▲ ▲ ▲

PONGAROA PASSING

Tom gently reined the big roan to a halt, leaned forward and rubbing his horse's silky neck, spoke softly, "Take a spell, old timer."

The horse gave a whinny as though in reply and immediately began nuzzling away at the sparse grass between the worn rocks protruding from the round knoll that was the summit of the Puketoi Ranges.

Tom stretched back and reached into his saddle bag for his makings and rolled a smoke. When he had got it going he squinted through the smoke drifting in the still air, surveying the hills, ridged like waves stretching away in the distance. He gazed to where the blue of the hills merged with the blue of the sea, and further out to the horizon where the blue sea met the sky.

He felt a deep sense of pride knowing that all of the land spread out before him was Pongaroa Station that had belonged to his family for close to a hundred and fifty years.

Though it was fashionable now for people to say that other people had owned the land before his great-grandfather, he knew in truth it was once long ago as good as empty of all human life. If anybody owned these hills and valleys it was the birds and the insects, the flowers and the trees, the tussock, bush and scrub.

It was his ancestors who had lived and died to make something of what they saw as an underused wilderness. Conservationists and others with the benefit of hindsight were critical of his family and said the land should have been left alone. He knew that then, as now, the human impulse to turn nature from merely existing into providing for the greater good was overidingly powerful.

He had no regrets; he felt no need to apologise or explain. Pongaroa Station had long proved the critics wrong. Even the Johnny-come-lately greenies couldn't argue with the success of the land stabilisation programmes started by his father when Tom was just a small boy.

Sometimes Tom thought he should bring the greenies and for that matter, iwi up here and let them look and see what a century and a half of sympathetic, conservative and wise husbandry meant to the land that made up the 2,600 hectares of Pongaroa Station.

Had he not felt it was none of their business he would have shown them the station's stud book and annual accounts going back as far as they cared to look. Not one year, not even those of the Great Depression, showed red ink.

For all that pride Tom did feel deeply sad. It wasn't his doctors much repeated advice that his smoking would kill him if melanoma didn't that worried him; he knew his time was coming to an end. His sadness centred on the fact he had no heirs.

Even if there was somebody in the family who could take over there were people threatening succession, who seemed to think they had a prior claim, becoming ever more strident for its return, just as the land became ever more productive.

Tom drew on his smoke and contemplated the blue haze and wondered if he should just give the land back. Then he visualised the sweat and tears and joy that had gone into making the Station what it was. It was inconceivable that a Morgan wouldn't be forever deeply involved in caring for the land. What did the more recent claimants ever do for it except take what they could without giving anything back?

Tom slid off the roan's back taking care to favour his gammy leg. He grunted as he limped over to sit on the smooth rounded rock that had become his familiar seat. Often lately he hadn't bothered dismounting because of the difficulty of getting back up. If the track up to his vantage point hadn't been so steep he might have ridden the quad. Everybody else did nowadays. Then when he was astride his old horse he thought, 'Nah, a quad bike is no companion.'

He chuckled when he thought of Vincent on a quad. Vincent became head shepherd in Tom's father's time and had never retired even when Tom finally took over. He had been vehemently against the bikes when Tom first brought one back to the station. The bike changed to good fun the chore of fetching the mail and supplies from the rural mail box down the road. The hands vied with each other for that job. Vincent shook his head when Janey took to the thing and said, "It'll end in tears." She, like the hands, raced down to the box trailing a plume of dust.

It didn't end in tears and eventually Vincent couldn't stand the ribbing and was persuaded to have a go around the yard. Tom smiled as he recalled after that they couldn't get Vincent off the damn quad. And now here Tom was all those years later, the only one who still preferred to ride a horse.

Vincent's capitulation had opened the floodgate to mechanisation. He realised the sense of Tom's argument, no matter both of them were reluctant converts. Both were happy there was still a place for horses on such steep country, but the shift to noisy machines sped up over the years.

From his rock Tom could see one of his helicopters, sun glinting from its Perspex canopy as it wheeled, appearing and disappearing behind a range of hills toward the south west. The thwack of its rotors drifted faintly to him, disturbing the silence even after the machine had dropped down behind a ridge. What would Vincent, had he still been alive, have made of the station having a couple of helicopter pilots-cum-shepherds on the payroll?

For all Vincent's dire predictions and, if they cared to acknowledge their own unspoken fears, it wasn't machinery that ended their hopes of leaving the station to the next generation of Morgans.

Tom and Janey's only son Jake, named after Jacob, Tom's grandfather, drowned crossing the headwaters of the Pongaroa River. Or that's what they surmised.

Jake was twelve, helping with the autumn muster, when he didn't come back. Tom and Janey clung desperately for weeks to the idea he was alive. They willed Meg, his favourite Border collie to speak, and lead them back to where she'd left her master. As puzzled by his absence as they were, she whined and refused to leave the vicinity of the homestead until she passed away, long before she should have, as though from a broken heart.

Reason prevailed just as recrimination and guilt, their own and that fed by well-meaning acquaintances, wracked their existence. They didn't find Jake's body until the spring on the banks of the Owahanga River not far from where it joined the Pongaroa, yet miles from where the chopper set him down above a flock of Merino.

Tom wiped his eyes, blaming the smoke from the fresh one he'd lit from the butt of the last. He let his thoughts wander back to Jake and how everyone had accused him and Janey, but mostly him, of putting too much on the boy at such a young age. Tom, in his guilt, had agreed with them at the time, but over the years on cool reflection talking it over with Janey as a subject they couldn't let go, they'd decided that cruel as it might seem his death was a kind of natural selection.

Tom had begun roaming the hills even younger than Jake. Tom's father, in turn, had been about the same age. It took a special sort of person to work the back country. Someone who was at ease with themselves, confident and neither brash nor reckless. Someone who didn't mind their own company for days, even weeks, at a time, seeing and speaking to no other human. Yet could display the utmost loyalty to others and gather in return their deepest respect.

Tom knew instinctively that he had those qualities that when invested in a woman paid the dividend of a fiercely loving commitment for life. Tom's father and grandfather had been the same, whereas his uncle, craving the company of men and the bright city lights had stepped aside for his father.

The Morgans didn't push their men into the responsibility; they found it themselves. Jake had shown all the signs at age twelve. He was too young then to keep up with the grown musterers, but was a good companion to Vincent and the older shepherds. He knew the wiles and ways of dogs and sheep and cattle. The following summer he would have gone away to secondary school and he was already talking about Lincoln.

Tom called to the roan grazing some distance down the slope. The horse pricked up his ears and came slowly back up as though to let Tom know he didn't appreciate being disturbed. Tom gave him a pat and reached out the oil-skin slicker he kept in his right-hand saddle-bag and spread it on the ground at the base of the rock he had been sitting on.

Groaning he eased himself down on the slicker so that he could lean comfortably against the rock. He tilted his head back and looked up at the azure sky. It had darkened since he had arrived and the high ridges were casting long shadows across the valleys. He realised he hadn't heard the chopper for a while and was surprised when he glanced at his watch to see that it was past knock-off time.

He didn't care. Neither did the roan, who'd wandered down the hill in the other direction this time as though he knew there was better grass there. Tom shuddered at the thought of the empty homestead waiting for him. The grand old house held no attraction for him. Other people raved about it; how big it was, beautifully crafted at the turn of last century from rimu milled on the station. The house boasted return verandas and Victorian embellishments inside and out. It was protected from the south west by a hillock on whose northern slope it was placed, and now additionally sheltered by trees planted by family over the years. The house faced across the river flats that made up the home paddocks that comprised much of the hay country of the station.

Tom thought about rolling another smoke then dismissed the idea. He had given up not long after he and Janey married when she was pregnant with Jake. A few reproachful looks was all it took and he'd not given the weed another thought. Until Janey passed away last year. He guessed that was why he was in no hurry to ride home; apart from the fact he considered himself home wherever he was on the property.

Janey was the love of his life, and he of hers. A cliché, he smiled to himself. True, nevertheless. They were cousins and he sometimes wondered if that was why they got on so well. Neither of them dwelt on their connection, though sometimes the subject came up when they sat on the front veranda at the end of a working week, watching the sun slide behind Puketoi, Janey with a gin and Tom nursing a beer.

Janey had grown up the daughter of her father's sister who had married an Englishman. Janey's father was something in the city. Her parents hadn't had a particularly happy married life. Tom's father rarely corresponded with his sister so Tom grew up barely aware of Janey's existence in a big city on the other side of the world.

Tom had to laugh when he recalled how it would be impossible to find someone who had appeared to be more unsuited to back country station life than Janey. Yet when they first met in her parents' front room and been introduced by his father and mother she'd thrust out her hand to his, a gesture unlike he'd been used to from Kiwi girls, he'd felt something like an electric shock. The frisson of her touch rocked him to the extent he knew nothing would ever be the same again. He wondered if she was similarly struck.

Both their parents tried to dissuade them so Tom eased their fears by setting Janey a test. He would return to New Zealand as planned with his parents and leave Janey to make up her own mind free of his influence. She would have to organise, arrange and pay for her own voyage out to New Zealand if she wanted to see him again.

As far as Janey was concerned that was the most ridiculous thing a man could do. She was as determined as he. And so it proved. Whenever the opportunity arose during their long marriage, Janey gleefully reminded Tom of how silly he was to 'test' her and Tom never ceased to feel slightly ashamed of his silliness.

Then he'd retaliate by retorting, "If that's the only silly thing I've done then count your blessings."

And she did, because in truth no one could accuse Tom of being silly.

Tom noticed a slight breeze had got up and the air cooled as the setting sun lost its influence. Although the shadows had lengthened, being so high on Puketoi he was still in the sun. He squinted to the east and thought he could just make out a pinprick of light in the deep shadow where the station buildings would be clustered. The homestead would be dark, but the men would think nothing of it, assuming he'd gone to Masterton or Wellington for the night or a few days.

He stretched out again and drew the slicker around him against the breeze. He couldn't see the roan in the gathering dusk, but wasn't worried; he'd come with a call. The coast and sea had vanished in the haze which had turned from blue to grey. Soon, Tom calculated, the sun would go down behind the higher Ruahines to the west and night would be upon him.

He was undecided whether to break the spell and head back or let the magic continue for a while longer. Being out in the hills in the dark didn't concern him at all; he knew the land as his backyard. Besides, his horse could find his way home without much help from Tom; something a machine could never do.

He decided to stay put; after all, Janey always used to say, "When in doubt do nowt," which always seemed to be good advice when a course of action was unclear.

Tom's thoughts returned to his beloved family. How those years right up to Jake's death had been wonderful. Those that came after weren't too bad either, he mused, once they'd got over the whole sad business.

Tom and Janey had procrastinated about having another child after Jake was born. Neither put it into words, but after their son was born perfect in every way they hesitated, as cousins, to chance their luck on a second. Then, when Jake was nine, Janey read an article by a prominent paediatrician that showed that the risk of congenital problems in children of cousin marriages was no more than for anybody else and less in some cases because the family history of both parties was probably better known.

Susan was only three when Jake didn't come back after that dreadful autumn muster. Too young to understand the grief that infiltrated the household, but not too young to miss the boy she idolised as an older brother. Tom wished it could have been otherwise, but he was aware that he and Janey had neglected Susan for a while, years probably after they lost Jake. She had withdrawn into herself as defence against what her young mind interpreted as disinterest.

As the pain of their loss receded, as much as it ever could, the balance was redressed. Probably too much Tom could now see. Susan grew up as an only child spoiled and cosseted to the extent they tried to keep her safe as though wrapped in cotton wool. They were terrified that an accident might befall her as had happened to Jake.

They fostered interests away from the station, frowned on Vincent's encouraging at every opportunity her interest in horses and the land. Vincent, being Vincent, effected not to notice. With the contrary pulls on her impressionable self she couldn't help growing up a free spirit or as Janey often said, 'a rebellious Morgan,' and 'Uncle' Vincent indulged her.

Partly out of necessity because there was no high school in the district, and mostly to get her away from the temptation of risky adventures on horseback and motorbike, Tom and Janey sent her away to boarding school at the same age Jake had been when he died.

Strangely enough, although predictable, they went through another period of mourning moping around a house empty of children for the first time in fifteen years. Vincent didn't help, grumpily making his disapproval known whenever he could. They realised Susan might interpret sending her away as either another sign of rejection or that her parents considered she could never replace her brother or, perish the thought, both.

The pity of it was she was right, sort of. What Tom and Janey failed to explain because they hardly understood themselves, was that their daughter was not meant to replace their son; she was a loved person in her own right. Rejection and unattainable expectation could not have been further from Tom and Janey's mind.

Tom sighed as he recalled the reports coming from the school that Susan had lost her bounce and had retreated into herself not at all like the 'rebellious Morgan' she'd been. Tom and Janey discussed at length whether to bring her back before deciding the die was cast and for better or worse they had to live with the spectre of unintended consequences.

They were relieved to notice that by her third year away she had recovered some of her joie de vivre. Even the sadness of her beloved friend 'Uncle' Vincent's passing didn't knock her back for long. She came back from the funeral a quieter, more thoughtful person as though realising that life even for someone as privileged as she might not all be a bed of roses. She missed her old friend deeply, when riding the hills during holiday time, more than the brother she could now barely remember.

Tom leaned his head back on the hard rock and marvelled at the brightness of the stars. As always even after all those years, he was surprised at how quickly dusk turned to night. Gazing unseeing at the Southern Cross overhead he thought about his daughter.

He thought about her upbringing and wondered if he and Janey should or could have done anything differently. It saddened him to dwell on the unavoidable fact she was his only living relative. He felt he'd been rather careless losing the other two, Janey and Jake. Well, three if you counted Vincent even though he wasn't related; they all considered him one of the family. Four, if you counted Tom's father, Susan's grandfather. Five if you included Grandma.

Tom stopped himself before he descended too far into maudlin retrospection.

The dear departed, he told himself, are part of life, the circle of life, whose memory was to cherish, not to dwell on for too long. He snorted out loud, the sound startling in the stillness. He forced his thoughts back to the living daughter who he surely loved even if he didn't fully understand her. Maybe she wasn't Jake, but she had the confidence born of her upbringing. She had shown that in her chosen career. It was with mixed feelings, knowing she would be safe, knowing also there was no-one to take over the station that Tom and Janey attended her graduation as an agronomist. By the time she got her master's and then doctorate they were past any feelings of regret and filled only with pride.

Tom was glad Janey had lived long enough to see their daughter happy and confident on the world stage attending conferences representing government and big businesses. It was a shame Susan had been too busy to be with her mother as she slipped away. On the other hand Tom was grateful she attended Janey's funeral. Susan said, "I've been to too many of these already in my life," and only stayed on Pongaroa for a day afterwards explaining that a major conference in Melbourne beckoned.

To Tom, Janey's passing had seemed bitterly unfair. He felt responsible and guilty for bringing such a vibrant, cheerful person away from her privileged life in England to the hard life of hill farming.

Janey got rheumatoid arthritis shortly after Jake died. Stress activated the disease, experts said, and it was usually hereditary, which surprised them both given they had never heard of anyone in either family suffering. Janey was only thirty-seven when she was diagnosed. She changed from being a person full of the joy of life and conveying that to all who came in contact with her. Lucky for them all, modern medication kept the disease in check and to all outward appearances Janey recovered her flexibility and life returned to much as it was before.

It seemed unfair that having beaten arthritis Janey should have to battle another insidious illness. Again the experts said it could have been hereditary. Again Janey and Tom knew of no family member who had succumbed to breast cancer. Tom let his thoughts dwell only briefly, the agony still too raw to contemplate for long, on his beloved's passing. He was realistic enough to accept that at their age one of them would have to be first to go. Still he wished with all his heart she could have hung on a few more years or that it could have been him who went first.

Tom closed his eyes and let the profound silence wash over him. He thought how good it would be to drift off and never wake up. His melanoma was going to get him sooner or later anyway and what had he got to live for? Somebody would find his body in a day or so. Who would miss him?

Not Susan; she had her own busy life. Get a grip, he told himself. There was Tony; he would be the 'somebody' that found him and he couldn't wish that on him. Susan would miss him, too, he realised; so what if she was busy? Good on her.

Tom hadn't given much thought to Tony. Now he realised with a start that made him sit up that he was fond of Vincent's nephew. Tony had come to the station long after his Uncle Vincent, his real uncle, Tom thought, smiling, had passed away. When the going got too tough for Janey, Tom had sought a manager and Tony had applied and turned out to be the best candidate by far. He had graduated from Lincoln and even been a Nuffield Scholar investigating better ways of marketing premium meats.

Tony cheerfully admitted that despite his academic qualifications book work wasn't his thing. Being out on the high hills was; like uncle like nephew he laughed.

Vincent's sister had caused a minor local sensation when she married a Kahungunu man from up near Wairoa. Tom recognised it was none of his business, but Vincent kept him up with his family's dramas, problems and progress. Tom had heard that Vincent's nephew was doing okay and was pleased when he applied to manage Pongaroa, even more pleased that he was able to offer him the job on his own merits. Tony's tribal affiliations meant little to Tom; Tony was Tony, who happened to be brown.

Tom drifted off to sleep lulled by the comforting thought that Pongaroa Station might be in good hands after all; not family, but damn close. Completely lost on Tom was the irony that a Kahungunu was back in control of the land. The breeze dropped as did the temperature. At this altitude it was cold enough to frost even in late summer.

Deeply dreaming Tom is surrounded by his family and friends. He knows he must be dreaming because he sits again on Grandfather Jacob's knee, is comforted by his mother and father. He is riding his first pony and plays with the collie that was Jake's dog's ancestor. He dreams of Jake as a teenager and the young man he would never be. Janey laughs and loves with him as she teaches Susan to feed her calf club pet. He sees Susan, the young lady already older than Jake can ever be, cantering towards the river with Vincent puttering to keep up on a quad.

Although they were never at Pongaroa at the same time he dreams Vincent is standing on the veranda of the homestead with his arm around Tony's shoulder, as though passing responsibility to him. Tom dreams joyously about them all. Somehow his joy is overwhelmed by an immense sorrow as though even in his dream he knows it must end and in his dream he is dying.

Jake's collie is licking his face as though intent on waking him. Tom forces his eyes open. There is no dog. The cold wetness on his cheeks are his tears turned to ice. He has been crying in his sleep, from joy or sadness in the instant of waking Tom cannot tell. The power of his emotion suggest sadness.

Tom struggled to his feet stiff with damp and cold, his leg throbbing with arthritis. Now he knew how Janey had felt all those years, he thought grimly. He couldn't see the roan anywhere and got no answering whinny to his call. Feeling a bit of a fool and more than a bit hungry he gathered up his slicker and hobbled down the track, thinking Janey would have called him more than a fool.

His spirits lifted with the sun's appearance above the horizon. His sadness evaporated as though his family, alive and dead, had visited him one last time to urge him not to give up.

He hadn't been hobbling down the track long when he heard the thwack of a helicopter beating its way up the valley. He saw it round the low ridge separating his view from the river flats and make a beeline for the summit he'd recently vacated. He stopped and waved his hat and the chopper altered course slightly towards him to land on a small flattish area only a few metres off the track.

Andrew, the pilot, who had been on the station since they'd first got helicopters yelled, "Mornin' boss. Need a lift?"

Tom was already clambering into the machine and for once resisted the temptation to joss Andrew about the virtues of horses versus choppers. When Tom had the helmet and mic on and Andrew lifted them off, dropping off the hill like an express elevator going down, he said, "How did you know I was up Puketoi?"

"When your old horse was standing outside the stables this morning at dawn looking a bit sorry for himself we knew you hadn't gone to town. So where else would we look? We know you're always going up to the top these days. Tony says that his ancestors knew you'd make the hill summit your special place. That's why they named it Puketoi."

Tom was a bit surprised that the men were aware of what he regarded as a private habit. He thought they were busy going about the station's business directed by the ever-cheerful Tony. In truth, he was mightily touched by their concern.

"Those Kahungunu elders must have been smart fellows," he growled to cover his emotion.

Tony did that running crouch towards the chopper that the whirling blades encouraged the men to adopt, even though standing upright they would miss by a mile. He shouted over the racket, "Breakfast at my place, Tom?"

He made no reference to Tom's night out in the open, as though it was an everyday occurrence.

They drew up to Tony's house, smaller though just as characterful, but only half the age of the main homestead, that Tom had had built for Vincent. Tom noticed a silver Grand Cherokee that was vaguely familiar parked next to where they drew up in Tony's ute.

"New wagon?" he asked.

Tony looked at him. "Nah, belongs to someone you know."

"Suzy! What are you doing here?"

"Dad, how lovely to see you too," she replied mock sarcastically. "I thought you'd be pleased to see your daughter?"

"I'm sorry. Of course I am; just surprised."

"I ran into this big lug a while ago at one of those conferences in Lincoln," she said linking her arm through Tony's and looking at him fondly. "We've been seeing each other off and on since, but I'm wary of committing because of ...well, you know."

"No, I don't know," Tom replied.

"What with Uncle Vincent being Tony's uncle as well and working here and all it seemed..." she hesitated... "a bit incestuous and then there's the Maori thing."

When Tom made no comment she continued, "Then, about midnight I had a strange feeling that I wasn't being fair to Tony. You see, weeks ago he'd asked me to come down to the Bachelors' Ball and I'd said no because I sort of thought you might disapprove. Then in the early hours I had a lovely dream about us all. I woke up feeling I needed to hear Tony's voice straight away, that I must speak to him. And something told me I needed to see you too. So I rang him and here I am, or rather here we are."

Tom, somewhat taken aback by this turn of events, looked silently at them both, inwardly amused that two supposedly intelligent adults could look so sheepish. The things he had been thinking and dreaming about last night on his lonely vigil on Puketoi ran through his mind again. He didn't know if Tony had told her where he'd been all night. He wondered if it was possible there had been some sort of telepathic connection between father and daughter.

Perhaps there was no need for guilt or recrimination. He silently considered the incestuous aspect simultaneously dismissing it as irrelevant. He examined the 'Maori thing' and realised he hadn't given a thought to Tony's connection to Ngati Kahungunu. It didn't matter a jot. He laughed out loud as he twigged the irony of it all. The iwi were going to get their land back after all.

"Believe me," he said, "There's nothing for me to disapprove of. In fact, the opposite."

A TOWN LIKE TAUMARANUI

With dusk came fog and the mercury dipped in sympathy.

Bob looked down the main street where the fog-haloed street lights barely illuminated a scene that could have been the result of an apocalypse. Apart from a car's headlights dimly penetrating the vaporous blanket, the place appeared deserted.

He lamented the Friday nights of years ago when the main street would have been jumping. Mums and Dads, kids in tow, late night shopping, mostly making it a social occasion after the working week. The lights strung outside the picture theatre pulsed as though keeping time with the energy radiating out from the screen within. The crowds, the well-lit shops, the Teddy Boys lolling over their machines, lent long ago an air of carnival to Hakiaha Street. Even in winter. Even then right down to the West End where Bob had his garage and workshop with its three pumps, Standard, Super and Diesel at the ready.

Bob shivered, whether from the creeping chill or memories of a happier time he couldn't tell. He watched the car emerge from the murk and his spirits lifted a little when he saw it was a Range Rover; thirsty petrol V8 he hoped.

"Fill her up," said the driver from his seat; window barely open. Even so Bob felt the waft of heated air momentarily caress his frozen face.

"That'll be Super petrol, sir?"

Bob couldn't help but feel intimidated by the supercilious attitude of the man, though angry with himself at his own subservient reaction, dependant as he was on the custom of twits like this almost certainly from the smoke.

"Diesel. Can't you see it says so on the fuel flap?"

The driver's window purred shut before Bob had time to reply. Bob's spirit sagged. Prospects of a big sale of expensive Super petrol evaporated. He hoped the couple of litres of petrol he'd splashed in prematurely, that now wouldn't be paid for, would be diluted by the diesel.

He hung up the diesel nozzle and tapped on the window, which slid down barely enough that Bob had to crane his neck to speak through the gap.

"Fifty-eight dollars, sir."

He hoped the man would hand him sixty cash and tell him to keep the change even knowing it was more likely the driver would want to pay by eftpos and keep the receipt for tax deductibility purposes. Bob was mildly surprised that the man who had towered over him from the lofty seat of the SUV turned out to be short and portly. An insignificant person whose greying comb-over placed him closer to sixty than fifty. Long strands of greasy lank hair flopped over his ear when his knitted bobbled ski hat slipped off. The ski-suit onesy he wore, which Bob imagined might be fashionable at those après ski parties he had heard about, failed to make the man appear anything other than a fool.

"Be a sweetie, Dickie, get me a cappuccino with cinnamon," a girlish voice requested from the vehicle's interior.

Dickie didn't look like a sweetie to Bob and when Bob told him he didn't do coffee of any sort, not even instant, Dickie proved it by snarling, "What sort of hick-town business do you call this? Baby will not be pleased."

Bob could only shrug. At least the man hadn't waited for his cash receipt.

The man swooped up his ridiculous beanie, now a soggy rag, and climbed into the Range Rover without another word. Before the interior light dimmed Bob saw Dickie and the svelte girl he guessed was Baby remonstrating at his inability to supply coffee. Compared to Dickie she *was* a baby, thought Bob, as the Rover was jerked into gear and spun away into the fog.

Bob stepped back into the dim light under the canopy and inspected the folded notes the objectionable little man had pressed into his hand. Bob didn't know whether to laugh or cry as he saw the fifty and five notes. Dickie had not only *not* tipped him, he'd dunned him out of three dollars.

"Just about the bloody margin on diesel," he spat into the gloom.

Bob watched the Range Rover's tail-lights become red pin-pricks until they disappeared, leaving only the dim glow of the street-lights to relieve the grey. Patel's dairy was the only other business open up the street. He considered texting him to send one of his boys down with a half-dozen assorted meat pies to replenish the pie warmer he'd neglected to fill. Thinking about pies reminded him how hungry he was since he'd scoffed the last pie hours before as it started to grow dark and the fog thickened.

Bob got out the Samsung his daughter had given him for his seventy-fifth birthday. He fumbled around with it, mouthing to himself the letters as he laboriously texted his order. To be honest, he could think of many better things he would rather have had for his birthday than a smart phone. But his daughter seemed to think it was a vital necessity and who was he to argue?

On her rare visits she seemed to be constantly tapping away or swiping it with her fingers as though it were a misbehaving toy.

"I had no idea being a librarian was so demanding requiring communication twenty-four seven," he opined once. Which got him a dirty look and an even longer absence until her next visit.

"Pressure of work," she said.

The single bar heater in his office provided barely enough heat to take the chill off. Only a couple more cars required his attention. Unseen in the mist on the lines across the far side of Hakiaha Street a freight train rumbled through without stopping.

As the empty pie warmer door stopped rattling from the train's passing, Patel senior turned up with the pies.

"Come in, come in, kick the door shut."

Bob leaped up to help Patel side-step his way to the pie-warmer.

"I was remembering how the trains used to stop day and night, and the passengers off the Limited would rush into your dairy because the station tea rooms were so full."

"What you talking about that old rubbish now for?" Patel huffed. He wasn't prepared for or expecting a conversation drifting down a past increasingly painful as its rose-tinted hue faded.

"Anyway, bloody good thing me and Mrs Patel don't have to keep shop open these days to two o'clock in the morning or later when the express from Wellington was late."

Bob, like everyone else in the town, had never thought to ask Patel if he had a Christian name, nor had one ever been volunteered by Patel. A mild-mannered man, respected in the town for his conciliatory manner among the main street businesses, he would, had he been asked, have refrained from pointing out that labelling his first name Christian was hardly appropriate.

"I thought you'd send one of your boys down with the pies."

Bob had picked up that Patel didn't view the past so rosily. He sought to change the subject and he knew Patel never tired of talking about his boys.

"Boys gone," said Patel. "Mrs Patel too."

Bob was aghast. He'd known the Patels for more than forty years. Nearly from the first day Patel had turned up in town as the new owner of the West End Dairy that most people didn't even know was for sale. About a week later Mrs Patel and Patel's mother arrived on the Limited from Auckland. Bob used to wonder what they made of the place, stepping down from the train at what must have seemed like some frontier town in a Wild West movie.

"Patel, I'm so sorry. I had no idea. I mean we knew your boys are doing well, but Mrs P…" Bob's voice trailed off.

"Do not be sorry. Not your fault. Mrs Patel decided to give up on this one-horse town. She says she only stayed for boys and when they go away to seek fame and fortune she decided to go likewise. She wanted me to also go, but I cannot."

Patel paused and took a reflective bite from the butter chicken pie he had helped himself to. He made a mental note to charge Bob for one less.

"I must stay to keep shop going for people of Taumaranui and also shop is my only asset and who would buy it now?"

Bob had no answer.

"Enough about me. What about you, what keeps you here? Seems to me not enough business these days for two garages especially if one is small independent like yours."

Patel could see Bob was considering his reply so he went behind the counter where he knew Bob kept his percolator permanently on the boil hidden from his customers. He wasn't a bloody café, he'd protested to Patel years ago. Patel poured a mug for Bob and then himself.

Bob absently thanked him, forgetting it was his coffee.

"My wife. She keeps me here."

"But she's been gone for years." Patel had an uneasy feeling Bob might have lost his marbles.

"For me she's still here." Bob nodded in the vague direction of the cemetery down Golf Road. "Anyway, where would I go? My crazy daughter and her current husband can't stay in one place for long. I've lost count of how many times they've 'upgraded' or how many 'rentals' they own. Beats me what happened to the notion of creating a loving family home like me and Mavis did here."

Patel, dismayed the conversation had taken a melancholy turn, sought to cheer up his friend.

"Maybe we should properly retire and go on luxury world cruise. Very fashionable now, I believe."

Bob laughed.

"What? You and me; a fat Indian and a skinny old white guy. We'd be laughed off the boat. Anyway, I get seasick."

Patel glanced up the street just as the local ambulance swirled silently by heading for Hospital Hill. The lights of his unattended dairy shone like homing beacons in the fog.

"Golly," he said. "Might be wishful thinking, but I think I've got a customer. I must go and we will continue this discussion forthwith."

"Forthwith it is, old mate. I'm closing up. Midnight is late enough for an old guy like me."

Bob began his ritual closing down the service station, pulling in the signs, locking up the oil cabinets and switching off the compressor and lights. He saw Patel's go out at almost the same moment. He was just about to padlock the back door when he heard a car draw up to the pumps on the forecourt.

"Christ, who the hell can this be?"

He didn't realise he was speaking out loud to no-one. He stomped back through the workshop and peered out to the darkened forecourt. Bob was relieved to see it was Jim Saunders, one of the local cops, and not some pushy arsehole run out of gas. Jim was preoccupied, talking into his radio, only giving Bob a wave when he noticed him. Knowing full well his services were about to be called on Bob unlocked the garage doors and backed out the tow-truck.

"Haven't got a pie have you, mate?" Jim asked easily, already heading to the pie warmer.

"Help yourself, everybody else does. What's the job at this godforsaken hour?"

"A couple of ski yuppies got taken out by a north-bound freight train on the Owhango level crossing. Apparently they'd broken down or stalled right on the crossing. Probably not a scratch to the train driver or the train. Train didn't even stop; doubt the driver knew anything about it."

"What about the occupants of the vehicle?"

"Not too bad. They've been taken to hospital for observation. An older guy and his dolly bird. Lucky they were in a Range Rover built like a brick shithouse. The train just clipped the rear, but the Rover's still a mess. Got shunted down the track a little way. Should be easy to pull out. The old boy was raving on about someone must have put in the wrong fuel because it had been running rough since leaving Taumaranui."

Bob gulped.

"Know anything about that?" asked Jim.

"Nothing."

Bob resolved to drain the Range Rover's tank if there was anything left of it as soon as he got to the scene.

"Help yourself to another pie, Jim, and make yourself a coffee. Take your time. I can handle the wreck."

By the time Bob had the wreck hooked up Jim arrived to escort him back to Taumaranui, strobe lights flashing an eerie warning to other motorists. Not that there were any at that time of the night. After Bob had dropped the wreck alongside a few other carcasses and secured the yard Jim gave Bob a cheery wave and shouted that he'd come and inspect the wreck in the morning. Bob could have sworn Jim winked at him. On the other hand they were both dog-tired and he could have imagined it.

Bob was still feeling pretty groggy when he opened up at seven. Even on a Saturday morning there was always a farmer who was still loyal to Bob, although he could have got whatever it was he wanted cheaper from the franchise on the by-pass. One thing he didn't have to worry about was Jim nosing around the Range Rover's fuel tank, crushed beyond recognition, its contents disappeared. Good job he hadn't charged comb-over for the little amount of petrol he'd put in by mistake.

By midday the fog had lifted and so had Bob's spirits. He was in the throes of closing down for the day and about to head up to Patel's to see if the old boy wanted to go with him to the RSA when 'Slant' Winiata's taxi drew up on the forecourt. Most people thought Slant got his nickname because his left eye had a curious slant. Bob knew better because one slow night Slant had confided in him he got the name back in the day when he favoured Chrysler Valiants for taxis and they had the famous 'slant 6' engine.

Bob's spirits reversed when he saw clambering out of the taxi the Jafa ski couple from the Range Rover. He knew it was them, because the man was on crutches and the girl had her left arm in a sling and sported a bandage on her forehead. She looked none too pleased.

"There he is, Dickie. That's the man." She pointed at Bob, sounding not at all as girlish as 'Baby' of the previous night.

"I want a word with you." Dickie endeavoured to sound authoritative, but his words came out a wheeze and ended in a weak cough.

"Get a grip, Dickie. You tell him we're going to sue." Definitely un-babyish.

"Sue me for what?" Bob wiped his hands nonchalantly on an oily rag.

"You know damn well what," Dickie croaked. "You put something in my fuel tank last night."

"You've got a nerve, mate. I put only fuel in your tank and I've got the till receipt to prove it."

Which was true, sort of. Anyway it was an honest mistake.

The confrontation took the stuffing out of Dickie, who sagged on his crutches. Baby got her pout back and said to Dickie that they should get their belongings out of the Range Rover, and turned to walk away.

"Your vehicle is out the back in my yard with the other wrecks," Bob called.

"Show us then," Baby demanded.

"No can do. Police have to give me the OK first."

"You mean you're the police impound facility?"

Dickie looked disgustedly at Bob.

"How are we going to get our luggage and get home?" Baby sulked like a baby again.

"You're insured, aren't you?" asked Bob. "They usually spring for a rental car."

Dickie hung his head.

"Only got it last week. Finance company owns most of it. Could only afford third party."

"Dickie, you creep. You told me you were rich. I suppose the finance company owns the boat and house as well?"

Dickie's silence confirmed Baby's guess.

"I'm leaving. Send me my bag when you get it. Don't bother bringing it around yourself!"

With that she marched off down Hakiaha Street towards the station.

"Good luck with a train," Bob mouthed.

"What?" Dickie croaked.

"Only one train a day and it's already gone. Mind you, the bus to Auckland is due any minute. You might be lucky."

Dickie glared at Bob, the effect spoiled by his weakened state. He hobbled off after Baby.

Bob watched them go, indifferent to whether or not they caught the bus, glad nevertheless that he had, hopefully, seen

72

the last of them. He knew he would be joined to their affairs, or Dickie's anyway, for weeks if not months as bureaucracy worked its way towards signing off on the wreck.

Bob finished locking up the workshop and looked up the street to see if Patel's dairy was still open. Patel leaned on the door gazing, for something to do, at the inter-city bus stop where an altercation was taking place between the driver and what Patel took to be father and daughter dressed in ski clothes.

Bob wandered up and tapped him on the shoulder.

"Come on, mate. Close up and I'll shout you a couple at the RSA."

"Ok, brother. Be right with you."

As they strolled the near deserted streets the early afternoon winter sun warmed their backs. Bob was content even though he was weary and knew he'd have to open up the next day, Sunday as the skiers returned to the big smoke. But for now he was where he wanted to be.

"I've had a bit of an idea," he said. "Wouldn't be hard to slow those fat-cat Jafas down when they stop for fuel. Amazing how delicate modern engines are to a splash of the wrong stuff. Maybe bring in a bit of extra business all round. After all, they're the ones making the decisions in their ivory towers that have turned this place into a ghost town."

Patel looked hard at Bob.

"Better go on that world cruise *before* we land in goal for the rest of our lives."

"Ok, mate. I'll get on my smart phone first thing Monday. World cruise it is!"

▲　　▲　　▲

PEOPLE,
ACTUALLY

The only good thing about tabloids since they shrunk from broad-sheet is that they are easier to read outside in a breeze. Quicker too, because the intellectual rigour of the contents has atrophied along with the size.

These thoughts were knocking about in my brain as I contemplated what was certain to be another fruitless search through the pages of what purported to be the nation's premier daily. I hoped my eye would land on an article I'd missed the first two times. Even if it was about rugby.

I *could* have stirred from the pleasant bench thoughtfully provided by the city fathers and, presumably these days, mothers. I *could* have given up enjoying the late summer sun on my back. I *could* have got up and wandered along the shops and pried my wife out of one of them. I *could* have sat awkwardly alone and mimicked the effete coffee drinkers in one of the many cafes. I *could* have trekked to the dairy inconveniently situated at the far end of the shops and bought an ice-cream and a magazine. Instead I chose to remain seated.

From my vantage point I occasionally glanced down the street with shops either side apparently containing things irresistible to people who, fortified by designer coffee, were beguiled by fashion, kitchens, bathrooms and antiques. I have noticed that these people tend to be women, of whom, thankfully, my wife is one.

I considered seeing Marjory happily wasting avaricious shop assistants' time worth the small cost of being bored by a newspaper whose content meant that strictly speaking it could only be called a 'paper. If there had been a bookshop I would have entertained myself browsing, wishing I could afford, for once, to buy brand new. Luckily for my fiscal position book shops are as scarce as broadsheets.

I knew my wife would end her foray empty handed. She was as aware as I of the parlous state of our finances. We'd agreed that a little window shopping was justified on our way home after the emotional challenge of pretending to be thrilled at Marjory's niece's belated marriage to the man who'd fathered her third child.

Every so often I caught a glimpse of my wife as she emerged, empty handed, from one emporium and headed like a cruise missile for the next target. If she caught me watching she gave a little wave. Who would have thought after all these years that simple little gesture, as though connected to my heart by electric wire, could cause it to miss a beat. 'I'm a lucky bugger,' I thought, considering.

"Mind if sit here?" A voice interrupted my reverie.

Actually I did, coveting my solitude amidst city bustle, but said, "Not at all. Here, take my newspaper if you want."

"What? That rag! There's never anything worth reading in it. All gossip and scandal."

I looked sharply at the voice's owner not sure how this person of indeterminate gender had read my mind.

"My thoughts exactly."

I studied my co-bench warmer, who was dressed in the sort of outfit that not even a self-respecting farmhand would wear. Even so I saw she was a female. I guessed she was homeless, therefore a drug addict, therefore a prostitute and no doubt a single parent. I had her pegged, despite the fact there weren't many of her sort down the Kiwitahi Valley. So I didn't exactly have a lot of experience to call on.

I was a little out of my depth, and foolish for feeling so. Nevertheless I couldn't help being slightly intimidated by the proximity of someone who, had she appeared on the doorstep of the Morrinsville pub, would have been as much of a curiosity as a visitor from Mars.

I wished Marjory would come back. She was good in awkward social situations. Unlike me. Nothing the farm threw at me caused me as much bother as social occasions, except the drought we were going through for the second year running.

I stood up.

"You off then?"

"I said I'd meet my wife along there." I pointed vaguely in the direction of the shops. I hoped mentioning my wife might choke off the girl.

"I'm going that way." She stood up. "I'll walk with you."

I sat down again. I didn't want to walk along the street in broad daylight with a vagrant, addict, prostitute. It wasn't Marjory I was worried about. She would probably think it funny then disarm the girl with genuine concern. It was the feeling that this embryonic encounter was out of my control.

I didn't like the feeling. I was used to controlling events often dire and dangerous as half tonne bulls whirled around the pens desperate to escape even if it was right over me.

"Not off then?"

I could hear the scorn in the girl's voice as she assumed she knew why I'd changed my mind.

Her question was rhetorical, and the next let me off the hook.

"What are you doing hanging around here for anyway?"

"Passing through." I was determined to keep her nose out of my business.

"Passing through from where?"

"Wife likes a bit of shopping when we come to the city. Window shopping actually." Which was the truth; although I could see the girl thought I was pandering to her destitution.

"Yeah, right," she scoffed. "Passing through from where?" she insisted.

"South Waikato near Morrinsville."

"Got a farm there, have we?"

"Yeah. Not much of one right now." I couldn't keep the bitterness out of my voice.

"Why's that?" She answered her own question. "Drought."

I nodded. "Second year in a row.

"Global warming, I expect."

"You'd know, of course." My turn for scorn.

My opinion of global warming was that it was a fiction trotted out when the effort of sourcing real hard news got too much for the mainstream media. I'd worked the land all my life and seen the extremes of weather come and go. The human race is insignificant compared to the power of nature. I would become a believer when sea levels rose high enough to bring forth another Noah. About as likely as the second coming.

"Well, no. It's just what rags like this rabbit on about."

She screwed up my newspaper.

Just then a skinny guy sauntered up to the girl and planted himself in front of her without looking at me. He was wearing drainpipe trousers, a white singlet and a pink boa draped around his neck and enough piercings that, for him, metal detectors would render overseas travel an impossible dream.

"What are you gassing to this old fart for?" he demanded of the girl.

A bit aggressively, I thought, for a poofter.

"Just trying to narrow the rural-urban divide," she said coolly. "As if it's any of your business."

Again I looked sharply at her. I couldn't decide if she was taking the mickey or what. If she wasn't so self-possessed and clearly unimpressed by the rude interloper I would have stood up yet again and then we would have seen who was an old fart.

I remained seated, interested to see what these city folk would do next.

"Come on Suze," whined the shirt lifter. "If we hurry we'll make it down the benefit before it closes."

"You go," she said. "I'm all right."

"Come on. Don't waste your time with this fascist." He grabbed the girl's arm.

I stood up and took a step towards him. He let go.

"Fuck you," he said as he minced off in a huff.

"Friend of yours?" I said.

"Not exactly. Just someone who hangs around here. Thanks for standing up for me. Pinky can get stroppy if his fix is a bit slow in working its way into his system."

"So, your name's Suze, is it?" I sat down.

I realised that despite my intention to be reticent she knew a lot about me. She knew I was visiting from our drought-stricken farm in the Waikato; that my wife was down the street shopping; that I didn't think much of global warming and was uncomfortable talking to her. All I knew about her was her name, or thought I did.

"Susan, actually. What's yours?"

I stood up again. It occurred to me that since my peace was disturbed I'd been hopping up and down like a jack-in-the box. I didn't feel right giving her my name. I'd given enough.

"What's the matter? Don't want someone like me to know your name? Frightened I'll put the hard word on you?"

"Well, Susan Actually, where I come from we take a little time to get to know another person. It's got something to do with that old-fashioned thing called trust."

I cringed inwardly at how pompous I sounded. For all my distrust of this alien creature, for some deep reason completely lost to my rational self, I still wanted her to think well of me.

At least not to think I was a typical pontificating, right-wing, rich farmer.

She looked at me speculatively as though she was about to say something, but thought better of it.

"Here comes my wife." At last.

Marjory had barely noticed the girl so was slightly taken aback when I introduced her. I was rather more surprised by Marj's reaction.

"Nice to meet a local, Ian," she said before turning to the girl. "What have you been talking about that kept my husband, known for his extremely short attention span, glued to this bench?"

She gave me a smile to take the sting out of her comment. I had expected Marjory to be off-hand, dismissive, perhaps, given the girl looked like a generic low-life.

"We were trying to close the rural-urban divide." I said, parroting the girl's earlier words.

The girl blurted, even though we hadn't asked her name, "My name's not really Susan."

I thought she was about to explain. Instead, she fell silent before saying enigmatically, "You shouldn't judge a book by its cover."

"Are you in trouble?" My heart-of-gold Marj couldn't ignore someone in need. "Is there anything we can do to help? You look as though you need it."

The girl, Susan – or maybe not – shook her head and stood up.

"Got to go," she said. "Places to go, people to see. Nice meeting you. Maybe in another life..." She let her sentence trail off.

We walked with her down the street to where our car was parked.

"This is us," I said. "Can we drop you somewhere, Susan Actually?"

She smiled and shook her head and we watched her amble down the street.

In the car creeping along embroiled in the city's afternoon rush hour madness I couldn't help thinking about the girl. From her silence I knew Marjory was too.

I broke the silence. "Strange place, the big city, with poor souls like Susan adrift and vulnerable. Not to mention Pinky, who you missed, thank goodness."

"I saw Pinky. I saw you protect the girl too. Fancy her, did you?"

Marjory's candour revealed her absolute certainty of my devotion.

"You know I've only ever fancied one person in my life and she's sitting next to me right now." I laughed and continued, "I think the girl could have been pretty under the grime and those rags she was wearing. If anything she reminded me of the waste of potential. She seemed way brighter than her situation would suggest. If she'd been our daughter she wouldn't have been out on the streets shooting up and prostituting herself."

"How do you know she was doing that?"

"I don't exactly. I'm letting my inbuilt bigotry and learned prejudice have free reign."

This time we both laughed, and that was the last we spoke about the girl.

Except, as we cruised down the Bombay Hill and could see the Waikato basin laid out before us in all its mediocrity of brown, but still cherished home to us, Marj spoke again.

"Meeting someone like that girl sort of makes me wish we'd had a girl. We could have been good parents; given her a good life or a chance at one."

"Or a boy," I said. "*And* a boy."

Every now and again when we least expected it the subject reared up. We'd learned long ago to leave this particular regret alone. The time for doing anything about it was long past. We'd never followed up just which of us couldn't procreate, preferring not to know and open the corrosive trail to blame. Maybe it was both of us. I hoped so.

"Yes, a boy as well would have been nice," she sighed then laughed. "Listen to me, getting all maudlin. Maybe it was seeing all those kids at the wedding. More likely because you wouldn't let me buy anything."

"As if I could stop you. Anyway I thought you said you didn't see anything you wanted?"

I was glad she'd snapped herself out of thinking about things that could never be.

"I'm so looking forward to getting home to the real world."

"Me, too." She reached across to take my free hand as she often did when we were driving. "Me, too."

As we nearly always did after the heat and dust of a working day, Marjory and I were sitting on the lounger under the veranda chewing over the day and planning the next.

Not that the day had thrown up anything much out of what passes for ordinary on our spread. The boys had brought in a couple of mobs of bulls without major incident as we continued to de-stock in front of the drought. Nobody had been thrown, the horses stayed on their feet, nobody cut, trampled or injured except Billy's pride when he'd scrambled for safety after being caught by a bull who decided a one–way trip in a stock truck to be turned into hamburger meat was not for him.

"Hello, who's this?" Marjory said spotting a car, too far away to make out, turning into the road gate.

The rising plume of dust marked its progress until it emerged from the avenue of trees that marked the fence line of the home holding paddock.

"Strewth, it's a cop car. Something must be up. Clive wouldn't be paying us a social call this time of day. Hope the lads are OK. They said they were stopping at the pub for a few quick ones on their way home."

As it drew closer we could see it wasn't a local police car. Slowing down, it rattled over the cattle-stop and onto the circular drive to pull up almost in front of where we were sitting.

I stood up as a uniformed police officer with sergeant's chevrons on her sleeves climbed out of the car. She seemed vaguely familiar.

"Mr and Mrs McCutcheon?" she said.

Her voice sounded familiar, too. We nodded, minds racing over possible scenarios of the disaster about to befall us. The hands hardly had time to get into trouble in town yet. Must be family, although I couldn't think of any close enough to warrant the personal conveyance of bad news.

"You don't remember me?" The officer looked expectantly at us then answered her own question. "Susan from Mount Eden shops a month or so ago."

"Right, now we do." I glanced at Marj for confirmation.

"Hello, dear." She greeted Susan as though it was the most normal thing in the world for a vagrant last seen on the mean streets to transform herself into a police sergeant and find her way to Kiwitahi.

"We're having a coffee. Please join us."

"If you are Susan what are you doing impersonating a police officer and stealing police vehicles?" I was only half-joking.

"I confess." She held up her arms in surrender. "I am a police officer, and my real name isn't Susan and never has been.... actually."

She laughed at her own wit.

"OK, then, not-Susan Actually, how did you find us? I don't recall giving you my name."

"Your car rego was easy for an officer of the law to track down. My real name is Justine. Justine Walker"

"What are you doing here, Justine Walker? Did we break some big city bylaw?"

"Come on, Ian," Marjory interjected. "Give the poor girl a chance. She's come a long way."

Marj beckoned the sergeant to step up on the veranda and bustled off to the kitchen to reappear with a mug of coffee and a generous slice of chocolate cake.

"Thank you so much," said Justine. "I'm famished."

Though envious – where had that cake been when Marj and I had coffee? – I gave her time to scoff most of it before I said, "You haven't answered my question."

"You've probably guessed. I was working undercover when I met you in the city. I was just about at the end of my tether. Undercover is exhausting and awfully lonely mixing twenty-four seven with the sort of people you'd normally avoid like the plague. Except to arrest them, of course."

She smiled.

"The bust came down a few days after that. Meeting you gave me the strength to hold out through the last phase. It made me remember that not everyone's a junky ratbag like Pinky. That there are normal people out there beyond the Bombays living proper lives, real lives."

"Still doesn't explain why you're here," I said.

"The way you stood instinctively to defend me when you clearly didn't approve of me, and you, Marjory, offering help to someone like me, or someone you thought me to be. Not one other person had done so in the three months I'd been undercover. That touched me deeply. You seemed a little sad and lost as though something was missing, despite your outward appearances."

She paused to take a breath and waited to see what we would say. Not inclined to give much away, Marjory and I said nothing.

"As soon as duty allowed I had to come and see for myself if you were real." She paused. "If you were all right," she added softly.

Marj and I stayed silent while we absorbed what seemed a confession of sorts from this person who'd emerged out of a chance meeting we'd almost forgotten. A meeting of such little consequence to us had, it seemed, meant much to Justine.

Marj, as usual, ended the awkwardness, topping up the girl's coffee.

"If you can stay the night," she said, "tomorrow we'll show you just how real our farm is even though it's not looking the best right now. Not much happens on the weekends, especially in a drought. The boys won't be here tomorrow so we'll have the place to ourselves."

Next morning with a sun bright enough to make the shade under the veranda a cool haven, the conversation flowed easily. Like the cups of tea we drank as we demolished a 'full Kiwitahi,' as Marjory called her breakfast of home-made sausages, bacon and eggs. We learnt more than we needed to know about the life of a female city cop, and were fascinated anyway.

Justine was equally curious about our life on the land. She repeated, as she scanned the horizon, how peaceful and lovely the farm was, how lucky we were despite the dust and brownness. We knew that, took it for granted, almost.

"Wonder what Billy's coming out here for?" I'd seen his ute, unmistakable even that far away, turn in the road gate in a power slide, scudding up a trail of dust.

"He's in a hurry," said Marj, as the ute came on raising a plume like a steam train at full throttle. "I'll get him a plateful. He'll be hungry. He always is."

"Billy's our top hand," I explained to Justine. "Well, he's more than that. He's my foreman. Been with us nearly five years. Came to us after he'd had a bit of bother with the law. Clive, our local copper, straightened him out and what with one thing and another Billy ended up here and never looked back. Never will now, I expect."

The ute that I knew was black under the dust slid to a stop behind Justine's police car. Out jumped Billy, his face troubled.

"Everything all right, boss?"

"Why wouldn't it be?" I couldn't resist stringing him along, with the police car plainly in view.

"Ran into Clive this morning. Said he'd had a call from Mrs Jackson. She'd seen a police car turn in here last evening and was calling to see if everything was OK. Clive didn't know. Is it?" He gestured at the police car as though ready to battle it with his bare fists in my defence.

"Settle down, lad. Nothing's wrong. The opposite, *actually*."

I glanced at Justine, acknowledging what had become our in-joke. She hadn't moved from her chair in the shade of the veranda.

"Come up here and have some breakfast and meet our guest."

Billy, adjusting to the sun's bright contrast, hadn't noticed Justine in the veranda's shadow. This morning she'd changed her uniform for jeans and T-shirt. She stood up.

"Billy, this is Sergeant Justine Walker."

Billy, as laconic as he was lanky and unused to being intimidated, was struck dumb. I had to laugh, and Marjory did too, recalling our first encounter with Justine as a vagrant and the impression she would make on the locals if she ever came down here. Now here she was and Justine might as well have come from Mars by the look on Billy's face.

"Ian and I were going to show Justine around the farm after breakfast, but I'm not feeling up to it." Marjory shot a warning glance at me to keep my mouth shut.

I nodded as though I was aware she was unwell.

"Would you mind standing in for us, Billy? After breakfast, perhaps."

"Be an honour, Mrs Mac," Billy found his voice.

We watched as the two of them, already deep in conversation, strolled towards the gate that led to the hill track behind the yards.

"I know what you're thinking," I said.

"I know you think you do." Marj gave me that wistful smile I knew so well. "But you're wrong. I'm not."

"Oh," I said, drifting into upsetting territory and unable to stop myself. "Aren't you hoping we might have given serendipity a little nudge?" I nodded at the rapidly diminishing figures striding up the track.

"You think I'm seeing those two as the kids we never had or even, for heaven's sake, the grandchildren that will never be?"

"Well...." I was hedging and she knew it.

"No, Ian. Those regrets are long gone. We can't keep saying 'if only.' Who knows what might have been. I *might* have died in childbirth, the child *might* have died, he or she *might* have become what we thought Justine really was. There are so many *mights* and *could haves* that it's pointless to go there."

She paused to catch her breath.

"We love it here. This is our life, and it only needs to have a good meaning for us."

Up the track the couple had disappeared over the ridge.

"Who knows what the future holds for those two? Maybe we'll be lucky and it'll be something that keeps us in the loop. And if not, it doesn't matter. I'm with you every day and every night and in the end that's all that matters."

I thought back to my encounter with the vagrant who turned out to be Justine. I remembered sitting in the sun thinking of all the things I *could* have done and doing none of them, enjoying the moment.

I looked at Marjory and marvelled. No matter how long I'd been with this person who was everything to me, knowing much of what was in her mind and even what she'd say next, it was always wonderful to hear her say it out loud.

"For someone who's supposed to be unwell you sure make a lot of sense."

I wrapped my arms around her and planted a smacker on her forehead.

"I'd better clean up the breakfast stuff. You put your feet up."

"Hah!" was all she said, linking her arm through mine as we headed for the kitchen.

EASY
MONEY

"Like a bit of the other, do you?" Joel, the gang boss, flirted with me as soon as the owner of the orchard left the harvest gang to it.

"Depends who with." I wished he would shut up and leave me alone. I also wished I'd had the nous not to respond from the beginning.

It crossed my mind that if I was going to have 'a bit of the other' it wouldn't be with a sweaty uncouth lech like Joel. I should have slapped the bastard on day one. But I needed the money.

The kiwifruit picking job had been advertised on the notice board at the backpackers. Also studying the notice board were a couple of German guys. Their Teutonic accent made me do a double take in case they were taking the mickey. This pair seemed genuine enough and said they'd made good money.

"How come sexy girl like you travels without friend?" asked the dishy one.

"My boyfriend's coming soon." I hoped that would choke him off.

In truth I'd been travelling alone since Brenda had taken off. I'd befriended the Aussie girl down the South Island and she'd taken off early one morning while I slept off a night out in Queenstown. She'd also taken off with my 'get out of jail' stash of the folding stuff. Bitch. Thank goodness for debit cards. Now I needed to give my balance a boost, and according to the German guys picking kiwifruit was how to do it.

If I hadn't been so short of readies I would've told Joel, the gang boss, where to get off. I've noticed how so many of the blokes I meet think us English girls are easy. Many are. Then so are Aussie girls if Brenda was anything to go by. She'd of shagged sleaze-ball gang boss up against a vine trunk by now. Still, she was shaped a bit like a tree trunk herself so couldn't afford to be picky.

"Ah, you haff boyfriend," said the German. "He is lucky guy to haff pretty fraulein like you."

"Thank you," I said, smiling sweetly.

If I had a boyfriend he *would* be lucky. I already knew I was pretty; I'd been told often enough. It *must* be right when you've heard it constantly ever since you were old enough to understand what being pretty meant. Who was I to argue when adults gave me things? And being attractive to men had its benefits though, for that matter, constant come-ons from greasy gang bosses, or Germans flirting with you, wasn't among them.

Picking kiwifruit or manual labour of any kind wasn't my ideal way of making money, but there didn't seem to be anything else on offer. Usually I managed to find bar work or waitressing, even the occasional hostess job at some event or other.

In this buttoned-up town there was nothing for it but to break the habits of a life-time, get up early and help bring in the harvest. Almost romantic, until the weight of the full picking bag strung like an apron around my neck threatened to drag me to my knees.

My first day on the job I watched as others furiously plucked the fruit, dropping them into bags as nonchalantly as though the bags were gossamer light. I struggled to stay upright.

I'd managed to pick a couple of bags full and tip them into the waiting bins on a flatbed trailer towed by a tractor when the gang boss sidled alongside. To be fair he did help me tip out the bag, sending the fruit cascading into the half full bin. I was so grateful I made the mistake of gushing, "You're a sweetie."

"Aren't I just? he leered, and ice broken, pestered me with ever more lewd suggestions. Mostly it was OK, because in the picking gang it was easy not be left alone with him.

In the orchard it was gloomy even in daytime under the dense overhead canopy of vines strung on wires above our heads. When we worked a bit later into the evening to finish a field it got so dark we could hardly see to pick.

This was when Joel took his chance and contrived to be alone with me. Laden with my picking bag and defenceless he came stealthily up behind me and put his hand up my shirt. He'd done it twice. Each time I spat at him, but he just laughed, certain I wouldn't do anything about it.

Through the gloom and partly obscured by the trunks of the vines, I saw him a couple of rows over, levelling off the fruit in the bins on the trailer. That's when I saw my chance as the tractor began to move. He couldn't see or hear me coming. I pushed him in front of the trailer wheels, yelling "Stop! Help!" as soon as the wheels had run over both his legs.

I was surprised at the fuss. This country isn't as laid back, 'she'll be right' as it seemed. The police got involved, and the workplace health and safety people, too. I thought that sort of officiousness was the preserve of those EU wankers.

Joel was in no condition to point the finger at me and who'd believe him anyway? It's never been hard for me to fake a few tears. In the end, it was put down to a 'work-place accident.' Thanks largely to Ralph. He was the German, who I'd labelled Goebbels because of his uncommon resemblance to that Nazi thug. He stuck up for me, said he'd seen the whole thing and the gang boss had slipped just as the tractor driver had called out to keep clear.

Ralph demanded I pay off my debt behind the locked laundry door of the hostel later that evening. 'No-balls Goebbels' certainly didn't apply in his case.

The next day the orchard owner introduced us to the new gang boss. A taciturn bloke, Rangi proved impervious to any attempt to charm him into lightening my burden.

"Must be gay," I whispered to Ralph. He wasn't amused. Germans have no sense of humour.

I had another go at Rangi, the new gang boss, after lunch. I was sprawled on the grass eating my sandwich and let my shirt fall open. There was a flicker of interest in his eyes as I met his gaze full on in that suggestive way that gets them every time.

"Why's a nice girl like you doing a crap job like this?"

A hackneyed line I'd heard variations of a million times before that still made me cringe.

"Travel funds, mate."

My fingers made slow progress buttoning up my shirt, and his eyes followed every move.

"Better get back to work, hadn't we?" I rose slowly stretching up my arms.

"Yeah," he stammered, cheeks flushed with colour. "Back to work."

Not so gay after all!

As the gang settled back into work after lunch, Herr Ralph contrived to work alongside me. By now I'd got into the rhythm of the task, hands dexterously plucking the furry brown fruit in a never-ending stream into my bag. Then off I'd waddle as if hugely pregnant to the bins for momentary relief before starting once again.

"Vot you vont to make the sexy eyes to that native person for?"

I laughed. "Ralph, I do believe you're jealous."

"Not jealous," he blustered, "it is not proper for girl like you to be talking in that manner with native persons."

"You can't be serious." I stared at him, astonished.

"Very serious. You must not......," he searched for a word, "... *entice* that black man anymore."

"I'll entice anybody I like, buster. Get that into your thick German blockhead."

I'd miss the laundry room that night, but a girl has to stand up, or should that be 'lie down,' for her rights.

I couldn't help flirting with the new gang boss. Power even at this pathetically low level always brought out the slut in me. Besides, it infuriated Ralph. He became more and more incensed. I imagined steam rising from his head.

He copied my ploy. He made his move at the end of the day when the gang boss was jotting down the tally and the rest of the gang were trudging back to the yard. I trailed along, turning as I heard a commotion and the two of them were exchanging blows.

"No, stop." I said quietly, deliberately waiting until they'd both run out of steam. Ralph had a cut lip and Rangi a bruised cheek.

Beyond my comprehension and annoyingly they appeared to make up after the fight and studiously ignored me. I resigned myself to buckling down, shoulder to the wheel, best foot forward, and all those other hilarious clichés my parents trotted out.

After a week or so I realised I hadn't noticed the weight of kiwifruit round my neck. I'd kept up with the gang, bag for bag, bin for bin. The German boys continued to ignore me, as did the gang boss. My tan was as deep as Rangi's natural bronze. I was fit and strong. Wouldn't go so far as to say the work was enjoyable, but it was satisfying. I'd earned my wine at night around the hostel dinner table. The other girls stopped looking at me with malicious envy. I'd become one of the boys for the first time in my life.

Things were looking rosy until Brenda turned up, the bitch Aussie who'd lifted my stash in Queenstown. We were deep in the middle of a vast orchard whose rows of vines stretched into the distance when the gang boss announced that another gang that had finished elsewhere was joining ours.

I saw Brenda straight away and laughed scornfully at her inept picking. She must have only just started with the other gang. She didn't seem to recognise me, and that was a puzzle until I realised I had changed out of sight from the pale and pretty girl I'd been. The sun and hard work had turned this English rose into Boadicea.

I contemplated giving her a gentle nudge like I'd done to poor old Joel. Easy as to make her lose her balance just as the tractor surged up the row with its full bins of fruit. Before I gave into temptation, I realised that apart from getting my money back I didn't care a jot about Brenda, and maybe it would cost me my job this time.

Ironically the Germans had forgotten their Aryan supremacy and were now best mates with the gang boss, freezing me out. I guessed they wouldn't be averse to dobbing me in for grievous bodily harm if I tried the same trick with the bin trailer.

I watched with mild amusement as the Germans and the gang boss tried out their crude charm on Brenda.

"Getting desperate, boys?" I taunted. "Be like fucking a hippo. Besides, she'll never fit into the laundry room."

They gave me a dirty look and said nothing. Didn't stop them laying it on for Brenda though. I could have told them they were wasting energy; she'd spread her legs for the asking provided there was something of the folding kind in exchange.

My prediction proved correct a few evenings later. First the gang boss, then the Germans, one after the other, exited the dining room, looking so innocent they had to be guilty of something. I had to chuckle. I followed the haughty, handsome

German, whose unlikely name was Herman. Sure enough the laundry door was locked and the sounds of debauchery came from within, though the grunting and groaning sounded just like hippos mating in the pen at Whipsnade Zoo.

This got to be a regular thing. To my disgust the boys, despite being obviously knackered, helped Brenda as the day wore on. They marked up her half-empty bags as full loads, cheating the rest of us in the process. I was the only one who seemed to notice. I tossed up whether to dob the cheats in to the orchard owner. On reflection I decided I'd get my money back first, with a bonus if the opportunity presented itself.

I waited until they'd locked the laundry door from the inside then for good measure clipped a padlock through the eye bracket on the outside. I couldn't stifle my mirth, but *no worries*, as the Kiwis say. Nothing distracted the hippos inside.

I made my way to Brenda's room, which the silly cow hadn't bothered to lock. The slovenly bitch had strewn clothes everywhere and the detritus of a backpacker's life overflowed from the rubbish bin. Beauty products, a lost cause in her case, no doubt filched from hotels, covered the surface of the vanity. I searched her bags and found what I was looking for, and some!

My two hundred quid was there all right, not to mention a stack of dollars, Kiwi, American, even a few Aussie ones. My conscience got the better of me (sometimes I surprise myself, it must have something to do with my British upbringing.) and I took only what she had pinched from me. She was probably too careless to notice.

All this had taken less time than I'd anticipated. I knew it would take the hippos an embarrassingly long time to attract attention and get that padlock unlocked. I decided to check out the Germans' room. I didn't expect to find anything and as soon as I saw how anally neat and tidy it was I knew that my expectation would be met. I left without bothering to open even one drawer.

The gang boss's room was at the end of the corridor. In for a penny, in for a pound. Not as tidy as the Germans, and any impulse to check out his stuff died as I glanced from the open door at his pathetic possessions. Then I noticed his tally book on the desk and out of curiosity took a dekko to see if my suspicions were correct that he'd been crediting Brenda more than she'd picked.

Sure enough he had and the Germans too, the bastards. From the daily tally they weren't skimming enough from us that we would miss it, but added up over time it would still amount to a tidy sum. The bins had to tally up with what was loaded out on the trucks so it meant he was dunning the rest of us in the gang by crediting us with less. I knew that the others lost track of the tally like I did. Every day I promised myself to keep score, but as the day heats up and the sweat flows everything blurs and it's hard to keep count.

I debated with myself what to do about the little scam they had running. I considered cutting myself in, but that would mean cutting everyone else short even more. Surely someone savvy would notice sooner or later. I could dob the bastards in. Or I could do nothing.

Or I could let them know I knew what they were up to and they'd better stop or else. For that I needed the tally book as leverage. I had a little think about the situation; examined my conscience, so to speak, and found it wanting. A full turnaround from five minutes before. So much for my British upbringing.

I decided they deserved to be cleaned out. So I headed back to Brenda's room and pocketed all the folding I could find. Then I did over the Germans, too. Their stash wasn't hard to find, tucked into a briefcase that might as well be labelled '*rob me.*' Lastly I returned to the gang boss's room and pocketed the tally book. This was for insurance should any of them consider following me or decide to sic the cops onto me.

On the unattended front desk I slapped an envelope with enough dollars to cover what I owed the hostel. I didn't want them on my case even though I knew my backpacking days were over, thank goodness. If I hurried to the stop down the road I could catch the next bus out of this dump that went to the city.

The bus driver said, "That'll be twenty-five bucks, sweetheart."

I knew that was three times the going rate and opened my mouth to protest, then shut it when I realised he thought I was doing a runner without paying the hostel bill. He'd seen it done before and made a little earner out it. On the other hand, ripping me off meant he was likely to keep to himself the fact he'd seen me.

"Shit, fuck!" I mouthed. "Aren't there any honest people left in the world?"

I got out one of Brenda's fifty dollar notes and said, "Keep the change, arsehole."

He did, and kept his mouth shut as he accelerated the bus away towards the bright lights of the city.

LONG AND SHORT

"Whaddya wanna hang out with him for?" I tried not to whine. I hate needy girls, myself included, but sometimes I can't help it.

"What's it to you?" Long could go from passive to aggressive in an instant.

Sometimes she scared the crap out of me. Like now.

"He's a dweeb." As if that meant anything.

"Who says?" She was dismissive. "You?"

"Well, he is. Just because he's in the first fifteen doesn't mean he's got anything between the ears."

"Who cares about the ears?" Long guffawed. "There's plenty between his legs."

I hated it when she embarrassed me by talking dirty. I didn't like to think about boy's anatomy, but Long's coarseness forced me to. She knew it did and enjoyed tormenting me.

"You should give it a try." She nudged me with her elbow. "I bet you've never ever squeezed a guy's nuts?"

Before I'd even begun to formulate the lie my answer would be, the dweeb in question came loping off the footy grounds grinning like a self-congratulatory hyena who'd robbed a lion's kill. He was such an idiot he had no idea that he was the prey and Long the lion.

"Whaddya hanging around for?" Dweeb had no qualms about making me feel bad.

"Leave her alone, you bully. She's my friend." Long deflated Dweeb and inflated me. No wonder I hung out with her.

Dweeb stared at Long hopefully, "I was hoping you and me could go down the domain on our own."

Briefly he turned to me, his twin machine gun eyes spitting bullets, then back to Long.

"Coach said I could finish early while he put the backs through their paces."

"Paces!" I laughed. "The only paces that lot's got are slow and slower."

"Why don't you bugger off?"

Dweeb swung at me the sweaty T-shirt he'd taken off ostensibly to cool down. In reality, to flaunt the torso that sported a few wispy downs of adolescent body hair. One advantage of being short is that I can duck. The sweaty garment swished harmlessly overhead.

"Now, now children." Long stepped in. "There's plenty of me for everyone."

Did she even realise the promiscuous implications of her word choice?

"Short, I'm afraid you will have to bugger off as Dweeby boy so nicely put it. I fancy a stroll through the domain along the river bank. I'll catch you later."

She patted me on the head. I felt like I was being jerked by electric shocks of jealousy. I watched them go. Even as the voltage subsided I had to admit they looked good together. Long, the tallest girl in school by a head alongside Dweeb, the school's star rugby player. They could see eye to eye, I thought maliciously, not only when they were lying down.

Once he had served his purpose Dweeb didn't last long, and neither did I. After years of being oddball friends thrown together by virtue of our disparate height, Long devoted herself to the opposite sex big time.

I was right about one thing. Long was not satisfied with boys her own age. Even one the size of Dweeb was too tame for her. She soon started going out with older guys outside of school; dangerous guys with motorbikes and greasy slicked-back hair. Guys who had jobs and money.

The last term of school was a boring trial for Long. Nearly every morning after assembly, from which her towering person was notably absent, the call came over the loudspeakers for "Caroline Long to report to the headmaster's office immediately."

By then I had fallen out of her orbit, involuntarily I admit. I had no idea whether or not she fronted up to the headmaster's office, but an ugly rumour went around the school that she did and unspeakable things happened behind his hallowed door. I found that hard to swallow. The headmaster was short for a man and bald; aspects that had previously evoked derision from Long.

By the time Long had put in a cursory appearance for the sake of getting her graduation certificate I'd taken up with Angela. She was smart and sexy and only a little bit taller than me. She didn't call me Short because I wasn't compared to her. She said she liked my real name.

"How's it going, Short?" Long ignored Angela as we stood waiting our turn to go on stage and accept our graduation scrolls.

"Quite well, thank you and my name isn't Short anymore."

"Oh yeah? What is it now then?"

Angela spoke up. "Her name is Jacinda, as you well know."

"Whatever." Long made the 'W' sign with her fingers and turned away.

That was the last time I saw Long. After the school holidays I didn't see much of Angela either. She went south to university. I got a job flipping burgers in the Burger Fuel on the corner of Custom and Quay down near the docks.

Some of the guys that came in all hours of the night were hard cases. Eventually I plucked up the courage to say yes when one of them asked me to step around the counter. The wolf whistles were enough to almost make me believe I was pretty.

Not long after that, one particularly handsome trucker offered to show me the tractor unit on his rig, complete with sleeper cab and just about everything required to live.

I found out I wasn't a lesbian which was something of a relief because after Angela I'd found it tough to make a connection. Clearly my heart wasn't truly inclined to the Sapphic.

I'm not ashamed to say I made up for lost time. In the early hours of the morning I was often the only one on duty. The back office, empty at night, had a day bed in case any of the staff were unwell. My regulars came in for more than a burger and I was happy to oblige.

With the New Year approaching, and my departure for university looming, some nights I spent more time in the back office than out front. I guess I was serving customers front and back. Some of my regulars were almost in tears when I told them all good things must end.

Every now and again I read in a fashion magazine about Long modelling. Her height and looks preordained her for that vacuous profession. Though, when I thought about her, which wasn't often, I did wonder how she reconciled her mercurial nature with the boredom that would surely accompany such a passive waste of time.

She must have managed because by the time we were twenty and me in my second year at med school, she was being touted as one of the great cat-walk models. I was pleased for her even though I could barely raise a yawn for her as I slogged away at matters of life and death.

Not that I was above dining out on our shared school days.

"Oh yes," I would say at any gathering that passed for a party, sharing cheap red among impoverished med students. "I knew Caroline Long before she became just Long; it was me who first started calling her that."

Occasionally someone was impressed and wanted to know more about her, but mostly their interest was fleeting. Med students are notoriously hard to impress, and rightly so. I would console myself with a second or third glass of cardboard red when yet another of my anecdotes fell flat.

Med school ground on and we all began to specialise. My student friends dispersed to be replaced by others. Consequently my stories about Long were ever fresh to my new acquaintances. And she helped by forever popping up in the media, often for some scandalous behaviour involving recreational drugs and someone else's husband.

True to my prediction, she did seem to tire of the glamorous modelling world, dropping out of the gossip pages. She resurfaced some time later for critical review on the movie pages of *Entertainment Weekly*.

The parts she got, by virtue of her notoriety, were little more than bit; whore, bar girl and early-in-the-episode murder victim. I went to the movies one precious off-duty evening to test if she'd stir any latent feelings of lust. Seeing her larger than life on screen was astounding.

I'd forgotten how much she resembled a dark version of Uma Thurman. Unfortunately the resemblance was the only thing they had in common. I hadn't realised how accomplished an actress Uma was until I saw Long in her second fleeting screen role. I was glad I'd saved myself embarrassment by going alone to see *Thunder on the Mountain*. Lust remained latent.

After what seemed both like a lifetime and a fleeting instant I became Doctor Jacinda. Something about night work must appeal because, as in my long ago burger days, I found myself volunteering for the duty known ironically among the staff as the graveyard shift of Accident and Emergency.

At Central the time of day made little difference. Every shift was as busy as the other. In an institution amply supplied with beds there was no use for them other than to accommodate the sick, the injured and the dying.

I liked to think my morals had become somewhat elevated since learning over and over again to appreciate the sanctity of life. Or it could have been I was too busy and too exhausted to contemplate shenanigans.

Long's film acting career didn't exactly take off. Despite that she remained in the public eye, not usually for any good reason. Months went by when I didn't give her a thought until a candid picture of her increasingly desperate face featured on the front cover of one of the scandal rags. I confess I ignored the salacious nag in my head and bought a copy telling myself my interest was concern for an old friend.

If the media were to be believed she had lost the haughty self-confidence of her high-school days and become a self-destructive Hollywood wannabe. I sent her a sympathetic email when I read of her melt-down after she bust up with her fiancé, Ben Lomond who was now enjoying a very public affair with his latest leading lady.

I deleted the long message I composed. When I re-read it before hitting the send button I sounded too much like a needy trying to get close to a celeb. Instead I wrote '*Anything I can do? Keeping it short from Short.*' I guess either there was nothing or she didn't remember me.

Two years into my stint at Central I was considered an old hand in the A and E. Although the work was entirely satisfying, when I was offered a promotion to general ward doctor I took it. A and E was all-consuming and I'd miss everything except the exhaustion. In all that time I hadn't given my private life more than a passing thought. No one among the staff had piqued more than a fleeting interest and, no doubt, vice versa.

While I was lazing on the beach the weekend after my last night-shift and before I started on the wards, I noticed a couple entwined on a beach towel a few metres along. I realised with a pang that I hadn't slept with a man since Doctor McNeish after the staff New Year party nearly twelve months before.

To be honest that encounter wasn't anything to write home about. It did remind me marginally of my tarty burger days, but no way enough to tempt me back into bad habits. Nevertheless I envied the sandy couple their passion and refrained from calling out 'Get a room.' I returned to my book until I could ignore them no longer, when I packed up and left the beach.

As I passed the corner dairy, I popped in on impulse and bought a gossip rag. I flopped onto one of the chairs set al fresco out front of the cafe next door and ordered an espresso. I opened my magazine and was confronted by Long's tear-streaked face. Her mascara had run and she looked old and ugly. Yet she was still only my age, thirty-two.

I felt sad for her. Sorry that her shot at the celebrity life seemed to bring her so much grief. The photographer had taken advantage by snapping the most unflattering picture possible of her drunken episode. Reading the gleefully malicious story made me weep in sympathy for my old friend. Or maybe I was sorry for how she'd wasted her opportunities and I'd done nothing to help as our lives diverged.

"Everything all right?" A man had stopped, casting his shadow over my table.

"Yes, sure." I took a breath, regained the composure I was hardly aware I'd abandoned.

"You're sure?"

"Quite sure, thank you."

Something about him was familiar although as I squinted into the sun I couldn't tell what. He didn't move.

"I was reading about my friend, my old school friend."

I pointed at the open magazine with Long's picture predominant.

"I used to know her too." He leaned forward to study the picture, then turned to me. "Hey, you're Short aren't you?"

Nobody had called me that for years. I put on my shades and inspected him properly.

"Good heavens! It can't be Dweeb, can it?"

I barely recognised the man grown from the boy who had been Long's plaything centuries ago.

"Dwayne." He corrected me gently, giving no sign he was offended at the disparaging name I'd used reflexively.

"Sad, eh?" He pointed at Long's picture.

I didn't remember him as being the type to be concerned with anyone other than himself but maybe we were all like that when we were teenagers. Most of us grow out of being self-absorbed to some extent, some more than others.

"She didn't manage to grow out of being a taker giving nothing back. Comes from always being the centre of attention, I suppose."

"Wasn't her fault she was so tall. Couldn't help but *be* the centre of attention." Dwayne sounded as though he was apologising for Long's fall from grace.

He brightened up.

"Look Short – Jacinda – I'm running behind a manic schedule." He nodded at a giant truck and trailer rig I'd barely noticed pull up in the parking bay short of the cafe. "I was heading into the dairy for a pie and thought you might be in trouble. Gotta run, but it was great seeing you."

With that he dodged into the dairy and out again, Four-'n-Twenty in hand. I marvelled at how such a big man could move so gracefully. He quickly had the rig started and easing into traffic with a wave and a farewell blast on twin airhorns.

"Bye, Dwayne," I mouthed to no-one as the rig was lost to sight in traffic. I wrote on the margin of Long's picture the phone number from Dwayne's truck door.

The barista brought me another coffee unasked.

"Thought you might need this," he said. "On the house."

Some days bowl me over. In the hospital I've seen so many miracles and as many sad endings that it all becomes a blur. Now here I was on a leisurely beach day minding my own business. Then out of the blue a person from my past showed up whom I hadn't particularly liked because I blamed him for busting up my school-girl crush. Yet he had shown compassion for me, while clearly still holding a torch for his long ago love. And then a stranger had seen my distress and proffered sustenance for no reward.

I had intended to keep Dwayne's phone number for myself. Now I'd pondered the situation. I got up and went into the cafe. There were no customers. The man who had waited on me was behind the bar writing something in a ledger. He looked up as I approached and gave me an encouraging smile.

"Don't suppose I could have an envelope and a stamp, if you've got them?"

He nodded, and stepped into the office behind him, returning with both and a notepad and pen I hadn't asked for.

"Good on you." He grinned as though we were old friends conspiring. White teeth lit up his brown face. "You're doing the right thing."

My heart skipped a beat, which as a doctor worried me not in the slightest. I made a mental note to ask the barista sometime soon, very soon how he knew exactly why I wanted stationery.

▲　▲　▲

CHRONICLE OF A HITMAN

When I was still at high school my mates used to say I could foresee what would happen next. For a few years I believed them and used it as a party trick, to be one of the gang.

By the time I left school I'd realised the trick came not from some cosmic gift, but from plain and simply watching and listening. In other words, paying attention. If you train yourself to observe and understand what you see and hear you come to realise what is happening right now generally gives rise to what comes next.

I'd developed the habit of not saying much, which meant I listened and heard things. My mates thought me quiet, which surprised me because I was constantly conducting loud conversations in my head. I kept my eyes open and noticed a lot. My friends never picked up on the fact that I chose my predictions, saying nothing unless I was sure.

Trouble was, predicting the future and being right most of the time meant the present began to bore me. What's interesting about living through everything twice? Maybe it was a self-preservation thing. No surprises; although hard to say which came first. Alertness to avoid surprises or the fear of surprises causing alertness?

I left school at sixteen bored to the back teeth. Mediocre marks in School Certificate except in the subjects that seemed to me to be of infinite interest like history and geography. My parents no more understood the value of my gift, that ability to pay attention, any more than I did. I acquiesced when they steered me into following in my father's footsteps. I was inwardly appalled, but couldn't think of anything better.

I'm not saying I despised my father's long public service, far from it. He'd had the mortal struggle of the Second World War to get through, surviving against all odds. He'd had enough excitement, and his job represented serenity and longevity.

I stuck it out in the public service for nearly two years until it all got too much. I was slowing down, losing my gift, alertness fading.

I joined the Army and signed on for the SAS. I was not yet eighteen, so my father, recognising that I had to go and fight my own wars, signed away his rights as legal guardian. I could have waited a few months and done it without him, but It seemed the decent thing to do.

I tell you it was a shock going into the army. Not at all the glamorous gung-ho crusade I'd imagined. Once I'd got past the self-recriminations of asking myself what the hell I'd done, I began to get into the swing of it. If anything is of value in the army it is alertness. Soon I was once more able to work out what was going to happen next, most of the time.

Basic training took three months, the same as for all recruits. Those of us signed up for the SAS were the butt of a few jibes from the regular force instructors, but that was all. At the end of basic training the Army held its aptitude tests to either prove the recruit's choice or steer them in a new direction. The tests reinforced my choice. Proficient in the skills of the ordinary soldier I was now set on the course of how to 'kill people efficiently' as the Army termed it. As though doing it at long range with artillery, rockets and rifle was inefficient.

For my nineteenth birthday I found myself crawling through the jungle bordering the track that called itself the main supply highway between Kesong and Milai where the Cong had battalions in reserve. Intelligence had indicated it might be possible to ambush a convoy and extract an officer who the boys back at base might be able to turn.

I became extremely good at it. The officers got to rely on my killer skills and I was often sent out on extraction missions completely alone. Trouble was the more I went out into the jungle or even into the towns and cities I became even more self-reliant, unable to accept the petty strictures of the military after the cat and mouse, life and death weeks observing, planning and executing whoever the bigwigs thought the Viet Cong could do without.

Eventually one particularly pompous American officer who thought he had jurisdiction over our forces required me to go out on another mission only hours after I'd returned from a ten day slog through the mire around Ke Sang. I was already angry because I'd failed, one of the rare times, and when it did happen it was usually, as in this case, faulty intelligence.

For a few days I'd trailed a group of Cong fabled at avoiding detection. They were supposed to be heading back to their supply dump where intelligence had reported they were manufacturing bombs destined to terrorise civilians in the city. I followed them to a village deep in a valley encircled by hills where they were obviously on good terms with the locals because soon after their arrival the rice wine flowed and a party broke out.

After two days of this it was clear they weren't going to re-arm just yet. I was in grave danger of being detected hanging around the outskirts of a busy village. I was close to starving and sick of living off bamboo shoots and precious little else. Fear of giving myself away meant I had to eat raw the few lizards I could catch. Hunger can be tolerated if alone or if everyone else is hungry, but was made worse by the Cong being close enough for me to smell their food and hear their carousing.

I refused the American's directive to go straight back on patrol. Luckily my commanding officer agreed with me and interceded. Still, my attitude had been noted, and had probably been for some time and forgiven, until the army deemed such individuality too much.

Gradually I was pulled back until I rarely went alone on deep penetration missions. There were always at least four or five in my squad, sometimes more. I hated this because even though the others were in theory equally proficient, to me they sounded like a herd of elephants tramping through the jungle. Must have sounded like that to the enemy, too, because our failure rate was near complete.

My discharge from the army was amicable enough, yet I could tell my commanding officer was glad to see me go. After five years of committing unspeakable acts in the name of righteousness protecting democracy I was free. Twenty–four years old and a trained killer by any method appropriate.

I had a few months off. Went home for the first time since the end of basic training. Nothing much had changed at home; it was as though the five years hadn't happened. It seemed time had stood still and all I'd been doing was a myth in my own mind. I enjoyed the peace and quiet for a few weeks, and certainly didn't miss the army bullshit, the orders and the pettiness, the dressing up of the sordid business we were engaged in with fine and noble words.

By the end of three months I was crawling up the wall with boredom. Besides, my father was dropping hints that he'd had enough of me hanging around, asking me every second day what my plans were. I didn't have the heart to tell him I didn't have plans. I was avoiding plans even while suffering boredom. So I told him that I'd been asked to join a private security firm in the USA.

I hadn't, and even if I had my opinion of Yanks was so low after Vietnam I could never work for them. I'd witnessed too many times their ineptitude in the field where their military solution was to throw ordinance to obliterate men, women and children. To hell with the consequences; collateral damage they called it. Self-reliance on individuals, despite that being a major part of their national ethos, was alien to their modus operandi.

Once I'd floated that as my next move, however, I decided I might as well go there anyway for a look-see if nothing else. My discharge pay was substantial and I hadn't spent much in five years so I had money in the bank.

On the flight over I was reading a *Time* magazine article about corruption. A wealthy business man was being hounded by the press over the fact he had bribed defence officials to get them to overlook the allegation his company had been cutting costs by taking shortcuts in the manufacture of plastic explosive fuses. It came to me that this was the bastard ultimately responsible for my friends blowing themselves up, which we had put down to their carelessness rather than equipment failure.

There wasn't much evidence left after these episodes. Jay had been killed outright, but Kay (names changed) was now a quadriplegic back home. I fumed as I read and reread the article and it came to me I could revenge my mates and at the same time bring jungle justice to the urban jungle.

It was a piece of cake. Within three days of arriving in Los Angles I had staked out the businessman's Sacramento factory, watched him face off against the press on TV and trailed him to find out where he lived. Though I felt a bit sorry for his wife and kids, I decided my purpose was more important. Statistics favoured it being an unhappy marriage. For all I knew, I was doing them all a favour.

When the automatic garage door rose up in response to a transmitter fitted to his car, I'd seen along the back wall of the garage the propane gas bottles that no doubt fuelled his family's domestic appliances. It was like old times for me to silence the house alarms and fit a small charge fused with one of his own. I hoped the greater voltage of his automatic garage door opener would trigger the charge rather than his wife's hand-held remote. To be honest when I thought of my friends who had made the ultimate sacrifice I wasn't too perturbed by the thought his wife and kids might cop it too. Their lives were about to be radically changed one way or the other.

In case there was no evidence remaining to show this was not a random hit but revenge for dealing in the death and destruction business, I made an anonymous call to the Feds implying the anti-war brigade were responsible. All my motel and hire car records were in the name of the Dutch tourist's passport I'd stolen.

By a roundabout route I arrived back in New Zealand. I dropped in on Kay again, who was surprised to see me so soon. I showed him the Sacramento newspaper with its report of the businessman's violent death by persons unknown, but suspected to be tied in with his manufacturing of explosive components for the military.

"So what?" Kay said.

So I told him what I had learnt about the faulty equipment almost certainly responsible for his winding up in a wheelchair.

"I decided to do something about it."

Kay didn't believe me. Said I was bull-shitting him, though glad the bastard had got his come-uppance. I didn't push it, but over a few beers Kay challenged me to do it again if I was so smart. Like, go and knock off that so and so who is in the news at the moment in Bosnia causing mayhem. We had a laugh and without thinking too much about it started talking about how to do it.

Next day when it wasn't the alcohol talking, Kay said, "Well?"

Knowing damn well what he was talking about I said, "Well, what?"

"Bet you can't. And I bet that wasn't you who did in the American guy."

Then I had to prove it was.

When I got back to Kay a few months later he had already seen it on the news that the Bosnian bastard was dead in a car crash. I showed Kay a newspaper cutting from the London *Times* reporting the death and a photo of the guy taken at a conference where he was in civvies. The tie he was wearing in the picture was the same as the bloodied tie I took from my pocket and unwrapped.

"How did you do it?"

Kay couldn't entirely believe that what had started as a bet fuelled by alcohol had resulted in a man's death halfway round the world in a war-torn country. A death welcomed by most from all accounts.

"Easy. Timer under the car."

That's how our dirty little revenge business started. Kay ran the home office. Who'd suspect that a man in a wheel chair living in a house fitted with ramps in Whitney Street, West Auckland was the controller of an assassination business with the ability to strike anywhere in the world?

We did good business although we only made a couple of hits a year. The rates we charged we could have lived well off one. Not that we charged the same for each. Some jobs we did for very little depending on the circumstances and the hirer's ability to pay.

With a New Zealand passport I could travel anywhere without raising eyebrows from local authorities. There had always been a Kiwi in even the remotest unlikeliest places before me to ease my way. Kay developed extraordinary skills as a forger. Why not, he said, it was only his legs copped it not his brain or arms. I soon became confident his perfectly forged documentation would not let me down whether I was crossing borders, hiring cars or anything else that demanded official papers.

In the early days carrying a gun wasn't much of a problem. Later on travelling across borders with a weapon was folly, especially by air. If you knew where to go, which we did, I could always pick up a piece or anything else I needed without hassle from people we could trust.

One of the high-profile jobs we did was the film star Bridgette Boyes who, as far as anyone knew, topped herself. That's what we wanted the world to think. It was an easy job, funded by a heavyweight political family who wanted her gone before her pregnancy became common knowledge and the scandal rags started asking who the father was.

Bribing the drug store chemist in Beverly Hills who supplied most of her prescription drugs was easy once I found out he had a penchant for underage girls picked up at the city bus terminal. Boyes was flirting with death anyway with the amount of anti-depressants she was ingesting. God knows what effect they'd have on the kid she was carrying. It was a simple matter to get the chemist to understand he was doing her and the kid a favour by upping the dose a little bit at a time.

In the early seventies South America was a happy hunting ground for us. Doing a major political like President Héctor Cáypara of Argentina took some extra organising, though presidential security was slacker in those days. The Peronist I'd set up to take the fall was soon caught, courtesy of my anonymous tip-off. Those who reckoned they had heard a second shot and espoused the conspiracy theory were absolutely right if they did but know it. I was a fraction late pulling the trigger. We were reluctant to take on this one because this president seemed to have his heart in the right place. Ultimately our client persuaded us he was a danger to stability in the region.

We weren't sure who commissioned this hit, though we had our suspicions. We thought our hirers had to be a government because of the elaborate, untraceable method of payment. Gold bars into, of all things, a deed box account at the National Westminster Bank, High Street branch, Peterborough in the east of England. About as anonymous as you can get without all that fictional spy story rubbish that demands a Swiss account. Incidentally, we felt bad enough about the job that the gold is still there. I use the account at intervals long enough to keep it active, though I never check in the strongbox itself.

The anonymous people who directed us on that job are most likely long gone, yet somewhere in the dusty record vaults of M.I.5 or the CIA I wouldn't mind betting there is a record of the transaction. If it was them. We figured out it was a proving job to see if we were any good. I mean, for most of our hits we were expert at laying off the blame. Therefore we found it difficult to prove it actually was our work. Only the hirer and us knew it for sure and we couldn't exactly ask for testimonials.

We didn't have to. Don't ask me how, I don't know the answer, our rep must have spread by word of mouth because we sure as hell didn't do any advertising. No doubt we made it look as easy as all things well done by skilled people. Our main secret, if we had one, was Kay's dedication to research. Not so easy in the seventies before technology sped up the process. Before that, our network had to be established face to face. This, while time-consuming and expensive, turned out to be a blessing. Even with the internet and the latest gadgets, we still vet resources face to face as a final step before making ourselves known.

We haven't had to eliminate a resource for years now. I guess technology has allowed us to get further down the research track than in the early days, while keeping our anonymity. I'd had to pop a couple of snitches who had sold us information and then tried to sell the information again. Unfortunately for the snitches they'd chosen to sell to associates we'd hired to test them. I suppose word got around that the penalty for crossing us was dire.

There is no doubt technology and the internet made our business simpler. Although we still rely on a network of contacts, mostly journalists, for information. Journalists are good because they're usually poorly paid and with a moral sense of right and wrong, convinced that wrongs should be righted and the world should know.

Most jobs didn't make it into the headlines, though not many went entirely unnoticed by the media, with a sidebar perhaps on the obits page. Our level of operation meant even a run of the mill hit didn't come cheap which meant the vic usually had some profile to justify the expense.

Many of the jobs involved eliminating a business rival who had crossed some sort of line like appropriating a design then altering subtle detail to avoid copyright infringement. The hirer had no other recourse. Sounds trite, but when you think of the numbers and revenue involved it becomes more understandable. For example, I scared the hell out of a board of directors of a toy factory that was stealing the designs of a rival then rushing into production ahead of the patent-owning company. The particular design that precipitated the hit went on to sell 14,000,000 units, all of which would have been lost if I hadn't put a stop to such antics. Unfortunately it took the deaths by car crash of the chairman and deputy before the board got the message.

It was inevitable given the price we charged that eventually only the wealthy could afford our services and that meant governments. We had no problem letting this myth take hold in the dark underbelly where secret services and political rivalries operate. Yes, we charged a fortune for a major political hit; yet a few million to eliminate an opposing head of state was cheaper than funding a war that might drag on for months or years and cost billions.

Governments and giant corporations always managed to get a message to us, generally by floating code double-speak that there was a job up for tender.

We kept quiet the fact we did some work for next to nothing, even pro bono if we thought the hirer and the cause worthy. The ordinary punter had no idea how to contact us, if he or she even knew we existed. Usually it was us who contacted the wronged party through one or other of the investigative journalists we trusted. They knew the drill and had checked out the veracity of the injustice.

These lower order jobs rarely resulted in a hit. Most people are surprisingly forgiving at heart even if they had publicly wished dire consequences on an adversary. When offered the chance of fulfilment of that wish they usually backed off and said they didn't mean it. I always respected their wishes and offered them a milder solution that while still revenge didn't result in permanent physical damage to the wrongdoer, but still hurt him or her, especially in the bank account. Again this was often accompanied by a little dirt digging and threats I happily acknowledged as blackmail.

The day came when it had to end. Kay and I were both slowing down even as contracts came our way in a never-ending stream. It seemed like the willingness of the unscrupulous and megalomaniacs to chance their arm would never diminish.

Maybe our ideals had been eroded over the years and we became less judgemental, less choosy.

Worse, my willingness to exercise my ability to concentrate and pay attention, anticipating what came next, was diminishing. Time was running out for us. Sooner or later one or the other would make a mistake and that would be it.

Still it was a shock for me to come back to the farm, which had long since replaced the Whitney Street house as our base, to find Kay slumped in his wheelchair, stone cold-dead. To this day I'm not sure he died from a heart attack despite what the autopsy showed. In our line of work, where we specialise in making sudden death explicable, paranoia goes with the territory.

Without Kay I had no desire to carry on even if I could find someone to replace him. I called it quits. Sold everything up and gave half to Kay's only living relative, his younger sister. She'd been fairly well looked after in a modest way over the years as Kay hinted that the farm and other business interests were doing OK. I still remember with a smile the shock on her face when I handed her the papers that laid out she was due almost thirty million dollars.

There was no way my restless nature would permit a quiet retirement. Neither would the numerous enemies I'd no doubt made over the years. I'd eliminated many threats to world peace and prosperity, and the newer breeds of terrorists were exhibiting most unforgiving and irrational tendencies. I could see no future in settling down in one place to be a target for the vengeful.

I bought a Farr 38 set up for single-handed, deep-water sailing and set off with Kay's old dog as my only companion on a shakedown cruise to Gisborne. Then I would see where the wind would take me.

▲

Postscript

Reported in the *New Zealand Herald*, 13th March 2010:

A trawler operating 25 nautical miles off East Cape found a yacht presumably abandoned. The trawler took the yacht in tow and arrived in Tauranga mid-morning yesterday.

The police say a dog in a severely dehydrated and distressed state was the only living thing found on the vessel. The dog was handed over to the RSPCA and is expected to make a full recovery.

Records regarding the ownership of the yacht are incomplete and the police say they are continuing enquiries into who the crew were and what might have happened to them. The vessel was set up for single-handed sailing and might therefore have been crewed by one person.

A Police spokesman says there was no sign of foul play but are asking that anyone who might have information regarding the un-named yacht's movements to come forward.

▲   ▲   ▲

REVENGE FOR
MRS ARKWRIGHT

Things weren't easy in the private investigation business. The major franchises were moving in and undercutting the independents by quoting low on the lucrative insurance fraud cases. To save overheads I'd had to move out of the high rise on Queen Street to a poky back office on Lorne Street. Forlorn Street, I called it.

Most of my time these days was spent on penny-ante jobs that any moron could do, like background checks for the institute on prospective real estate agents. To be honest, that was a nice little earner because often I could clip the ticket coming and going. The institute would pay me the agreed fee and the agent a century or two depending on what was in their background that didn't need bringing out in the light of day.

If a juicy job came in, I took it for myself. That was logical because firstly, I couldn't afford to turn anything down and secondly, I was my only employee. Except for Leonie who was my receptionist although she had aspirations to be much more. Leo was a large woman from Rarotonga. She was only a girl really, twenty-five I think she wrote on her job application a few years ago. Her size made her look older until you got up close and saw how smooth and fresh her skin was. Not that I ever got up that close, but I'd seen a few try who Leo settled down with a remarkably swift blow to a man's vulnerable anatomy. They learned the hard way that she wasn't just a pretty face.

On a day when there was so little happening I was helping Leo with routine background checks on applicants for private school jobs, out of the blue a juicy job walked through my door. To be frank it was the person who was juicy; the job I had yet to hear about.

I recognised her from the tabloids as Mrs Arkwright, ex Mrs Kilpatrick, ex Mrs Moore, ex Mrs Wilson, and probably ex a few more for all I knew. Before Mr Arkwright, who appeared to have no sporting affiliations whatsoever, she'd been married in quick succession to one well-known sportsman after another. With each disappointment she seemed to favour union with exponents of all the major codes starting with rugby, league, tennis and cricket.

Sordid details of her marital failures were laid out for the world to savour. No one professed to be interested yet every messy episode resulted in the gossip rags being snatched off the racks faster than hacks could pen the next instalment. It was as if the media took delight in turning on one of their own.

Under her radio byline, Kitty Turner – presumably her maiden name – she was renowned as one of the country's most accomplished radio personalities, reducing politicians and other sorry officials to reckless fury as she relentlessly honed in on the truth.

Little was reported from her side of the story, but we were told she'd cheated on each of the sportsmen she'd wed, who without exception remarried vacuous bimbos while Kitty Turner's radio career continued as though nothing had happened.

In contrast to the media frenzy surrounding her earlier nuptials, her marriage to Mr Arkwright in the early part of last year had passed relatively unnoticed. This time Mrs Arkwright dropped out of the public gaze. Now here she was, wanting to speak with me, a private eye.

"Hello, Ace," she said.

We'd met before not long after I'd parted company with the police. Then she was Mrs Kilpatrick and I worked for Ace Investigations before I went freelance. There'd been a bit of a mix up over some marital property and she'd hired some muscle to retrieve it. I was the muscle.

"Nice to see you again, Mrs K," I said. "I'm sorry, old habits die hard. Mrs A, I meant to say."

After that gaffe I thought it wiser not to add some wisecrack about starting again on a new batch of husbands with surnames beginning with A.

She shot a glance at Leo diligently tapping away, absorbed by the spreadsheet on her computer screen.

"Can I talk to you in confidence?" she said.

"No worries, Mrs A. Leo is so busy I doubt she can hear us. Can you, Leo?"

Leo didn't deviate from her tapping and kept her eyes glued to the screen.

"Fire away, Mrs A. What can I do for you?"

"I want you to find out if my husband is cheating on me."

I was mildly surprised at this abrupt statement. I'd assumed, primed by the media, that it was she who 'played away.'

"I know what you're thinking. Contrary to the slander that I was the unfaithful siren, I loved my husbands, who seemed to fall rapidly out of love with me. It suited their competitive sportsmen's egos to blame their shortcomings on me. As long as they didn't expect a handout, I didn't mind their antics."

"It's none of my business, but why did you keep tying the knot with sportsmen?" I had to ask.

"A good question that I used to ask myself. In truth, in my position, I couldn't marry a nobody, could I?" She laughed dryly. "I guess I'm a slow learner. It took me a while to find out that not only are the egos of accomplished athletes huge, they're also extremely fragile. Besides, they believe they're who the media says they are. That, I found out to my cost, was far from the truth. Still, I'm an optimist and lived in hope the next star would be Mr Right."

"So you're like the rest of us; human, as opposed to your radio persona."

"Got it in one, Ace," she said, a little ruefully. "But I'm not here to go over my life story. It's my husband I'm worried about. He's so different from my exes I was sure we could be happy and I don't want to lose him. I couldn't bear it if he let me down."

For a moment, I thought she was going to cry. But I guess you don't get to be a feared radio personality by giving in to the weepies. I gave her a moment to compose herself then said, "For you, I'll see what I can do, Mrs A. Or should that be Ms Turner?"

"Mrs A is fine, Ace," she said. "My husband is managing director of an import company. We used to go out for lunch three or four times a week when he didn't have a business meeting. Now I'd be lucky to join him once a month. He's become evasive, though his explanations, taken individually, are plausible enough."

"Hate to pry Mrs A, but that's my job so can you tell me how things are in the ..." I searched for the phrase ... "um, marital bed."

She coloured, which surprised me. So hard-boiled journalists do have feelings. Maybe she did love her husband. As though to confirm this, she said, "There's nothing wrong with our sex life, if that's what you mean. I love him and I thought he loved me."

"OK, Mrs A. I'll be in touch as soon as. My usual fees are..."

"I'll pay whatever you think appropriate. I trust you, Ace."

She rose and exited the office. The door closed softly behind her.

Leo gave up her pretence of being immersed in her work and leaned back in her chair.

"Did you get all that, Leo?"

"Does the Pope eat fish on Fridays? Of course, I was *so* busy I only heard all of it! Fancy trusting you of all people to be fair with your fee. Maybe that's her problem; too trusting. Us wahines wouldn't trust no man no way."

"Yeah, right." I was sceptical. "Better not tell that to that great hunk you're married to who tells me you're the love of his life. Can't imagine why."

Leo laughed, "Except him, whom I do absolutely trust." A rare confession and she continued briskly, "I suppose you're going to leave me to slave away while you swan off to do the juicy stuff?"

"Right again, Leo."

Next day around midday I nursed a flat white, no sugar, in a coffee shop opposite the office tower where Mr Arkwright managing directed whatever it was his company did. Mrs A was vague on what exactly her husband imported. If I'd had the smarts to delve a little deeper, I might have put two and two together and come up with five a little quicker.

Thing was, it seemed simple enough to trail an errant husband, and discover what else, besides eating sandwiches, he was doing in his lunch break.

Arky, as I thought of him, was an easy mark to follow. Even in the business district a tall, athletically-built man (I could see where Mrs A was coming from) power-suited in dark blue pinstripe with a contrasting red tie was easy to tail. I kept a discreet distance behind and I was sure he had no idea I was on his case as he headed for the railway station.

City Central is a cavernous mausoleum of a station that does double duty as a downtown shopping mall. A few of the town's prostitutes hang out there, even during the day. These tended to be the married ones who had to pick up kids after school or be home to cook hubby's dinner in the evening. They were daylighting, rather than moonlighting, for a little extra cash.

So that's what he was up to. Not getting enough at home, I suppose. Although Mrs A is a stunner, she's getting on a bit and maybe her 'nothing wrong with our sex life' might not be the same as her husband's take on it.

Arky walked in through the station entrance. To my surprise he brushed aside the pros. He marched as bold as brass up to the ticket office and bought a single stop ticket on the Eastern Line. I did likewise, in a suitably covert manner.

Within a few minutes he alighted and strode across the street to a row of low-rise office buildings. Without hesitation he marched into the foyer of a building that was occupied by a multitude of small businesses. He certainly knew where he was going as he stabbed the lift button without consulting the wall-mounted directory.

I was close enough behind to see that the lift had stopped on the second floor. A glance at the directory indicated seven businesses with offices on that floor and wary of losing him I didn't have time to read what or who they were. So I raced up the stairs to the floor indicated. Opposite the lift, wooden-framed glass double doors were swinging closed. In classic gumshoe style I peeked through the glass, and sure enough, Arky was in the arms of a woman.

She was much older than him, but slim and athletic. I did a double-take at the printing etched on the glass swing door, which read *Madam Vetriano's School of Salsa*.

Clearly there was more going on here than the horizontal rumba. He probably didn't need any lessons in that, if Mrs A was to be believed. He was polishing up on the vertical. Arky wasn't such a naughty boy after all. I was relieved for Mrs A's sake.

She'd had a rough time of it from the trousered half of the population if her side of the story was true. Before I shared the good news that hubby was on the up and up, and hoping to surprise her with his dance moves, I decided to check on him a few more times. Besides, it wasn't often a client handed me a blank cheque.

Arky followed a similar pattern when he emerged at lunchtime every second or third day. The fourth time I'd followed him to Madam Vetriano's I was so bored I was about to clear off and leave him to it. My conscience at taking Mrs A's money was nagging a smidge, and I was sick of the lukewarm flat whites served up by my stake-out cafe.

I was on my third frothy excuse of a coffee when I realised Arky had previously emerged from his salsa lessons midway through my second. I checked; he was half an hour overdue. I exited the cafe and crossed the road to Madam Vetriano's. I peered through the glass door expecting to see twinkle-toes pirouetting around the dance floor. The place was empty.

Cautiously, I entered and edged towards the glass-fronted office at the far end of the room. Inside Mrs Vetriano, at odds with her glamorous facade, was chomping on a well-filled sandwich that she put down hastily when I tapped on the glass.

"Buena journo, senor. 'ow eez it I can 'elp?" Her attempt at an Italian accent was pathetic.

"Excuse me, are you Madam Vetriano?" I always start with an easy question.

"Velly solly." She had drifted confusingly into a Chinese accent. "There's no actual Madam Vetriano, but I am proprietor of this establishment." Now she had no accent at all.

"You wanta learna the salsa?" Full circle back to Italian.

"Notta me." I got into the spirit of the exchange. "Ima privata eyea lookinga fora informazione."

"Oh, fuck it. You've sussed me out. The punters like a bit of the exotic, you see, when they come to learn Latin dance."

"Your secret's safe with me." I leaned forward. "Just tell me what happened to your last punter?"

"Oh, sometimes he doesn't stay long. Says he has urgent business to attend to and slips out the back." She sniffed. "None of my business, I'm sure."

"Thank you for your time, Madam...?" I left the question hanging.

"Mabel Jones." She spoke forlornly, a human version of the street where I had my office. "Just Mabel Jones."

I had been going to couch my report to Mrs A in vague terms so as not to spoil her husband's intended surprise. Something official along the lines of 'Mr Arkwright was going about an innocent activity that might be of benefit to you both.' Now, with Arky's vanishing act, I wasn't so sure.

I shouldered open my office door. Leo immediately picked up on my preoccupation when I didn't snort with disapproval to find her lounging behind the reception desk, cigarette in one hand and the phone in the other as she murmured a final Rarotongan endearment before hanging up.

"What's up, boss? Sleuthing too much for you?" she mocked.

"Yeah. Sometimes things ain't what they seem. I hate to be the bringer of bad news to Mrs A. She's such a doll."

"Why? She's used to being shafted by bastards, isn't she? One more won't break her."

"You're all heart and sympathy, Leo. I was going to call off the investigation today because it looked as if Arky – Mr Arkwright – was sneaking off to learn fancy dance moves. Now I'm not so sure that's all he's doing. Today he disappeared from the dance studio and not for the first time."

"Sounds like more sleuthing is required. Mrs A can afford the fees and you owe it to her to find the facts, nothing, but the facts, ma'am." Leo parodied the hard-bitten cops from *Dragnet*.

"I've finished those background checks you left me with and another batch is coming from those fancy real estate brokers in Parnell. That'll keep me busy while you make like a detective and get fat on flat whites." She grinned, and looked me in the eye to make sure I got the blatant racial reference.

"I much prefer long blacks myself."

Next day instead of following Arky as he left his high rise I waited until he'd crossed the intersection at Albert and Victoria heading in the direction of the station and Madam Vetriano's. Once he'd been swallowed up in the lunchtime crowd. I entered the office tower and approached the pedestal encased in speckled white marble that seemed more suitable for a cathedral than a receptionist station. The haughty receptionist clearly thought herself worthy of deification.

"Mr Arkwright's office, please."

She looked at me as blankly as she had at her computer screen.

"One moment."

She tapped Arkwright's name into her computer, then told me frostily, "No one of that name is employed in an executive capacity for F.F C."

"F.F.C.?"

"Fleece Finance Corporation." She gestured towards the giant stylised ram sculpture in the lobby.

"You can't pull the wool over my eyes," I quipped.

Her blank expression remained.

"F.F.C. has the first six floors. There are at least twelve other tenants in the building. We have no record of who is employed by them."

Signalling my dismissal she pointed in the direction of the lifts, where a fancy board displayed names, office and floor locations.

So Arky didn't work for the large corporation as I'd been led to believe, as had his wife, apparently, though she hadn't exactly said so. Fleece Finance certainly wasn't in the import or the export business, nor did it have anything to do with fleeces or animal products of any kind. Unless you'd call bloodsucking, parasitic bankers animals.

I searched the board, but there was no Mr Arkwright to be seen. The multiplicity of tenants meant I could wander the floors and corridors with impunity, pleading lost if anyone asked me my business. In the event I was ignored with hardly a civil word from any of the harried, pale and sorry-looking types who voluntarily spent their working lives in this office tower.

I had just about given up finding I had no idea what exactly. Some vague notion had lodged in my brain that if I could have a look around Arky's office, I might learn something. I'd worked my way back down from the sixteenth to the seventh enquiring at the various receptionist's desks if they were manned, which they mostly weren't.

I pushed through the swing doors facing the lifts in the seventh floor lobby to be confronted by the sour face of a spotty youth purporting to be the receptionist for a business importing toiletries. Hardly the province of someone as pre-eminent as I'd been led to believe Mr Arkwright to be. But you never know.

"Yeah, mate. Whaddya want?" Clearly Spotty was no graduate of Kiwi Host.

I was tempted to proffer him immediate promotion to the role of punching bag. Discretion overrode temptation. Even this cretin might remember who punched him and who I was asking for. I confined myself to a direct enquiry.

"Mr Arkwright work here?"

"Don't fink so, mate."

I was about to walk away when he redeemed himself.

"There's a geezer works on his own out of an office down the end. Back out our doors and turn right down the end of the corridor, mate."

"Thanks, *chief.*" I loaded the word with irony. Completely wasted. He had no clue that being addressed as 'mate' annoyed me unless the addressor *was* a mate.

I glanced back as the doors swung shut. Spotty was preening himself as though I'd paid him a compliment. The young are so damned thick.

The office down the end of the corridor was locked. No surprise there. What was unusual was that there was no sign, no name, no indication of what business the occupant of the office undertook. Through the glass top half of the door I could see an outer reception area and a partly open door to an inner office.

There were no posters or charts or anything else that might hint at the daily commerce enacted here. There was no sign of any commerce at all: no papers on the outer office desk, no mail piling up, no inbox or outbox. There was a name plaque on the desk of the inner office, but the partly closed door blocked all but the last few letters from view. I palmed my smartphone and zoomed in, managing to make out the last three letters of the name – 'ight.' Ok, four. I took a few snaps while I was at it. I've no idea why. Somehow it seemed what a detective ought to do.

I didn't bother going back to my office. I had a date that night with a detective constable who considered she owed me. I'd rescued her from making a fool of herself on a burglary case we'd worked together – her for the force, me for the vic, a few months ago.

So it wasn't until the next morning that I saw Leo.

"Mornin,' boss," she greeted me, with her usual sunny Polynesian demeanour. "Kia-rana."

The Herald rustled as she raised it up.

"Seen the morning paper yet or the news last night."

"No. I've been a bit tied up."

A momentary recollection of the detective constable in handcuffs sprawled across my bed flashed before my eyes. I must have smiled because Leo cackled.

"Ho, ho. Been up to a bit of hanky panky, eh, boss?"

"Mind your own business," I huffed, an attempt to regain my dignity, impossible where Leo is concerned. "What's so important in the news anyway?"

"One of Mrs A's exes, that cricketer Wilson, topped himself yesterday. The cops say it's suicide, but it's under investigation. This is the third of Mrs A's exes to croak and they're wondering if there's a link."

"Wow. Pass me the paper, please."

The story had little to add to what Leo had told me. There were pictures of two of the deceased: Kilpatrick, the rugby international and Moore, the tennis player. Moore's picture was taken from when Mrs A was married to him. Both were grinning at the camera. There were no pictures of Wilson.

I realised that the Wilson 'suicide' as reported had occurred the day before yesterday, the day Arky cut his dance session short and disappeared. Like any sleuth worth his salt I had a hunch. I gave Leo the dates Mabel had confirmed, bless her. She was meticulous in charging half fees for the lessons Arky didn't stay for and had recorded all neatly in her ledger.

"See if any sportsmen or minor celebs snuffed it on any of these dates. No need to go back beyond early last year."

I left Leo to Google deaths and dates. Leo called me as I boarded the Eastern Suburbs train. Sure enough the three now very ex-exes had expired on dates Arky had cut his lessons short. Curiously they had died in the alphabetical and chronological order Mrs A had married them. Two or three other deaths also fitted the pattern, except those deceased seemed to have no connection with Mrs A or her husbands as far as I knew.

Circumstantial evidence. Flimsy, even; but I didn't need the same level of proof as the cops. I decided to confront Arky. First, though, I'd cross check a couple of the dates against Mabel's ledger.

"Oh, fuck it, it's you." Madam Vetriano defaulted to Mabel making no attempt at an Italian accent.

"Bon journo to you, too." I spoke lightly, though I'd picked up a bad vibe. "Yes, Mabel. It's me. Were you expecting someone else?"

"No," she said sourly, "It's just that since you came poking your nose into my business I've been burgled."

"Much missing?" I had to ask, though I thought I knew the answer already.

"Only the petty cash."

So my theory was rubbish then?

"Oh, and for some weird reason my ledger has gone. Why an earth would anyone steal that?"

There it was! Theory not so rubbish, after-all. I knew why, but I kept that to myself. No need to check dates now. The fact the ledger was missing confirmed that Arky's truancy had led to the permanent AWOL of some of the city's most prominent personalities. Not necessarily the good, the bad or the exes of Mrs A, but including all or some of them.

"Sorry to hear you've had trouble." I mustered as much sympathy as I could.

"Can't see why my visits had anything to do with you being burgled," I lied. "Maybe I'll come back and learn the rumba." I lied again.

Mabel brightened up and her Latina miraculously returned as she exclaimed, "Pleasa do. Youa mosta welcome."

On the downtown train back to the CBD I called Leo and laid out what I knew and the conclusion I had come to.

"I feel bad for Mrs A," I said. "But if you don't hear from me or I don't get back to the office by knock-off time call Detective Constable Hill."

"That would be DC Victoria Hill, would it, boss?"

I ignored Leo's probing into my private life.

"That would be her," I confirmed.

By early afternoon I was back in the familiar foyer of Fleece 'em Corporation. As before, I was largely ignored. There was a different girl on reception but with the same blank look. She might or might not have registered my presence at the lifts.

I punched in seven and stepped out carefully, hoping to avoid Spotty. I wanted my presence in Arky's office to go unrecorded and my luck was in. I palmed my Beretta and racked a round into the chamber before sliding it back into the holster to the rear of my right hip. It occurred to me that I was being melodramatic? Then I remembered all those sudden deaths, ostensibly from natural causes or accidents.

This time the glass door to Arky's outer office swung open to my push. I could hear music playing softly. Barbara Streisand in duet with Barry Gibb singing 'Guilty.' An odd choice for a man I reckoned was a killer, but there's no accounting for musical taste or a person's sense of humour, two things I'd never associated with a violent profession. Though he must have good taste for Mrs A to be attracted to him.

"Ace, or if you prefer, Mr Dunn. Please, come in."

I reached for my weapon and spun around.

"Come now, Mr Dunn, no need for that. As you can see I am unarmed."

Arky sat behind the desk in the inner office, arms outstretched, palms upwards empty of weapons.

"Ace is reserved for Mrs A. You can call me Mike." I was beginning to recover my composure. "How did you know it was me? I haven't seen any CCTV cameras."

"Technology, my friend. I know this isn't the first time you've been in my office, and I'm hoping it won't be the last."

He pushed a button on the arm of his chair and a curtain pulled back to reveal two wall-mounted screens. One was recording in real time, and the other clearly showed me taking cellphone photos through the outer doors. I shifted uncomfortably.

"What an earth were you up to? You should have got in touch, invited me out for a drink. Which reminds me, I've forgotten my manners – Scotch and soda, isn't it?"

Arky's manner was so pleasant, that I nearly dismissed my intention of confronting him with my suspicions. Despite his affability it seemed a kind of threat that he should know so much about me, including my tipple of choice.

"Yes, scotch is fine," I said. "Look, I think I know what you do for a living and I'm not stupid enough to come here without letting someone know where I am. The police will be alerted unless I say not to. It's Mrs A I'm concerned for."

"Me too, my dear chap." He handed me my whisky. "I'm a simple importer of sporting guns and high tech security equipment."

"You're something else as well, aren't you?"

"Oh, I've been involved with security forces in the past and I still have contacts, of course. That explains why I've known from the first you've been rather too interested in my movements."

I was beginning to see that Arky or Mr Arkwright, as I was now thinking him, was not going to be easily shaken.

"I have seen Madam Vetriano's register that shows you weren't there when at least two of your wife's exes expired prematurely."

"So what?" Mr Arkwright shrugged, half-smiling. "Show me the register and I'll check my diary and maybe I can tell you where I was if you really want to know."

"Mr Arkwright, you know damn well neither Madam Vetriano nor I have the register. I'm certain you stole it in case the law decided the deaths were more than a coincidence."

"No need to be formal, Mike," said the man affably. "Call me Allan, please."

"All right, Allan. I'll lay it out for you. Mrs A came to me worried you were 'playing away.' She really cares for you, you know, and after her run of marital errors was hurt and afraid you might turn out to be another. I know your wife from way back, and my regard for her is high, despite her bad press. Leo checked back through some of the dates when you cut your lesson short and found nearly every single time someone in the city snuffed it. Then the register disappeared. Coincidence? I don't think so."

"What an imagination. And I thought you were just a dimwit gumshoe. Appearances can be deceiving, can't they?" He laughed to take the insult out of it.

I didn't mind. I'd been called much worse, and couldn't help admiring his cool.

Allan leaned forward in his chair, and swirled his whisky before taking a sip.

"I love my wife and will never do anything to hurt her. You and I are on the same page on that. As for the untimely expirations, I admit nothing except, if you care to check, they all deserved to die." He lounged back in his chair. "Yes, for one reason or another they needed to be removed from civilised society. Especially the exes who were despicable characters intent on further damaging my wife's good name unless she funded their hedonistic lifestyles."

"You know this how?" I was sceptical. "Who appointed you both judge and executioner?"

"As I said I'm admitting nothing although in my import business I do hear things and consult with the rich and powerful on – let's say – matters of security. It's surprising what the conversation gets round to where guns are concerned."

"What about Madam Vetriano and her register?"

"Oh, dear old Mabel." Allan laughed. "I might have been a bit sloppy there and won't be so predictable in the future. You might not believe me, but I started off with Mabel learning to salsa to impress my wife, who's already good at it."

I couldn't think of anything else to ask him. He'd as good as admitted he was a hitman for hire. Money didn't seem to be his motivation; there was clearly no shortage of wealth in the Arkwright household. The only evidence that might start a police enquiry was missing, probably destroyed by my suspect.

I stood up and held out my glass to clink his.

"Cheers. Thanks for your time and good luck."

The thought crossed my mind that I, and possibly Leo, would be on his list if he had doubts about what I would report to Mrs A or the cops. As though reading my mind he said, "Up to you, Mike. I trust an old friend of Mrs A to do the right thing, whatever that may be. You have nothing to fear from me."

I made it back to my office shortly before five to find Leo anxiously checking the time, hand poised on the phone.

"Jeez, boss! I thought the crafty bastard had offed you. I was about to call DC What's-her-name. What took you so long?"

Leo collapsed in her chair.

"He's crafty, but no bastard or not where Mrs A is concerned." I laughed. "He's not a bad bloke. We had a drink, more than one; even so, I think I'm right. He's a hitman. He admitted it without admitting it, if you know what I mean."

"What are you going to do now?" asked Leo. "Tell Mrs A of your suspicions or tell the cops? Either way the unfortunate lady's life is stuffed up yet again. And we can't have a killer on contract roaming the city." Her eyes widened as she realised the implication. "I guess we're a danger to him now."

"I don't think so." I was as reassuring as I could be. "I didn't exactly put that to him in so many words, but I got the impression he would leave us alone no matter what."

"Hope your impression is correct. Pity you didn't get him to sign an affidavit to that effect while you were at it. As if he would!"

Leo headed for the door.

"Hope I see you tomorrow, boss."

By next morning when I pushed through the office door I still hadn't resolved my dilemma of what to report to Mrs A.

"Wow, are we early or what," Leo mocked. "Both of us still alive too, eh? That's a bonus. Your impression must have been correct."

"Good morning to you." I ignored Leo's banter. "Mrs A is due here any minute. I need to finish my report."

"Oh, yeah, what's it to be? The facts, ma'am, nothing, but the facts."

"Dunno."

With a mug of Leo's coffee in hand I settled behind my desk to await my client.

It wasn't long before Leo called out in her best officious manner, "Mrs A to see you, boss."

She held a chair for Mrs A then handed her a coffee unasked. Mrs A murmured, "Thank you."

I decided not to beat around the bush and skipped a long preamble reporting how I'd spent her money over the last few weeks. Maybe I would not even bill her. I still wasn't sure what my conscience would determine I say to her so I let my mouth do the talking.

As I was about to speak, Mrs A leaned forward, smiling.

"Before you begin, I must tell you Allan is moving us for business reasons to South America."

That settled it. Contract killer on the loose; someone else's problem.

"Mrs A, I'm sorry because he wanted it to be a surprise. I'm grieved and relieved to reveal to you that your husband is … learning to dance."

MIKE DUNN, SLEUTH

Chapter 1

"Customer coming up, boss, better put the whisky away." The intercom clicked off cutting short Leonie's chortle.

'Very funny,' I thought, smiling as always at Leo's irreverence for my exalted position as her employer, which never had cut any ice with her and which she maintained was a figment of my imagination. She was right, as she was about most things.

I hadn't yet got the bottle out even though it was late Friday afternoon and business was as slow as it had ever been; like, dead in the water. I had my feet up on the desk and was gazing out the window of my office at the signs above the shops opposite and wondering what they meant in Chinese and Vietnamese or whatever.

Where had all the Kiwi businesses gone, I asked myself. A fruitless exercise that I'd indulged in periodically over the years especially when business was slow, which usually ended with me wondering if I should go too.

To get past Leo the customer must have made a reasonable case; either deserving or more likely, their ability to pay. I'd shortened Leonie's name from day one as she reminded me of a lion, or lioness in her case; protective, clever and strong.

She'd seen my ad for a general dogsbody in the downstairs office window. Sick of the job rejections, which she suspected were connected to her Polynesian appearance, large and brown, she decided to 'try *me* out.'

Five years down the track she maintained she still hadn't made up her mind whether to stay in my employ or not.

"Please come in," I said to the woman I assumed was the customer as she peered into my office.

"I understand from the…ah…lady downstairs that you are a detective?"

If her manner hadn't been so tentative she would have been striking; medium height, late thirties or early forties, boots over jeans and a fluffy polo-necked jersey glistening with raindrops.

"I am, although some ill-informed ignoramuses would dispute that."

"Oh," she stuttered. "Then perhaps I've come to the wrong person."

"Apologies, ma'am, I was trying for a little levity; a bad and inappropriate habit of mine." As usual I'd gone too far too soon, as Leo was fond of pointing out.

"I am a fully qualified and licensed private investigator at your service. How can I help?"

"I don't know where to begin," she almost whispered.

"How about beginning with your name and then what it is that made you confront that brown harridan downstairs?"

She laughed. "Oh, she's no harridan; she's a sweetie."

I laughed this time. "Yes, she is, isn't she? Don't tell her I said so. She wouldn't want her cover blown. Now, your name?"

"Joan Withers and I'm here because my husband is trying to kill me."

"OK. Mrs Withers, what makes you say that?"

"Oh, I know you'll think I'm being silly. We seem to be having too many accidents. Luckily, so far, I haven't been hurt nor has my daughter Evelyn."

"What sort of accidents, Joan – I may call you Joan?"

"Yes, please do. I can't prove anything, but we've had two car crashes, both when Harold, my husband, was driving with me in the passenger seat. I think he lost his nerve in the first as we just missed the power pole, but we still ended up in a ditch. The second time was almost identical, except he drove into a tree. He didn't miss, but in the new car the airbags saved me, apart from a few bruises and bumps."

"What did the police have to say?"

"They weren't involved in the first one. Harold got a farmer to pull us out of the ditch. The car ended up being written off. He told the insurance company he'd been startled by a dog running across the road. I'm sure there was no dog, though he insists there was and that I must have been shaken up by the accident. He told the police after the second accident that he must have dozed off and they breathalysed him, but found nothing. He was fined for careless driving."

"Did you mention your suspicions to the police?"

"Not then because I didn't have any suspicions."

"So tell me, Joan, when did you start thinking your husband was trying to murder you?"

"After he tried to drown Evelyn and me." She looked imploringly at me as though aware how far-fetched her story sounded yet willing me to believe her.

"It was as though having failed with cars he gave boats a try. He insisted on buying a small aluminium dinghy, a 'tinny' he called it. Said he wanted to teach Evelyn how to fish. He knew neither of us were strong swimmers or had ever said we wanted to go fishing. He must have known I've always been afraid of the sea. I went along with him as I thought he might at last be taking an interest in Evelyn even though she is only his step-daughter.

"The weather was a bit changeable when we went out, but Evelyn was excited and I didn't want to spoil it for her so I said nothing. I did ask where the life-jackets were and he got angry and said they were in the locker under the front seat and anyway the forecast was good. Yet the weather turned rough almost as soon as we got out near the heads. There wasn't another boat in sight and the shore had disappeared in the rain. I was frightened by then and so was Evelyn.

"I clambered over the seats to get the lifejackets and the locker was empty. He just looked at me and I swear he sort of smirked and said, 'Oops.' I screamed at him to take us back, but he ignored me. The boat was filling with water, sinking I suppose. I couldn't see why as only a little was coming over the sides from the waves. He yelled the bung must have come out and he couldn't get the motor started. I thought we'd had it."

As she relived her ordeal, she became increasingly agitated.

"Take it easy."

I got up and poured her a coffee from the percolator. She took the mug gratefully, holding it in both hands as though to warm them.

"Thankfully you haven't had it because you're here. What happened next?"

"Unbelievably a big launch almost ran us down. I suppose at first they didn't see the grey tinny in the murk. They made quick work of dragging us on board including the dinghy. The man steering the launch said they'd seen something on the radar, but didn't think anything that small would be out so far in such weather."

She managed a half-smile.

"Luckily for us they decided to check anyway. I saw Harold fiddle around near the back of the dinghy and I think he was putting the plug thingy back in. The launch men were angry at him for what they called stupidity at going fishing in those conditions and without lifejackets."

She sipped her coffee, then continued. "They said they should notify the coastguard and police. Harold had a joking explanation for everything and they put us ashore with a warning not to be so irresponsible next time. As if there ever would be a next time."

"That's quite a story, Joan. But wasn't your husband in deep with you, if you'll pardon the pun?"

"I know what you're thinking; why would he risk himself to murder me? I don't know the answer. All I know is, from the hateful way he looked at me when I saw there were no life jackets, that he had planned it. Worse, I realised it wasn't only me he wanted to get rid of; it was Evelyn as well."

She lapsed into what would have been silence except she was hunched over with her head in her hands, gently weeping.

I'd always felt awkward around crying females. Some sort of latent guilt for being the oppressor gender, I suppose, or that's what Leo informed me was the reason. She walked in the door as I was about to call on the intercom to ask her to come up and tend to our customer. I remembered she usually listened in to my interviews with clients on the open intercom unless I asked her not to, and no doubt she only heeded that instruction if it suited her.

Leo shot me a reproachful glance as though it was my fault the lady was distressed. She put her arm around Mrs Wither's shoulders and handed her a tissue.

"You must think I'm crazy, imagining everything. The fishing incident was nearly a month ago now and since then it's as though he doesn't care about making it look like an accident anymore," she whispered.

Leo looked at me as though she knew I thought Joan Withers was crazy so I gave her the nod.

"Mrs Withers, Joan, what has happened since the boat rescue?" Leo spoke softly.

By way of answer Mrs Withers pulled up the sleeve of her jersey to reveal deep bruising from shoulder to elbow. "There's more all over my body if you want to see."

"How did that happen, Joan?" Leo helped Joan pull her sleeve back down.

"I was carrying a big load of laundry and he waited until I was nearly at the top of the basement stairs on the little landing then he flung open the door. I took an awful tumble right to the bottom and landed on the concrete floor."

"What about Evelyn – is he abusing her?" Leo still had her arm around Joan's shoulder.

"Not physically, but he completely ignores her most of the time. He does say horribly sarcastic and hurtful things to her if she annoys him in some way."

Leo stated the obvious. "With those bruises to show you could go to the police or social welfare."

"Why would they believe me? It's not as though Evelyn has been harmed yet. He has such a plausible way of explaining things that they would believe him before me. Besides if I did report him he would know I knew what he was up to."

"Why do you think he wants to, ah, do away with you?" Leo can be delicate at times.

The poor lady started sobbing again.

"I don't know. I've been as kind as I know how for the six years we've been married. His first wife died in an accident about a year before we met."

Leo gave me a sideways look to be sure I'd picked up on that comment.

"He was nice to me and caring of Evelyn at the start. Later his attitude altered, slowly at first. Perhaps all marriages cool off."

"So you can't think of a reason why he wants to murder you?"

If she noticed my attempt at shock tactics, which brought a frown from Leo, she didn't show it. Just shook her head in the negative.

A bit of her spark surfaced. "What is it exactly you want me to do? You're the detective. Can't you find out what he's up to without him knowing?"

"Not as easy as you might think, Joan. Why don't you leave it with me over the weekend? I'll ponder your problem and get back to you soonish."

Leo ushered her down the stairs and held the street door for her. Over the intercom I heard Leo say by way of goodbye, "Don't worry, Joan. My boss is good at this. He'll help you."

Presently Leo reappeared with her body rigid and arms aggressively folded. Experience told me I could tell she was intent on speaking her mind.

"You don't believe her, do you?"

"Not all of it. Maybe it's a domestic, not my line of work, or yours."

"What! It has to be murder before it's our line of work?"

"Come on, Leo. I said I'd think about it and get back to her."

"You said ponder her problem and you would get back soonish. I know you, soonish means maybe, sometime never in your language."

"Yeah, well, you're right. I can't help being more concerned with those insurance fraud jobs we've got piled up that you're supposed to be working on with your magical computer research skills. Forgive me if I put corporate paying jobs, which pay your wages by the way, before tin-pot domestic quarrels."

"So money's everything now is it?"

"While we're on the subject of money, can she pay? Has she got any?"

"Boss, you know damn well that was the first thing I asked her and you know damn well the answer is NO."

"Yeah I know. Domestics are always pro bono and you always sucker me into taking the case if *you* think it's the right thing to do. Look, I said I'd think about and I will."

"OK, I hear you, I hope you do. Right now I've gotta go. Hubby will be wondering. I'll get onto the fraud stuff 'soonish' come Monday."

"Very funny. Say g'day to Jim for me."

"Will do. It's late. You should go home now too boss."

As Leo departed I reflected that our disagreements never lasted long. I would hardly call them disagreements, more slight differences of opinion in an otherwise fine employer and employee relationship. Funny how her opinion always was the one that seemed to count though. To hell with it, I mused, it's Friday night and the weekend awaits. I shut down the percolator, flicked the lights off and went out the street door, into the neon garish world of what might have well been called Chinatown. I happily whistled Dire Straits *Sultans of Swing* and gave Joan Withers and her problem not another thought.

▲

Chapter 2

It was too early to go home. There was nothing there anyway. My house was on the edge of the city's central business district, not exactly the suburbs, but just as dismal in the early dark of a wet winter's night.

I headed downtown, parked the Chrysler in a loading bay that surely wouldn't be needed this time of the evening, left my police parking warrant in clear sight on the dash just in case. I strolled up High Street to the Civic where if I was lucky Mac and some of the city's finest would be celebrating their survival after another crime fighting week.

"Hey, hey, look what the rain just washed in. Our city's top numero uno private detective come to wise us up on how it's done!" Mac raised his glass. "You're a couple behind, mate. Been fighting the triads out there in Chinatown? Or has Leo been keeping you late again?"

"Smart bastard," I said. "Leo never keeps me or anyone else late, except maybe her husband. Anyway, how come you and your fellow defenders of public order aren't out busting the triads, if there are any?"

"As a Chief Inspector it behoves me to direct others."

"Behoves, eh? I can tell you're a C.I., I suppose you and Andy and Gordon and the others are here in conference about some weighty criminal matter?"

"Of course. We're all commissioned rank here including Vic over there, who I don't believe you've met."

Mac gestured at a woman sitting back to the wall on the far side of the low table the cops had made their own for the evening. The plain trouser suit she wore looked a whole lot better on her than the similar cop outfits of the others. She looked far too young to be an officer, which was why I had overlooked her when I'd come in, thinking she might be a girlfriend of one of the other cops.

"Well, pleased to meet you, Vic," I had to raise my voice over the bar's din. To which she nodded coolly.

"Talkative type." I turned back to Mac. "All this banter has made me thirsty. Got me one in yet?"

"Now who's the cheeky bastard? Inspectors don't buy drinks for private dicks; it's the other way round. Make mine a double."

So I did and the conversation rippled out from crime and police work to the usual blokey stuff, but always coming back to crime and police work. Everyone had an opinion about everything. Except the female cop. Not that she remained aloof. When spoken to she responded with a nod or a few words. Her presence didn't seem to inhibit the men. Mind you, they'd all been around the block a few times; you didn't get to be an officer in the force if you're a sensitive shrinking violet.

She piqued my curiosity, yet I knew if I made even the most oblique reference to her the others would show me no mercy. Although a little taller, Vic's stature reminded me of the distressed woman who had come in late to my office. In every other way they couldn't have been more different.

Vic, despite her reticence, exuded confidence and self-reliance. I couldn't see her sobbing with self-pity or succumbing to a brute of a husband.

"Have any of you guys come across a Harold or Joan Withers?" I asked the gathering in a conversational pause.

"Not me." Mac shrugged. "Anyone else?"

No-one answered and the hubbub resumed.

"Why, what have they done?" Mac asked.

"Domestic, if anything."

"Not your scene, is it? I thought you were making a fortune collaring those insurance cheats?"

"I wish. The wife, Mrs Withers, came in off the street with a major sob story. Thinks hubby Withers is going to off her. Leo thinks she is genuine and I should do something about it."

"If Leo thinks you should, then so do I. Tell you what, if I remember I'll run their names through the computer Monday morning, see if they've got a history. Right now I'm off home to my dearest and a quiet weekend."

Mac left and the others drifted away, including Vic who left with one of the younger cops, confirming my earlier assumption. After another round of desultory conversation I left Andy and Gordon contemplating the sea of silent empties covering every inch of the table.

"See you guys next Friday maybe. Don't let those crooked bastards get you down."

Outside the city had had its Friday night shift change from day people to night people. The rain had stopped, although the pavements still glistened and the cars swished through gathered water. I'd stayed a bit later than I'd intended at the bar, but keeping in with the boys was no hardship.

Mac, older than me and always a couple of jumps ahead on the promotion ladder had been my mentor and still was where police matters were concerned. We'd become more like equals since I'd gone solo.

Andy, Gordon and I were classmates at police college back in our early twenties. They'd only recently come into my orbit again when they joined Mac's Serious Crimes Squad after various postings in other cities.

Our careers had been level-pegging until my voluntary exit from the force. I'd never bothered analysing or questioning our relationship since. Maybe it was more mutual benefit than friendship.

My car was where I'd left it, unmolested. The police parking warrant could work both ways as an attractant or repellent to unwanted attention, but as far as I know nobody has yet spotted that it officially expired years ago.

▲

Chapter 3

"Late again, boss." Leo grinned as she stated the obvious.

"Yeah, well, the game on Sunday was a tough one."

I must be the only employer in this town who feels required to explain their actions to an employee.

"Don't know why you play that game, I'm sure. More like a brawl than a game," Leo sniffily opined.

"Give me a break, Leo. I've heard your opinion about rugby ad nauseum."

"Ad nauseum? Wow, this is going to be a highbrow week. Speaking of which, you've got a visitor."

Leo never let anyone into my office when I wasn't there except Mac. Even so I knew he wasn't above 'updating' himself as he called it. So I clumped up the stairs to give him plenty of time to put back whatever he was 'snooping' at, as I called it.

"Learn anything?" I headed for the coffee percolator which Mac had thoughtfully switched on and helped himself from.

"I had no idea insurance fraud was so profitable. Makes me wonder if I should quit the force and take up your line of work," he said not bothering to deny he had been snooping.

"Nice of you to drop by. Glad I can offer some career advice, though I doubt, you being a highly experienced police officer and all, that you've come here for advice."

"I notice that you haven't done anything about the Withers case?"

"What Withers case? There is no Withers case."

In truth, I had not exactly forgotten Joan Withers. After all, Leo had asked me about progress a couple of times over the past fortnight since Mrs Withers had paid me a visit. I had put any idea of checking out her claim on the back burner. I didn't think I could do anything unless she was willing to bring charges against her husband. Then it would be a police matter.

"Has she made a complaint?"

"She can't; she's dead."

"Bloody hell! Now that does make me feel bad."

"So it should. About as bad as I feel. I forgot, what with the weekend and family stuff and then on the Monday the squad took on a couple of high profile cases like that low-life on parole dropping another kid on her head you've been reading about in the press."

"Uh, oh. Leo's going to have an attack of 'I told you so' any minute now."

"Don't worry; I've already turned the intercom off." Mac got up to refill his coffee.

I held out my cup. "Don't mind if I do, seeing it's mine. What makes you think I can help?"

"I did remember, when the commissioner dropped the case on my desk this morning, that you'd mentioned their names a couple of weeks ago. I was hoping you could tell me why Mrs Withers came to you in the first place?"

"Sure. From memory, she reckoned her husband, Harold, was trying to murder her. Why, she had no idea or wouldn't say. Seemed likely she was being pushed around. She had no real proof, which is why she didn't come to you guys even though I urged her to do that."

"Well, she didn't. I wonder why?"

"Like most abuse victims, frightened I suppose. She would have been afraid for her daughter, Evelyn. Who's looking after her?"

"She doesn't need looking after. She's had her throat cut, too."

"Jesus wept!"

"Yeah, well, he oughta," Mac got up. "Look, I've got to go down the morgue, pick up the coroner's report. Come if you want, take a look at mother and daughter, maybe think of something relevant."

If it wasn't for the macabre purpose of the trip I would have enjoyed the ride. In defiance of the force's public relations policy Mac wasn't above using an occasional growl on his unmarked cruiser's siren to ease his path through the city's chronic gridlock. I had to laugh.

"No wonder you get around Gotham faster than Superman."

"Don't know about Superman and I've never been to Gotham. I certainly don't give a shit for public relations when murder is the go and especially where double murder including that of a minor is concerned."

"G'day, Maude. Is the sawbones in?"

Mac smiled at the lady behind the front desk, who had melted at his approach.

"Good morning, Chief Inspector. Please, go right in."

She almost simpered, which was entirely wasted on Mac. I'd seen the reaction he evoked in women many times before and not once had he ever acknowledged the lady's reaction let alone taken it any further. He was well aware of his appearance and charm and didn't hesitate to use it to get his way. Like the siren on his cruiser.

He'd been married for more than twenty-five years to Mary and remained devoted to her and their three kids, all now studying at different universities around the country. Not only an honest cop, and ruthless when circumstances demanded, but moral.

"Morning, Doc. I see my people are already on the job."

Mac nodded towards the woman who had been talking animatedly to the man Mac had addressed as Doc.

164

"Whaddya reckon, Vic, anything new?"

"Been sexually molested."

"Mother or daughter or both?"

"Daughter. Doc's going to run some more tests, see if he can pick up some foreign DNA."

With that she turned and, with a wave that included Doc and Mac, but pointedly excluded me, left the cold room.

Mac turned to me.

"You met Vic a couple of weeks ago at the Civic, didn't you?"

"Yeah. Is it just me or does she freeze all men out?"

"Pretty much, so don't take it personally. With your gentlemanly charm and manners you might break through one day though, take my advice, I wouldn't hold my breath because she doesn't like big ugly brawlers like you."

"Her loss. What's she doing here anyway?"

"Same as us. Vic's taking a look at the vics, no pun intended. Seeing if she should get involved. She's my child abuse expert."

"Bloody hell, no wonder she doesn't like men!"

I consoled myself that her indifference to me wasn't personal.

"OK, Doc. Let's have a look at what we've got."

Mac handed me a white coat and mask and donned one himself.

Doc flicked back the green rubber sheets that covered the two cadavers and began in a monotone explaining the injuries. I'd seen this sort of thing a few times before, though not so much since I'd gone big on insurance fraud.

Even so the brutal way the throats had been slashed and the bruising over much of both female's bodies was hard to take. I could see the sweat on Mac's forehead and realised that no matter how many times or how recently you had seen this brutality you never got used to it.

"Amateur or in a hell of a hurry." Mac tried for lightness, the only response possible in the circumstances.

"Or both," I replied. "Or a professional trying to look like an amateur."

"Yeah, OK, smartarse. What else?"

I moved around the table to get a different angle on the bodies.

"Left handed, tall or tallish, above medium height anyway."

"Very good," said Mac. "Or it could have been a right handed, short person trying to look like they weren't."

"Yeah, OK now we're both smartarses. I suppose the husband is an ambidextrous, shortish tallish person. He has to be first in the frame, doesn't he?"

"No wonder you're a top private detective. Yeah, he's in the frame all-right. You'd expect as normal his prints and DNA to be all over the house and even on the bodies. After all, he is, was their husband and father or stepfather. But there is none on the bodies where you'd expect it to be and no semen or any other fluids."

"Well, if doc keeps looking he'll surely find something that puts the husband's hands where they shouldn't be."

"Maybe," replied Mac. "Trouble is hubby's got an alibi that an eight point earthquake couldn't shake."

▲

Chapter 4

I had nothing to help the case move forward. I left Mac to it with his promise to keep me informed if anything developed. Nothing must have because I heard nothing from him for a few weeks and I'd had other fish to fry, bringing a number of fraud cases to a satisfactory end. Being busy meant that unusually I'd missed two consecutive Friday evenings at the Civic.

Then midway through the third week I got a call from Mary, Mac's wife, inviting me to dinner with them the following Saturday night. Mary had elected herself as my surrogate carer after Susan passed away. I had nothing planned and I probably would have accepted even if I had. Mary was a damn good cook, which would make a welcome change from the TV dinner that was my usual Saturday night feed if I wasn't having pie and chips at the footy club after the match.

"Come on in out of the cold, big boy," Mary stood on tiptoe to plant a kiss on each cheek. "Mac's out on the deck firing up the barby. We know how much you like a good steak. Go on through while I finish up the salads."

"Good to see you, Mary and thanks for the invite." I handed her the bottle of Turtle Cove pinot gris. "Anything I can carry through for you?"

"No, no, dear. You know the way. I'll be along shortly."

The beauty of Mac's place was that the deck was almost fully enclosed. Provided the weather was reasonably benign, which it was even though it was the middle of winter, barbecues were possible any time of year.

"About time, mate. We're getting hungry here." Mac grinned broadly at me as I stepped onto the deck.

"You will live out here in the boondocks. Why, I can barely see the lights of the city from here; makes a city boy like me feel insecure."

I laughed too because we both knew I'd been raised on a farm and had far more claim to be countrified than he had as a true blue Westie. I turned as a woman spoke, her voice laden with sarcasm.

"Excuse me for intruding, I'm sure. If Mac isn't going to acknowledge me I'll say good evening myself."

"Excuse you? Why, leaving already are you?" Which smart alec response I instantly regretted when I saw it was Vic, the female cop.

"I'm sorry. I didn't see you sitting over there in the dark."

"Mac said he was inviting a friend this evening. If I'd known it was you, I probably wouldn't have accepted."

"Well, don't let me stop you leaving now. What's Vic short for anyway? A man's name, I bet. Victor?"

"Whoa, kids, come on. Saturday night with Mary cooking is no time to be squabbling. Let's start again. Vic, Victoria, this is Mike. He used to be in the force and now he's a P.I. Mike, this is Victoria Hill, our newest detective in the Serious Crimes Squad. Her father, you might recall though it's slightly before your time, was my first station commander and retired last year. Now shake hands and be polite to each other at least."

"Sorry, Mac. And apologies to you … Miss, Ms, Mrs? … Hill." I offered my hand. "I'm not sure how I've offended you. Perhaps we can start again?"

She returned my handshake firmly and without the least hint of apology.

"Victoria, or if you must, Vic. like most people around here."

She shot an angry glance at Mac as though he was responsible for anointing her with a sobriquet of which she didn't approve.

Or she could have been, for all I knew, irritated at Mac and Mary's blatant attempt at match-making. I know I was, and it wasn't the first time. They'd promised to desist after the debacle that was the last jolly evening we had endured nearly a year ago.

The lady in question was the widow of an innocent victim caught in the crossfire of one of Mac's more spectacular busts. To Mac and Mary she seemed to tick all the boxes and therein lay the trouble. She reminded me of a lesser Susan and it seemed I reminded her of her late husband and so she wept throughout the evening.

I realised then that even after nearly a decade it was always going to be too soon. I asked them to cease and desist their kindly efforts.

"I know what you're thinking," Mac spoke up. "Mary and I have set this up to bring you two together. You're right in one way, though not in the way you think. I wanted to run the latest on the Withers case past you, Mike. Vic, you've been the most involved from our crew. I thought you could fill in any gaps."

"Dinner's ready, Mac, if you'll bring the steaks in." Mary was oblivious, or pretending to be, of any awkwardness out on the deck.

I let myself be seduced by Mary's vivacious good cheer and delicious cooking. Everyone played it safe and kept the conversation light. As usual I couldn't help myself confirming what I perceived as Vic's opinion of me as a macho misogynist thug, which, from their frowns, pained our hosts. Even that, perversely, pleased me because it proved, if I needed proof, that Mac and Mary knew me well enough to know that that wasn't the real me.

"Not a rugby fan then, Vic?" I enquired after extolling at length the manly virtues of the game.

"Not for me to say."

"Oh? I thought I saw you frowning just then."

Why the hell I couldn't shut up I had no idea.

"No, no. If you think smashing into each other to cripple and end up brain damaged is sport, that's your affair. Don't ask me to watch or approve. I see enough mindless violence as it is."

"Don't want to come and see me play then?"

She gave a little shudder. "Thanks, but no thanks."

And that seemed to be that. As we watched Vic climb into her car I said to Mary and Mac, "Nice try, and thanks for the meal."

"Time you moved on, big boy. Vic's a lovely lady, you know, and ten years is a long time," Mary said wistfully.

"Yeah, I know. I'm a bloody idiot but I can't help it. Maybe one day."

With that I departed, the lights of my big Chrysler failing to illuminate more than the red pinpricks that marked the taillights of Vic's sleek Alfa Romeo.

▲

Chapter 5

"Boss, you've got a visitor on her way up. I'm out for a while and won't be back today," Leo's voice came softly over the intercom.

"Ok, Leo, see you tomorrow." I was happy to be interrupted. Insurance work might be lucrative, but it gets a bit tedious. Sure, Leo was an expert researcher and she had an excellent rapport with the companies. Clients still liked to see my input somewhere in the process.

When I heard footsteps on the landing, I got up and opened the door ready to welcome a new client.

"Oh, hello," I stuttered. "I wasn't expecting you."

"Who were you expecting then?" asked Vic.

"I'm sorry, no-one in particular. Just not you."

What was it with this woman that caused me to blurt out things like a gauche schoolboy? Me who could supposedly defeat villains with one hand tied behind my back, never bested in a fight, and, most impressive of all, maintained a cordial working relationship with who many considered the most formidable front office Poly in the city.

"Well, it's only me, and I'm sorry if that's a disappointment for you."

"Not at all What can I do for you?"

I resolved to keep my lip buttoned and stick strictly to business. Evidently Vic had decided the same thing, but it was hard to tell. So far she hadn't said much whenever I was around. Her lips seemed permanently buttoned.

"You recall the Withers case?" she said eventually.

"Of course, and I've followed it in the papers. Mac said in passing that you hadn't got far with it. I thought it was open and shut, down to the husband?"

"Yeah, that's what we thought, too, but the husband's got a cast iron alibi. We can't shake him and there's no-one else in the frame. Mac suggested I come and see you."

I think she nearly added 'goodness knows why' before she stopped herself.

"He thinks you can do things we can't, especially in such a high profile case."

"You mean he doesn't want to remind the powers that be of the force's recent police brutality faux pas?"

'I don't know anything about that. He just said you'd been on the right side many times over the years and wouldn't mind helping."

"Depends. What do you want me to do?"

I'm not sure, so how about I lay out what we know? Maybe we'll come up with an idea between us what to do next."

"Well, well, this is a new spirit of co-operation between us. With due respect, I owe Mac a lot and I'd help wherever I could, but don't take that as an insult to you. I'm happy to help you, too."

She shrugged as though indifferent and hurried on.

"You know the basic facts. Two weeks after Joan Withers came to ask you to check on her husband's activities she and her daughter Evelyn were murdered. We had the husband for it. His vitals were everywhere in the house, but that wasn't any use as evidence; they weren't estranged. There were no body fluids where there shouldn't have been on or in either of the vics."

I noticed she pinked up a tad as she spoke; not as detached as she'd like me to think.

"Anyway, he was miles away down south in Hamilton on a business trip. We've checked his story and 'phone calls and they're all kosher. The bastard even had a hooker in his motel room and she corroborated."

"Sure you're not trying to fit him up just because he clearly is a bastard?"

She glanced at me askance. "What kind of amateur cop do you take me for?"

"No offence intended, but look, you wouldn't be much older than my daughter if I'd had one, so I've got no idea if you're an amateur or not."

Damn. Mouth open and foot inserted. Again.

"If I was your daughter, heaven forbid, I would only be about sixteen. It may surprise you, but you have to be a bit older than that with qualifications and a lot of experience to get on Mac's Serious Crimes Squad." Vic spoke softly with only a hint of sarcasm.

I recognised she'd made a valid point. "Look, I'm sorry. Of course, you have to be good to be invited to work for his outfit." I paused. "Damn it, I always seem to be saying sorry to you. That's it. No more. And from now on I'm going to call you Victoria even if no-one else does, if that's all right?"

It sounded lame, even to me. To my relief a half-smile played upon her lips.

"I would be pleased if you did." For the first time she met my gaze directly.

"Great! That's settled. Now, Victoria, what does Joan's hubby do for a crust?"

She had the grace to pretend she didn't notice my experimental use of her name.

"He's one of those commission salesmen. He works for himself as a rep for plumbing supply companies. So he's away from home a lot. IRD records show he's doing OK with it.

Seems fairly well-off, though he seems to have kept the family on a tight rein."

"What about motive?"

"Nothing definite yet. We're working on it. Could be an insurance scam, so right up your alley. Maybe he was a sexual deviant meddling where he shouldn't."

"Could he have come back anytime during the evening after the vics were last seen alive and before witnesses put him in Hamilton?"

"Mac had one of the traffic guys replicate the trip, same time of evening, weather conditions and similar powered car even if he had to use the brights and siren a couple of times. He was ages slower than the time hubby would have needed to get to the family home in the Western suburbs and back to Hamilton in time to connect with his next alibi."

"Which was?"

"The prostitute turning up for her trick."

"Charming. So we reckon this person drove like a bat out of hell for what – three hours or so – then calmly had it off with a hooker."

"He could have used Viagra."

I laughed. "That wasn't what I meant, Victoria."

"I know." She laughed too. "I was making a joke."

"Joke, eh? Things are looking up. I can see why hubby's sticking to his story; it's pretty tight. So where does that leave us?"

"How would you feel about coming the heavy on the bastard? I mean, you wouldn't have to hurt him, just threaten him with grievous bodily harm."

"Sure, no problem. I like a bit of GBH now and again."

Victoria regarded me with distaste.

"Joke, Victoria. My turn."

She almost smiled.

"Hey, it's Friday and I'm about to lock up. Leo's long gone. The Civic awaits along with your intrepid crime-fighting comrades no doubt. How about we shock them all and put in an appearance?"

"Sorry," she said. "Prior engagement."

I hoped I'd concealed my disappointment.

▲

Chapter 6

The Withers house had been released as a crime scene so it was reasonable to assume Harold Withers had moved back in. The house was a stucco, executive style bungalow on a brick basement garage, set back from the road. Sited in a quiet street of similar houses on quarter-acre sections, it dated from a time post-war when it was considered necessary to provide children with outdoor play space.

There was a Ford station wagon of the type travelling salesmen drove parked nose in to the closed garage doors. I ran the Chrysler up behind it rather than park on the street. Might as well intimidate from the get-go. I noted the V8 engine option badges on the Ford.

I banged heavily on the front door, eschewing the bell push. There was a scurry of sound, more than you'd expect from one person, and then a man answered the door. From the headshot Victoria had given me I knew it was my man. The photo, and one or two I'd seen in the press flattered him. He was big all right, but size had turned to flab; a penalty of being a sedentary salesman, I supposed.

"Mr Withers?" I spoke as officiously as I knew how.

"Yes," he answered dismissively.

"Mr Harold Withers?"

"I've already said I'm him."

"I need to speak with you about …ah, recent events."

"Look, pal, I haven't got time right now to speak to you or anyone for that matter, especially if you're media. I've said all I'm going to say to them and the police."

"I only need a minute of your time. It's about insurance."

I considered shoving the door hard and stepping over him, but there was a fair chance a neighbour was watching, fascinated by what went on in a house where a double murder had been committed.

He wavered at the possibility 'insurance' meant a payout for him.

"Ok." He stood aside and swung the door wide. "I'll give you a few minutes."

"I'm investigating a policy held by Mrs Joan Withers. Certain aspects could rule against the company paying out."

"Oh yeah. I didn't know she had any insurance. How much is it worth?"

"I'm not at liberty to say, though probably be in the high six figures."

I let that sink in.

"The coroner has ruled death at the hand of person or persons unknown. You, Mr Withers are entered on your deceased wife's policy as beneficiary. Quite clearly the company cannot pay out such a substantial sum to you if you are a suspect in her demise."

Besides being lucrative, working on a multitude of insurance fraud cases had another benefit; I'd picked up the jargon.

He was immediately combative. "I'm not a suspect. The police have exonerated me."

"That may well be what they've told you. I happen to know from my police contacts they're still highly interested in you. Until their interest ceases the company cannot proceed with forwarding the payment to her estate."

There was a cough from a back room.

"I'm sorry. I didn't know you had company."

Harold was furious. "I told the bitch to keep quiet when anyone came to the house."

He rushed out of the room and I heard a slap and yelp of pain from a female.

I took a punt. "No need to take your predicament out on Miss Desiree from Hamilton. Not her fault you can't collect unless you can prove your innocence, is it?"

He exploded. "Get the fuck out of my house you fuckin' creep."

He grabbed my arm, assuming because he was bigger than me that I could be forcibly ejected. Big mistake. I waited for him to open the front door with his free hand then as he turned I sucker-punched him in the solar plexus.

"What the fuck!"

He screamed in shock as he went down on his knees. I grabbed a handful of hair and jerked his head up so his eyes met mine.

"We were getting on so well and you blew it, sunshine. Tell Miss Desiree goodbye from me."

I raised my voice. "Miss, I know you can hear me. If you've got any sense you'll put as much distance as you can between yourself and this arsehole."

I turned back to Harold. "And you, pal, I'll be seeing again soon and I won't be half as patient next time."

With that I gave him a moderately firm kick in the ribs, stepped around him and placed my card on a table by the door. I sauntered down the front steps, with a friendly wave to the curtain twitcher across the street.

▲

Chapter 7

"Keep up the good work." I tapped Leo on the shoulder as she hunched over to concentrate on her computer.

"Whoa, hang on a minute there, boss." She surfaced just as I'd almost made it out the street door. "Where are you off to, if you don't mind me asking?"

"Out. Business."

"Oh yeah, what business?"

"Business business."

"Paying business?"

"Not-paying-a-lot business," I hedged. I've never lied to Leo and she always sees right through any attempt to stall her.

"Ah ha, pro bono then." A statement not a question. "I bet you're involving yourself in that Withers murder. Why?"

"Ok, I am, so what? I feel bad about dismissing her story. If I'd taken her more seriously, like you suggested, things might have been different. Maybe I'm trying to make up for my professional lapse."

"Wouldn't be the first time and you'll notice I haven't said I told you so. Sure you're not in it to get closer to that Vic piece of skirt?"

"Leo! How could you suggest such a thing?" I adopted a tone of mock hurt. "You know me. I'm not interested in that sort of thing."

"I know that, boss, and I also know that sooner or later there would come a time when you did become interested again in *that sort of thing*."

Leo drew speech marks in the air.

"Maybe later has arrived, if you know what I mean." She waved me off. "Get outta here. I'll hold the fort as usual."

I grinned at her and waved as I stepped out. Already she was tapping away rapidly on the keyboard.

I gunned the Chrysler down Dominion endeavouring to make up time for my now late meeting with Mac at Central. The lights had other ideas and I caught every red. While I waited, I mulled over what Leo had said.

I don't know where she got her insight from; maybe something to do with her island roots and the wisdom of Poly rellies. Generally, she was right and I had come to trust her implicitly. Her double degree and the fact she was a smart lady helped, too.

I had told her the truth. I was doing the Withers case out of a sense of guilt, but Leo's comments made me realise that similar cases had happened before and I'd let them go. Hindsight is illuminatory and I couldn't pursue every case like a knight in white armour, or was that shining armour on a white horse.

Anyway, my Chrysler was black. Maybe I needed to re-examine my motives on this one, but not right now. I was committed, to Mac if not the dead, and that was that.

"You know the way." The desk sergeant waved me through the security door.

Mac was on the phone and he gestured for me to sit down as he hung up. He had a can of soda on his desk.

"What, no coffee machine?" I taunted.

"Our budgets are kept for items that progress the forces policy to protect and serve, not fritter on fancy coffee machines."

"Too bad. I could have used a cup."

"You'll survive. Now cut the backchat and tell me how you got on with Mr Withers."

"Sure, but shouldn't Victoria be in on this?"

"Victoria, eh?" He gave me a hard stare before he picked up the phone and pressed a button.

"Vic, got a minute?"

I related what had transpired at the Withers house. Except for the rough stuff as I was leaving; no need to show myself in a bad light. Not that Mac would care, but then it wasn't him I was thinking of.

"What a good idea to pass yourself off as an insurance investigator although I suppose that's what you do most," commented Victoria. "Did his wife have a policy?"

"No, not exactly."

"What if he makes a complaint?"

"Why would he? He still thinks he might have a substantial payout coming. Anyway, who's he going to complain to? You? The insurance company? I never mentioned any company by name. I left my card more in case his lady friend had a rush of self-preserving conscience. If he does come back to me he's going to find a legitimate private investigative business. He'd never get anything out of Leo."

"Is he left or right handed?" asked Mac.

"I dunno. He tried to hit me with his left, but opened the door with his right. I neglected to ask him or his lady friend and I didn't offer to shake his hand when I left."

"Speaking of his lady friend," said Victoria, "he must be a real low-life to be having it off with her when his wife and daughter are hardly cool in their graves."

"Yeah well, just because he's a rat-bag doesn't make him guilty of murder," I said. "Especially if he's got an alibi."

Mac sighed and sat up. "Where to from here then?"

"I'll have another crack at the hooker," said Victoria. "She's kind of elevated herself to accomplice status if she is the same one that was part of his alibi."

"I realise you guys have replicated the drive there and back in the time available, but I've seen his car. It's capable, big engine. I'd like to see if I can do it in mine. Same night of the week, weather, time, everything as near the same as possible."

"What makes you think you can do better than our man?"

"I'm not saying I can do better, but your guy is a policeman driving a police car. There are only so many risks he would take even with his brights and siren going. Also, maybe the motorway is the shortest and fastest on paper. This guy is a travelling salesman who probably knows all the back roads with almost zero traffic that on a quiet Tuesday night are less likely to be patrolled."

"If you do, be it on your own head. I'm not sanctioning any risk to public safety, and I'm assuming Detective Victoria Hill will volunteer to accompany you as police liaison officer to smooth things down when our traffic patrol catches you."

"If that's an order, Mac – ah, sir."

"Next Tuesday it is then," I said.

Mac couldn't resist it. "Sounds like you've got a date, Vic, with this big lug. Must be his first."

He grinned at my embarrassment and, I presume, Victoria's as we left his office.

▲

Chapter 8

"What makes you think this old crate can get us to Hamilton and back let alone break the land speed record?"

I retorted, "Because this old crate is a fine piece of machinery."

Victoria snorted.

"Looks can be deceiving, Victoria. You should know. You're a cop," I said.

"Looks don't deceive me for long, buster."

"My Chrysler 300C may not be the most beautiful of cars, but this one's got the big engine and performance options that makes it a wolf in sheep's clothing. It may look like an old ewe to you. It's anything but."

"All right, no need to get shirty. Men and their cars!"

The drive to Hamilton was uneventful and largely silent. We pulled up outside the motel Withers had stayed in. We got out for a breather and a stretch. Then I checked my watch.

"Right. Now I'm going to concentrate for as long as it takes us to get to the Withers house, so I'd appreciate it if you could keep chat to what's necessary."

"Shut up, in other words."

"Victoria, that's not what I meant. You're hardly garrulous as it is. The thing is, I doubt Harold had company, assuming he made the trip, and we're attempting to replicate it as much as possible."

"Gotcha." She made a zipping motion across her mouth.

"His last physical contact was with the motel owner ostensibly to get more milk at what; ten past eight?"

"Yep."

"Then what? The cell call that routed through the North Hamilton tower to an escort agency ten minutes later?"

"Check."

"Then nothing until just before midnight when he was recorded buying gas in a local service station, having dropped the hooker off nearby, so he said."

"Right."

I suppressed a chuckle to conceal from her I knew she was taking the mickey.

"So we've got to get from outside the motel to the western suburbs, park out of sight of the house, run in, murder a couple of people, drive like crazy back to Hamilton, pick up a prostitute, fill up with petrol all within slightly more than three and a half hours?"

"Correct."

"The police driver did it in three hours and forty-five minutes using the motorways, and he did it in reverse direction from the city to Hamilton. He didn't start from Hamilton?"

"Roger."

"Well, I'm going up the state highway, not the motorway. There'll only be a smattering of local traffic for the first hour and there certainly won't be any cops patrolling on a winter Tuesday night. Unless you've found out there are?"

"No."

"Is that a no, there are no cops or no, you've not checked?"

"No cops."

"Right then, we're off. All set?"

"Uh, uh."

I burst out laughing. "Ok, you win. Talk as much as you like. I may not answer, and that's not being rude, just concentrating."

"I didn't think you'd noticed I was being verbally economic. By the way, I'm impressed with a private investigator using long words like garrulous and ostensible. Maybe you're not the macho thug you make yourself out to be."

"Maybe you're not the buttoned up career cop you make yourself out to be either?"

We were both laughing now, though as I accelerated the car into its high speed cruise mode as we left the lit suburbs of Hamilton behind, we settled in to what struck me as a companionable silence.

The headlights on high beam bored through the darkness. Our speed, well over the limit, made it seem we were rushing through a never-ending tunnel. Victoria must have realised the mesmerising effect of this because every now and again as though checking I was still alert she made an inconsequential comment that required me to answer.

We rejoined the motorway system at the southern outskirts of the city to take us across town to the western suburbs. Even then there was little traffic.

I broke the silence. "How long does it take to murder two people?"

"He couldn't risk parking in his street in case a neighbour recognised his car. There is an all-night dairy on the main road just before you turn into his street. I reckon he probably stopped there. We could do the same and get a bite and drink for about the fifteen or twenty minutes it must have taken him. Let's say twenty minutes to give him the benefit of the doubt."

We pulled up outside the dairy one hour and fifty minutes after leaving the Hamilton motel. That meant we'd used up slightly more than half the time available.

"Maybe your police driver was right. We've still got to go and commit murder and get back to Hamilton."

"I know," sighed Victoria. "Is there no rest for the wicked? Come on, the department will spring for a couple of pies and coffee."

We sauntered into the dairy. The Indian shopkeeper recognised Victoria from when she'd been making enquiries about the double murder. He was obviously surprised to see her.

"Detective Officer Hill, what can I do for you and your gentleman friend at this late hour?"

She raised her eyebrows at the 'gentleman friend.'

"This is my associate, Mike. We're on the job and in a bit of a hurry. We'd like a meat pie and a coffee each, please."

"Meat pies coming up. Sorry, no coffee from machine. I make you instant coffee out the back. OK? No customers this late anyway. Come."

We followed him behind the counter and through a curtain to a large room warmed by a potbelly stove with a steaming kettle on the hot plate. His family, watching TV, turned to look at us, expressionless.

"Police people want coffee."

They turned back to the TV as though this was a common occurrence. Maybe it was.

"Sit, sit, officers, please." He offered us chairs away from the TV audience.

"Thank you," I said. "We've only got a few minutes. Pie and coffee are just what we needed."

Victoria picked up a long, blonde wig.

"Doing a bit of cross dressing Mr Patel?"

"No, no." He missed Victoria's humour completely. "I picked that up outside my shop a few days ago. Some kids must have found it in the rubbish bin when they were looking for bottles to redeem. It made me remember that one night I saw a big lady get out of car then she didn't come into shop. I forgot about her until I found wig that looked very much like big lady's hair."

Victoria looked at me.

"Can you remember when that was Mr Patel or even what night of the week?" she asked hopefully.

"Very sorry. So many nights and so many people."

"Our time's up, Victoria. Maybe Mr Patel would let us take the wig?"

We made the trip back to Hamilton faster than the trip up. Traffic had evaporated. The night was clear and cold. The Chrysler hummed. Victoria nodded off.

I let the car have its head and we swept through the night at a speed that would have seen the car impounded and me in jail if the force had so desired. If the force had put on an appearance, and if I hadn't had my insurance snoring gently beside me. I pulled into the service station with time to spare. The sudden silence woke her. She yawned and stretched.

"We made it then? Not bad driving, Mr P.I."

"Okay, we've proven it can be done but right now I couldn't care less. I've got to drive all the way back to the big smoke we call home."

"Move over. You've done enough for one day. Three trips and now it's my turn."

"You're welcome. While I remember; did you follow up with Miss Desiree?"

"Couldn't find her. She's apparently disappeared from the face of the planet. Withers said he paid her after your visit and she left by taxi, which checks out. Taxi driver says he dropped her off downtown corner of Queen and Quay and that's where her trail ends. Incidentally, the escort agency Withers rang on the night of the murder heard nothing more from him after his phone call. Desiree wasn't on their books. Withers said he picked her up on the street not far from the motel around about 9pm on the night. Appears this went unwitnessed."

The conversation petered out and so did I as Victoria drove the Chrysler smoothly through the night as we headed north once more. ▲

Chapter 9

Leo looked up as I arrived shortly before ten.

"Morning, boss. How did the trip go, or should I say trips?"

Ten o'clock had become by habit our catch-up morning break for coffee. 'Conference,' Leo called it, if she had to fob off any calls during this half hour, which had become sacrosanct between us on the infrequent occasions we were in the office together.

"What, no digs about my punctuality?"

"Not this morning, boss. I know you were racing up and down the intercity all night. Thought you deserved a bit of slack. What did your girlfriend think of your first date?"

"There it is. I knew you wouldn't be able to resist. Victoria's not my girlfriend and it wasn't a date."

"Ok, keep your shirt on."

Leo got up and made us coffee from her machine, which to my consternation always tasted better than from mine upstairs.

"For your information the night went well. We proved that Withers had the time to do it and that's about as far as I can go. We found a wig that a local witness might tie into Withers if the DNA doesn't. The cops can't figure out a motive beyond wanting to rid himself of his wife. Why kill his step-daughter? And murder seems a drastic solution to a domestic dispute when divorce would be just as effective, if a little protracted."

"Sounds like it's time to drop it and let the force plod on in their usual methodical manner. No one's paying you for this and I've had a couple of calls that deserve your attention." She pushed the files across her desk. "Nice simple, juicy background checks for a couple of corporates."

"You're right as per, Leo. Seems like I'm letting poor Joan Withers and her daughter down, but the cops can move things along without me."

I stood up, files in hand intending to head upstairs to my office.

With a crash that threatened to smash the glass the street door burst open to reveal a couple of gorillas masquerading as human beings.

"Come in, why don't you?"

The leading thug was ugly enough to give simians a bad name.

Ignoring Leo, he said to me, "You be Dumb, that smart-arse private dick?"

"It says 'Dunn' on the shingle and no mention of smart-arse. And I prefer private investigator."

He took a few moments to process what I'd said, then decided I'd admitted to being the man he sought.

"Listen, dick-face, I don't give a shit about shingles or what your name is. My boss says for me to tell you to lay off that Withers prick. Otherwise…"

"Otherwise?"

The thug punched a fist into his other open hand then held it up.

"That'll be your head."

"Yeah? Now who's the smart-arse?"

He was flummoxed at my refusal to be intimidated, and decided to keep face in front of his fellow thug by turning on his heels.

"Come on, Ritchie. Let's leave smart mouth here to his black bitch. If we have to come back, she gets it too."

With that they were gone, giving my street door another hiding as they left. Leo let out her breath.

"Nice company we keep, boss. Friends of yours?'

"Sorry about that, Leo. No, never seen them before. And to think I was about to give up on Joan. What was I thinking!"

"Does that mean you're back on the case?"

"Never left it," I yelled as I raced for the door. I looked south towards Balmoral Road, the direction the two heavies had taken and saw neither. Then as the lights changed at the intersection behind me, backed-up traffic rolled forward. A curtain-sider hung back to let a black Chev with tinted windows out of a parking space into the slow moving traffic. The Chev crossed the intersection on the amber and as it slowed to go left I made its plate.

"Any luck, boss?" Leo looked up from her computer.

"Maybe. Bit of a long shot, but I got most of the plate of a Chev Caprice departing in a hurry. Couldn't see who was in it, but it looked out of place around here amongst all the rice burners."

"Worth a punt then, boss. Leave the number with me and I'll run it past my old friend Mavis down at Vehicle Registrations."

▲

Chapter 10

"Crikey, that was quick,"

I spluttered into my coffee as Leo's voice boomed out of the speaker.

"Mavis is still grateful for that little problem you sorted off the record with her neighbour's thieving teenager. Apparently the kid is doing well since you put the frighteners on him."

"That's good," I said. "I've been to a couple of his footy matches since and made sure he saw me so he knows I'm interested. It was good of Mavis to nip his bad behaviour in the bud. Pity more people aren't like her, but on the other hand then we'd be out of a job."

"Anyway, she's got an owner and address for that Chev Caprice. It is registered from new to a Mr Tuia Fatilofa at 1037 Angel Avenue, Penrose."

"OK, Leo, thanks for that and thank Mavis for me too, would you? I'll take a drive and see what Mr Fatilofa has to say for himself."

"You take care, boss. The name sounds like he could be one of my countrymen and you know how *mean* those south-side Poly gangs can be."

Penrose belied its name. There was nothing rosy about it. Whoever named it clearly had other aspirations for the area than the mixture of light industrial and endless tract housing estates it had become.

No doubt once, long ago, the oily water of the inner harbour that marked the suburb's southern boundary, with its floating trash thick enough to walk on, had once been pristine fish-filled foreshore.

The industrial area wasn't too bad with the expediencies of commerce keeping a lid on overt criminal activity, during daylight hours at least. The housing estates were another story altogether. Even the cops were wary of venturing into the area.

If they did it was never alone and always in a police cruiser fully marked and lit. Unmarkeds left unattended were inclined to be stripped, as was any other car whose owner was foolish enough to leave it parked for long without a minder hovering.

If it wasn't for my GPS I would have taken an age to find the address. The houses and streets were equally as drab. Number 1037 turned out to be tidier than its neighbours and recently painted, even if only a dismal grey. There were no partly dismantled cars in the driveway, nor the usual half-naked dirty kids running around, seemingly impervious to the cold.

Instead, parked each side of the street were a couple of gleaming black cars. They made a sort of chicane that anyone driving down the street would have to slow down to negotiate. Neither car was a Chev Caprice but both had a dark-suited Poly lounging on the bonnet, both wearing dark glasses and suits like uniforms of the sort favoured by TV hoodlums.

As I drew up outside number 1037 the suit from across the road sauntered across and planted himself close to the driver's door, making it impossible to open. Close up he blocked out the sun as though we were experiencing a sudden eclipse. Discretion being the advisable course in this case, I slid the window down.

"Good morning." I spoke as politely as I knew how.

"Fuck off, whitey. Whatever you're peddling, we don't need any here."

"Excuse me." Still maintaining my manners. "You don't know what I'm doing here so how about being a little less hasty?"

"Look, pal, I know you're not a cop driving this shit heap." He kicked the Chrysler putting another dent in the door panel. "So as I said, FUCK OFF!"

I didn't mind being abused verbally, it goes with the job. I do mind it when an ignorant, impolite arsehole damages my car. I know it doesn't look much on the outside, but my car was special to me.

"My friend," I said mildly. "You shouldn't have kicked my car. That wasn't called for and is a bad-mannered thing to do."

"Yeah? As if I give a shit. If you don't fuck off I'll do more than kick it."

"You should give a shit." I pointed my snub-nose straight at his flabby, round face. "If you don't back off this little beauty will make a big hole in your head. About which I don't give a shit either."

The thing with firearms is that the sight of a barrel long or short creates instant panic in the target. In my experience, I have yet to observe anyone, no matter how tough or what side of the law, maintain a cool demeanour when confronted with a gun pointing in their direction.

Fatso was no exception. He stumbled backwards as though I'd pushed him, tripped and fell, legs splayed as his backside hit the wet tarmac, as helpless as a stranded whale.

I got out of my car, still pointing my gun at the floundering bully. The Poly from the other car had been strolling towards his mate. I'd noticed him coming in the mirror. When he saw the gun, he turned and ran back to his car.

"Stay in it and don't come out," I yelled.

I got a nod, though he was fiddling with his cellphone. I turned back to the heavy still sprawled on the road.

"Now, sunshine, you need to learn some manners so why don't we start again. When I say good morning you say, 'Good morning. How can I help you.' Got it?"

I stomped on his shin. "Good morning."

He howled, then said through gritted pearly whites, "How can I fuckin' help you?"

"Good enough I suppose, but could do better." I pointed at the grey house. "I'm looking for a Mr Fatilofa recorded as resident at this address."

At that moment the front door opened, presumably in response to the cellphone call from the other thug who, from his car, gestured frantically towards me. A portly Polynesian man came out and stood on the porch, staring.

"Does this bozo belong to you?" I pointed at the heavy sitting on the tarmac.

"Who's asking, if I may be so bold?" he countered, his speech quiet and refined.

"Dunn is my name. I'm looking for a Mr Fatilofa. Would that be you?"

"Ah, Mr Dunn. I am indeed Mr Fatilofa. Please come in."

"I will if you would call off your dogs."

I still had my pistol handy, though no longer pointing directly at the heavy on the road, and kept it where I could aim at any of the three.

"Come, come, Mr Dunn. There is no need for guns. My man is enthusiastic. He takes his duties a little too seriously."

Mr Fatilofa rasped out a string of Samoan that seemed to contain expletives. The thug on the ground got to his feet and retreated to his car. I heard the locks clunk as he locked himself in.

"There he will remain until I tell him otherwise. You're safe now, Mr Dunn. Please, do come in."

Mr Fatilofa led the way back into the house. I left the door open just in case. He noticed and smiled, but said nothing.

I decided not to beat around the bush; see if he would deny the connection? "I don't recognise those two out there as the thugs who busted into my office yesterday."

"I have many men in my employ. Usually they all look alike to you white people. The two to whom you refer are, um, gainfully employed elsewhere today."

"What, scaring the shite out of elderly convenience store owners by protecting them. Is that what you were trying to do to me yesterday?"

"Mr Dunn, I apologise for yesterday's error. My men were instructed to merely observe activity in your street. I forget that they are not well-educated and most anxious to please. Sometimes they read more into my instructions than I intend. They will be disciplined, as will the fat fool outside."

"Why are you interested in Harold Withers?"

"I'm sorry, Mr Dunn. That is a matter between Mr Withers and myself. My men's advice to you to forget about him was sound. I urge you to take it."

"You must know that Withers is the prime suspect in the murder of his wife and daughter. Even if I back off, the police won't."

"That is so, and the police require a much greater level of proof that, incidentally, they'll find impossible to reach. Whereas you, on the other hand, do not and will not. The consequence may lead you into areas I would prefer you not to go. For all our sakes."

"You mean I'll take the law into my own hands if I think it, ah, appropriate?"

"Mr Dunn, I'm sure it comes as no surprise that you're well-known to us here in Penrose – and I'm sure in other districts of this most intriguing city – as someone who has, shall we say, a loose interpretation of the law, but one that my associates and I find difficult to agree with. Now that is all I'm going to say to you other than good day. It would be advisable to rapidly exit the area by the main motorway on-ramp, which you will find first on the left at the end of the avenue."

I resisted the temptation to call him on his barely veiled threat.

"Good day to you, Mr Fatilofa, and thanks for your time."

I eased out of the still-open door and saw the thugs had remained in their cars. Nobody followed as I took the man's advice and soon I was on the south-western motorway connecting with the city.

Whether I took his other advice to leave Harold Withers alone and forget about Joan and her daughter didn't take much thinking about either.

▲

Chapter 11

"Not a lot," I replied to Leo's question as to what I'd learned from Mr Fatilofa. "One thing, he isn't a civilian. He has heavies out front who didn't exactly roll out the red carpet. The house is ordinary from the outside like a thousand others in the Penrose estates. Inside, it's another matter. His idea of interior decoration isn't mine, but money has certainly been spent."

"Sounds like it could be gang headquarters and he's the head man," said Leo. "I'll run it past Jim when he gets home tonight. He hears all sorts of things as he gets about in his truck."

"OK. Thanks, Leo. I'll be upstairs if you need me."

I fixed myself a coffee and nursed it while gazing out my window. What possible connection could there be between a Poly gang, a white plumbing goods salesman and two murdered females?

Add in the disappearance of the street walker Desiree who seems to have walked right out of the picture and I had a nice little mystery. Or it would have been nice if two innocent parties weren't dead.

Like all good detectives, especially those not locked into the department's eternal quest for good stats, when things don't make a lot of sense I start again. Sort of like shaking the bough so the cradle will rock and maybe baby will fall.

Shaking Mr Fatilofa's tree seemed a bit foolhardy just at the moment. Especially when there was a less hazardous option. I decided for the moment the cradle was the Withers house and the baby Harold Withers.

I called his home number. No reply. Probably off on one of his regular sales trips. I tried his business number and he answered on the second ring.

"Oh, it's you."

He didn't bother to conceal his disappointment.

"What do you want now?"

"Same thing as last time. Information," I said. "Do you want your dear departed wife's insurance payout or not?"

"I've told you and the police all I know. I'm still in mourning and you harass me on what grounds?"

"I'm not as easily fobbed off as the police, my friend. I can prove your alibi is a load of crap that will make your claim a goneburger. I need to see you about the bad company you keep and I'm not talking about Desiree."

There was silence before he answered.

"I don't know who you're referring to. Anyway, I'm tied up with appointments today and tomorrow and won't be home until Thursday."

"I can wait. Where are you speaking from now?"

"Palmerston, if you must know, although what it's got to do with you I don't know."

"Now be nice, Harold. I'll be waiting for you when you get back."

So I had two whole days to toss the Withers house. I headed downstairs to be met by Mac coming up.

"G'day, Mac. Leo didn't tell me you were here. This is a pleasant surprise,"

"You were on the 'phone so she said go on up. Off out, were you?"

"Yeah, but it can wait. What can I do for you?" I backed into my office, holding the door open for him.

"I dunno. Maybe I can do something for you or maybe I've dropped by to be sociable." He looked at me keenly. "Which do you think?"

"Mac, I've known you for a long time and I've never known you, a chief inspector no less, to drop by to be sociable. Not in working hours, which are 24/7 for you anyway. So, what can I do for you?"

"I'm thinking of a little mutual co-operation. You know, the scratch each other's backs kind. Although that comment raises an ugly image, especially in your case."

He laughed at his own wit and I tried not to.

"I know from my usual sources that you're still sniffing around the Withers case. Maybe I can do you a favour and you can reciprocate."

"Reciprocate?" I interjected. "Only a chief inspector would use a word like that. I'll have to go and look it up."

"If you'll shut up for a minute and let me finish you can get on your way sooner. We've reached a bit of an impasse on the case in question. Yes, we will pick it up again sooner or later when some new development prompts us to, if it ever does."

I contemplated telling Mac about the run-in I'd had with the Poly gang from Penrose. I decided not to because I hadn't got anywhere and no doubt I'd have some explaining to do concerning guns and violent behaviour. I thought it prudent to avoid mentioning that little fracas following my recent altercation with Harold Withers.

Mac continued. "Until then, or if something develops, which is maybe never, we've got other fish to fry. Somewhat easier fish too, usually. All I do these days is write reports and make up budgets and fill out the most inane forms you can imagine. I never get to do any proper sleuthing to get the chance to show my junior officers some of the stuff that isn't in the police manual. That's where you come in."

"What! Do you want me to come back on the force?"

"No, dummy. I want you to let one of my officers come with you, if appropriate, and learn a few of the finer tricks of the trade."

"Whoa, Mac. That isn't exactly my style as you know. I prefer operating alone. That's partly why I left the force in the first place. And some of my methods aren't exactly legal."

"Having an officer of the law with you would make some things legal, such as breaking and entering. If that's the sort of thing you had in mind."

He looked at me keenly through narrowed eyes; something he'd been doing too much of during this visit. That look always made me, a hardened P.I., feel guilty of something, so I could imagine how a real criminal felt when faced with that flinty stare.

"Maybe," I said, "though I'm doubtful I can teach anyone anything. Have you got anybody in particular in mind?"

"Detective Victoria."

He smiled. Mac knew he had a deal clincher.

▲

Chapter 12

"What do you want a bimbo like that traipsing around after you for?" Leo sounded almost sulky.

"Do I hear the tone of the green-eyed monster?" I teased her.

"Me jealous," she scoffed, "of a skinny white girl? No way. Isn't it a bit irregular for a cop to partner up with a P.I.?"

"The way Mac put it Victoria is anxious or ambitious, however you want to look at it. She's been pigeonholed into the department's child crime section, so she often gets pulled off juicy Serious Crime Squad jobs. She's missed out on major crime detecting experience and has threatened to transfer if she doesn't get some variation."

"You're telling me there was no one in the force she couldn't partner up with?"

"Not in Mac's squad, apparently. Budget restraints and all that."

I didn't confess I found the arrangement a bit unusual myself. No way could I contemplate any other officer accompany me and I had to ask myself the question; why her?

I didn't have an answer.

None I was willing to articulate, that is.

As though on cue the office phone rang and Leo answered it sniffily. "One moment, please," She handed it to me with a curt "For you."

"Somebody not in a good mood today, Mike?"

"Hello, Victoria," I said. "That somebody is feeling a tad left out, though I can't imagine why. Especially as I was considering giving her a raise in view of the excellent work she's been doing on the insurance fraud cases."

I stared pointedly at Leo, who affected not to notice.

"I may have to reconsider. She already gets paid more than most CEOs and her manners leave something to be desired. Oh, one moment, please, Victoria. I think Leo is trying to tell me something."

"Come on, boss, you know I was only kidding."

"Sure, and so am I. About reconsidering, I mean. I was hoping it'd be a pleasant surprise for you at the end of the month. You might as well know now. I put the bank variation order through yesterday."

"Gee, boss, you're all heart," said Leo, with a grin and only a trace of sarcasm. "I promise from now on I'll be extra nice to that bimbo, I mean police officer."

I spoke into the phone again.

"Sorry to keep you waiting, Victoria."

"Problems?"

"Industrial strife averted successfully, though somehow it's cost me yet again." I laughed. "Now, what can I do for you?"

"Mac told me you asked if I would help you on the Withers case. Sort of lend legitimacy, like when I came on the Hamilton speed test."

"Did he? I understood it was more the other way around. He asked me if I would help you."

I left out the bit about helping Victoria get some experience. That might be a blow to her pride too much.

"Well, whatever. I haven't got much on in the child abuse field at the moment so if I can help?"

"As it happens, I have a little venture planned for tonight and you're welcome. If you do come it would be good if we could borrow your car. Alfa, isn't it? Mine's been seen in the area before and I would prefer not to go in a police cruiser."

"Aha, sounds like this might be illegal." She chuckled.

"Who says you're not a good detective? You're welcome to come around to my place before we head out, or I could come to yours."

"See you at mine for a bite to eat at about eight. OK?"

"OK," I said, but she'd already hung up.

Her abruptness caught me anew each time, and took a bit of getting used to, though I kind of liked how it spoke of her self-confidence and the fact she wasn't intimidated by me. My size and manner intimidated most people whether I wanted it to or not. Sometimes I wanted it to, of course, when dealing with low-lifes. I was glad Victoria, like Leo, seemed completely unimpressed.

Leo was watching as I hung up.

"Careful, boss, this'll make a second date. You'll be marching up the aisle soon, I bet."

"You may mock, my dear. Strictly professional, just like the first time, as you well know. What's it to you anyway?"

"Just your welfare at heart, boss. Susan was a long time ago. I've got my Jim to keep me warm at night, and you should have someone too. Just make sure it's the right someone."

I suppose it was inevitable I'd come in for some mickey-taking where Victoria was concerned. Seemed like my friends were intent on drawing her to my attention.

Not that she needed their help. How could I not notice her? Yet I couldn't ignore the age gap. I picked her to be in her late twenties, a lot younger than me, or I thought so anyway. And then there was my loyalty to Susan, who was with me still.

▲

Chapter 13

I'd been to Victoria's house before when I'd dropped her off after the Hamilton alibi trips. Or rather, she'd dropped me off as she'd driven the car back while I dozed. That had been in the early hours and I'd neither the time nor inclination to give her house more than a cursory glance.

"Nice house," I told her, when she answered my knock. "Not what I expected."

I followed her into the hall.

Victoria's home was a two-storied villa bricked to the first story then white plaster with a dormer roof. A style beloved of wealthy middle-class professionals around the middle of last century. The leafy streets of Mount Albert had elevated the desirability of houses like this to stratospheric heights that even wealthy professionals might be pushed to afford.

"How does a cop own a house like this or even rent it?"

The interior as she led me into the lounge – sitting room, she called it – matched the period. Dark-stained wood and beamed ceiling with sculptured plaster inserts. A glass-fronted gas fire burned brightly, installed in what had once been an open fireplace.

"Oh, it's mine," she replied, which didn't exactly answer the question.

I followed her into the kitchen, which screamed modernism, unlike the parts of the house I'd seen so far. There was enough stainless steel to re-equip the kitchen of the 3,000-seat convention centre being built downtown.

"We can eat in here."

Victoria indicated a chrome and glass table and leather covered tubular framed chairs. Obviously, she didn't intend to satisfy my curiosity about ownership. No matter, I was a sleuth wasn't I?

As soon as she finished stacking our dishes in the dishwasher and departed to get changed for our escapade, I made a quick circuit of the living rooms with its medley of photographs.

In a maudlin fashion, this documentation of her family's history saddened me. Victoria's framed photos emphasised how empty my life had been made by Susan's death. No family pictures in my house.

I must have drifted into reverie because I didn't hear Victoria return. Not surprising because she was now dressed, complete with rubber-soled black Nikes, like a cat burglar. She moved like one too.

"Answered your own question yet?" she asked.

"I'm sorry. Old detective habit. Can't help being nosy."

"Don't apologise. If I didn't want my family photos noticed, I wouldn't put them out for the world to see, would I?"

"Good point. Are you going to tell me who they are? Though I think I can guess, certainly the ones you're in."

"If you can guess, no need for me to tell you. Time we were off, isn't it?"

There was that abruptness again like a full stop, whenever the conversation threatened to become personal. Mentally I shrugged. What was her private life to me? We were professionals, with a job to do.

"Ready if you are."

Victoria led the way through the internal door to the garage. I was surprised when we went past her red Alfa Romeo to an older nondescript saloon whose battle scars testified to its age. She slid in behind the wheel as the garage door hummed open.

"What's this?"

She nodded at the red car. "Unprofessional to draw attention to ourselves in that. This old girl is my daily driver; the other's for special occasions only."

"I see." I must have sounded doubtful, because Victoria turned and grinned at me,

"Don't let appearances fool you. This is an Alfa too although you'd have to be a fan to know it. These Milanos were built as race cars in disguise, especially these big-engined models."

She patted the dashboard as though it were a pet.

"Makes your scepticism about my fine Chrysler a bit like the pot calling the kettle black, doesn't it, Detective Hill?"

"Ah, what a memory for detail you have. Some would say petty."

That closed the subject for now.

Once considered the back of beyond, Henderson had now been completely swallowed up by this land-hungry city. The new cross-town motorway made getting there from inner city Mount Albert to Henderson an easy run that didn't take long. Especially with Victoria obviously intent on demonstrating how much better her old Alfa was than my Chrysler. She drove with the fluidity and awareness of a good police driver, rarely breaking the law yet always positioning the car to take any gaps that presented themselves. The car's power helped, too. I kept quiet about how much I was impressed.

"Drive past the house at normal speed," I said as we turned into the street. "Let's see if anything looks out of place."

"Like what?"

"I don't know, but I'm sure we'll spot whatever if it is. Just like the clues we'll find inside."

Victoria spoke sceptically. "What sort of clues would they be?"

"Clues aren't exactly labelled as such, Victoria. We'll have to hope we know one when we see it, especially if it links Withers with Fatilofa."

We drove past the house and everything was what you'd expect in a suburban street on a mid-winter Thursday at the late end of prime-time viewing. Lights were being switched off, including in the houses either side of the Wither's residence.

Victoria's was the only car moving. The few cars parked on the street were unlit with no exhausts giving off tell-tale fumes.

"OK, go back again, slowly this time and I'll take a closer look, make sure nobody's home."

The street lamps shone dimly through the cold mist that had descended. There were no lights on in the Withers' house and the blinds and curtains were undrawn. The driveway was empty.

"Looks like Withers was telling the truth when he said he was in Palmerston. Park across the street, Victoria. Make it a little harder for anybody who notices the car to tell which house we're visiting."

We sat in the car for a minute to get a feel for the place. There were no late night dog walkers or fanatical keep fit joggers. No dogs barking either, making the silence complete. Except for a few TV stalwarts the last house lights were flickering out down both sides of the street.

I'd noted on my previous visit a path up the side of the house furthest away from the neighbours. When we got to the back door I produced my burglar's kit and on the second try with my first choice pick I heard the Yale lock click. In the gloom I saw Victoria shake her head in disapproval. Only mock, I hoped.

Knowing there was no alarm, I pushed open the door and stepped inside. Victoria shut the door behind her and we got out our flashlights.

"You go that way," I whispered, pointing towards the kitchen and living room. "I'll take the other end."

Victoria surprised me by giggling. "Why are we whispering if the house is empty?"

"Top detective procedure in this kind of situation." I suppressed a laugh of my own. "Truthfully, I've got no idea. Stops us frightening ourselves, perhaps."

The long house had a central narrow hall with bedrooms either side. The small bedroom at the far end, next to the master bedroom, was used as an office. Besides a desk, devoid of paperwork, there was a three-drawer filing cabinet. I stepped into the room and my burglar's kit earned its keep for the second time that night.

Soon I was engrossed in Withers' financial affairs because a credit card receipt from a petrol station put him in the vicinity of the Fatilofa house in Penrose. Flimsy evidence, maybe, but enough to keep me delving into Harold's files.

I'd just started to figure out that he seemed to be making an unbelievable amount of money from his plumbing supplies business when I heard a muffled thump from the other end of the house. I put it down to Victoria moving furniture about, hunting for a hidden safe and therefore paid it no mind.

Until there was a crash and the sound of breaking glass. I thought she was being a little too diligent breaking into a china cabinet so I dropped the files back and closed the cabinet and headed back down the hall to check what she was up to.

Even with a flashlight the going was slow. There was no beam of light in the kitchen-dining area. I pushed open the connecting door into the living-room.

"Victoria," I called into the silence.

The light from my own torch fell on shattered glass, and blood on the carpet. There were no other signs of a struggle and the room was empty. The front door was unlocked when I rushed out. No movement on the street. No sound except the faint engine noise of a powerful car accelerating away on the main road out of my sight.

I made a rapid circuit of the house in case Victoria had gone out the back door where we'd come in. There was no sign of her. I locked up both front and back and checked her car in case she'd gone back to that for some reason. Yes, I was clutching at straws and the blood on the carpet had me worried.

The car was empty, as I'd known it would be. Victoria had the keys and my burglar's tools didn't work on a car lock. I called a taxi company on my cell and had to pretend my car had broken down to coerce them to come. I was freezing by the time it arrived, and my mood of self-recrimination wasn't improved when the taxi driver said, "Shouldn'a bought one of those Italian shit-heaps, mate."

▲

Chapter 14

In the taxi I thought about calling the cops. Dismissed the idea when I tried to work out what to say. Thought about calling Mac, but what could he do at five minutes to midnight?

In the end I left voice messages on Victoria's cellphone and landline. I'd have been surprised if she'd answered, and it helped to do something, no matter how useless.

I didn't sleep much, analysing the previous night's fiasco and arrived at the office the same time as Leo.

"Morning, boss. What brings you out at sparrow's fart?"

"I had no idea you'd be so cheerful so early," I retorted.

"Oh, so gloomy. Date didn't go well, eh? Early night, was it?"

"There was no date, Leo, as you well know. How could there be? My partner in crime disappeared. I suspect she was abducted."

"Have you told the cops?"

"What would I tell them? That I was illegally tossing a house aided and abetted by one of their own who, by the way, might have been abducted with violence. Or she had an attack of conscience and split and isn't answering her phones or returning calls after a lovers' tiff. That would be me, would it, and maybe I hit her over the head and what were we doing in the house anyway?"

"OK, boss, take a breath. I get the picture. You do have a problem. Mac knew more or less what you had planned, didn't he?"

"Yeah." I sighed. "I'll call him now. He's going to be thrilled."

"I don't want to state the obvious, boss, but maybe whoever snatched Vic didn't know she was a cop. Like they said when they busted in here, this is their warning to you to back off. They probably thought Vic was me in the dark."

"I shouldn't have agreed to take her along."

"You're right." Mac breathed hard down the phone. "You shouldn't have and I shouldn't have suggested it in the first place. We're both at fault here so what are we going to do about it, apart from getting her car towed back to her place?"

"We don't know for sure it's Victoria's blood on the carpet." I said optimistically trying to make the situation a little easier.

"I'll get the lab boys onto a sample pronto, then we'll know."

"There is something that I was going to tell you." I hesitated, knowing Mac would blow his stack when I did.

"Yeah, what?"

"There's a Penrose Poly gang mixed up in this somehow."

"What! You didn't think to share this with me before I okayed Vic going along with you?" Mac growled down the phone.

"The connection was kind of tenuous. I'd hoped to find something in Withers' house last night that would firm up the link, if there was one."

"Did you?"

"Not exactly, Mac. I did find that Withers seems to make more money than you'd expect as a plumbing goods wholesaler. And he has spent time in the Penrose area. Not exactly cut and dried, I admit. Victoria's disappearance kind of distracted me from looking further."

"If you're right and a Penrose Polynesian gang is involved then the Withers case is much more than a domestic male on females murder case. Poly gangs are the octopuses of the underworld; they've got tentacles everywhere."

Prudently I refrained from pointing out that eight tentacles could not possibly *be* everywhere.

"I'll take a run out to Penrose and see if I can shake up Mr Fatilofa."

"So you've got a name you also didn't think to pass on to me," Mac said testily. "I won't ask how you got it. I'd be pissed if it wasn't a sure bet it's a fake. I'll check the name out anyway and I'll let you know if it's Vic's blood in Withers house."

He broke the connection.

"Whew!"

I grimaced at Leo, who'd been perched on my desk listening.

"Not a happy cop, but not as angry as I thought he'd be."

"Lucky he seems to think a lot of you."

"I dunno. Maybe he thinks a lot more of Victoria."

"What now, boss?"

"Back to Penrose for me."

Leo watched as I got my gun from the belt holster, took the clip out and checked it was full before sliding it home and racking a round into the chamber. I checked the safety was on before slipping it back into its holster on my right hip.

"Take care, Mike," she said. "I mean, boss. Take care, boss," she softly repeated.

▲

Chapter 15

I might have known. When I turned into Angel Avenue, spectacularly misnamed on two counts in my view because of the remarkable lack of both angels and trees, the street was blocked by fire trucks. Fatilofa's house was a blackened roofless ruin still smoking as the firemen dampened down the ashes.

I drew up next to the uniform leaning on the door of his squad car, whose flashing red and blue lights reflecting back off the steam and smoke and faces of the curious lent the scene a festive atmosphere, at odds with sombre reality.

"What's up?" I asked the officer.

"What's it look like?" Clearly not a man overly concerned with politeness.

"Is anybody hurt?"

"Who wants to know?"

"I'm just a concerned citizen," I lied, annoyed at his attitude.

"Yeah, mate, I'm sure you are." His tone heavily sarcastic. "Don't get many around here."

I didn't want to reveal that I had any connection to the house, let alone knowing the occupant's name. Too difficult and time-consuming to explain.

Then the cop, as though taking my silence for umbrage, and thinking perhaps I *was* a concerned citizen said, "I'll tell you, mate, two stiffs have been barbecued in there. One of each gender. Now move along, please."

I winced at his choice of phrase. Thank goodness I wasn't a relative or friend learning a dearly beloved had been barbecued. Though it worried me deeply that one of the deceased was female. With difficulty, I pushed images of

Victoria's body, charred and twisted out of mind and drove back to the office.

"Whoa, boss, you're looking peaky," Leo piped up as I walked in. "Don't tell me you had a shoot-out with Fatilofa and his brown gang?"

"Nothing like that. His place burned down and they found two bodies inside. One male and one female."

"Uh oh." Leo was immediately subdued. "Could they be who you think they are?"

"Gotta be Harold because he hasn't turned up from his Palmerston trip. I hope to God the other isn't, wasn't, Victoria."

"We'll find out soon enough, I guess. Too early to jump to conclusions," said Leo. "That girl could look after herself from what I heard. No point worrying about something that might not be true. You aren't even sure it was Fatilofa and his crew who took her."

We both jumped when the phone rang. Leo picked up and listened for a minute then passed the handpiece over.

"Mac," she mouthed.

He spoke without preamble. "The uniform you had a conversation with this morning thought you might want to know what happened out at the Fatilofa house."

"How did you know I was out there?"

"Cop's not just an ugly face, mate. He ran your plates, recognised your name and connection to the SCS's missing officer and phoned it in to me. Efficient, eh?"

"I'm impressed."

"Yeah, you should be," he growled, "though it would have landed on my desk sooner or later."

"I take it since you mentioned missing officer, said officer is still missing?"

"Unless Vic is a well-endowed, brown-skinned Polynesian with Desiree tattooed on her neck we can take it she is still missing," he said dryly.

"Mac, that is a relief. Tough on our dead prostitute though."

"Yeah, tough for her all right and don't let's forget Vic is probably in the hands of some ruthless types."

"Sure," I said, coming back to earth. "Anything on the male?"

"Not yet. There wasn't much of him left to make a visual. Prelims suggest cause of death wasn't the fire. Autopsies will give us something later on and no doubt matching will tell us who the male was and confirm that Desiree picked the wrong client this time."

"I'm not sure where I can go from here except make a nuisance of myself. Rattle a few cages, piss someone off, provoke a reaction."

I was betting Mac would take up the slack. He did.

"While you take the bull in a china shop method of police work we'll do the technical stuff. By the way, the blood in Withers' house was Vic's, as though there was any doubt. I've got Andy and Gordon on the forensics there to see if they can pick up any latents or whatever. They're going out to do the same at Penrose tomorrow. The entire SCS is in on this now, not to mention the force is heads up with one of our own in jeopardy."

He hung up. Though it was Friday, I had a feeling there would be no conviviality in the Civic bar that night. If there was, it would be without me.

"See you Monday," I said to Leo, and went home.

▲

Chapter 16

The only cage I rattled was my own. Normally my house is my sanctuary. Usually the view from the Ponsonby rise over the concrete jungle that is the central business district and the harbour beyond put the day's tribulations into perspective.

I put Muse on loud, only to become agitated at the hard-edged rock, something I normally enjoyed, winding up the volume until the floor-to-ceiling glass on the main windows vibrated. I replaced Muse with Edward Sharpe and the Magnetic Zeros; much more soothing.

I went to sleep wondering where and what Victoria was going through. The only thing I could think to do was go back where my trail had ended; the burned Fatilofa house out at Penrose.

Not much point going back to the Wither's house. Mac's boys had trolled through that. Tomorrow they'd be going through the remains of the Penrose house. I would join them there. No footy for me tomorrow.

I was early enough, but the boys of the SCS were already on the job. The property was cordoned off as a crime scene and a uniform sauntered its perimeter to keep away the non-existent curious. He clapped his gloved hands together in an endeavour to keep warm in the crisp morning air. I was relieved to see he was a different cop from the day before.

At a nod from Andy he lifted the tape for me to pass under.

"Morning, mate," said Andy. "Didn't see you in the Civic last night. Probably a good thing. Some of the boys are a bit upset about Vic. Sort of blame you for leading her into this."

"Yeah, I sort of blame myself too. The crims probably didn't know she was a cop. Why would they, considering what we were up to. I'm sure it's supposed to be a warning to me."

"No point in crying over spilt milk. Help yourself to a suit and boots from the back of the wagon. There's gloves, too." He pointed to the police van parked on the footpath to which one end of the crime scene tape was tied.

I suited up and rejoined Andy who was on his hands and knees sifting through a pile of ash that had once been an office desk. Gordon, on the far side of the building's skeleton, his white overalls already filthy, gave me a perfunctory wave before returning to the laborious task.

"Glamorous police work, eh?" Andy grimaced.

"Guess somebody's got to do it," I commiserated. "Where are you at with this?"

"The bodies were removed yesterday about mid-day. Should have some prelim autopsies later this week. Both badly burned but scene of crime reckon they were already dead. Fire boys say it was a deliberate torching. They found signs of accelerant in the area of hottest burn, in the middle of what was probably the lounge. Strange place for a fire to burn the hottest unless it was started deliberately."

"Why do you reckon the vics were already dead when the fire started?"

"The ligature marks on their necks. The fire had only just begun to sear their upper bodies when the fire boys got on top of it. That's how we could make out the tattoo on the female's neck; presumably her name. Secondly neither vic had made any attempt to crawl away to somehow escape the flames. They would have tried even if they were eventually overcome by smoke. I'm betting the autopsy will show no smoke in the lungs."

"Christ almighty! Then this is an attempt by Fatilofa to dispose of a couple of bodies and erase evidence of his connection with Withers."

"Looks like it," said Andy. "Wouldn't be surprised if the male turns out to be Withers. The corpse as far as we could tell was the right size and colour."

"Whatever it is we've been doing has put the frighteners on Fatilofa."

I didn't voice my thought that by now Fatilofa almost certainly would know Victoria was a cop. Even if he didn't, he would be unlikely to leave her alive given the lengths he'd already gone to protect whatever racket he was involved in.

"We've got to find him or Victoria pronto."

Andy nodded and bent to his task.

I was tossing up whether to get my hands dirty and win a few brownie points back with Andy when Gordon gave a shout and held up an object like a cigarette lighter.

"Memory stick stuck in the elbow of the dunny."

He kicked the blackened porcelain bowl free-standing, devoid of its plastic fittings, on what had been the bathroom floor.

"Computer's in the van," he added. "We might be lucky."

Andy clicked his way through the contents and we stared without speaking at the screen, relieved at finding something yet dreading what it might be.

A long list of names came up, most of them pseudonyms unless there truly are people out there with names like Juvylover, Kidgroper and Freshmeat or worse. Each name had a dollar amount entered beside it that was probably a running total of monies due, according to the date at the top of each page.

As Andy kept on scrolling, our glee at being handed evidence on a plate for the police forensic I.T. guys to have a field day with turned to grim silence. Thumbnail head shots of young girls flickered on the screen, page after page of them.

"Hold it," I yelled. "Scroll back, I think I recognised a face."

There she was and as Andy hovered his cursor I said, "That one."

Andy double-clicked and the girl's headshot enlarged to become unmistakably Evelyn, the daughter of Joan, step-daughter of Harold. His charred body had recently lain at the foot of the toilet bowl that had given up its secret to us.

"Too much of a coincidence for Withers and the stick to be found so close together," said Andy.

"Maybe that's why he was offed. Maybe he wasn't meant to record anything like this." I gestured at the screen with its obscene images. "Maybe this is why he killed Evelyn and her mother. Maybe he killed them because he was afraid if he didn't Evelyn would spill the beans to her mother. Maybe she already had."

"Lot of maybes," offered Gordon. "Though I wouldn't be surprised if maybe becomes definitely."

Andy clicked off Evelyn and double-clicked on another thumb at random. Again a full body shot of a young girl came up, clearly dead and clearly abused. Usually I have no trouble divorcing myself from gruesome sights or making some inappropriate comment to lighten the moment whether real or pictured, but these had shocked all three of us into an uncomfortable silence. The photos were so horrible in their terrible fascination none of us could look away.

Andy let out a low groan of mixed rage and grief as he clicked to bring up another distressing image. This time some of the shots showed a girl still alive being forced into extremely lewd poses. The captions, like the others we had viewed, were numbers that didn't take much working out would be referenced to the names at the beginning of the document. Prices that could be for viewing vicariously or for real.

Andy clicked through to exit, saying, "I think this memory stick better get to Mac and the forensic computer wizards pronto."

He leaned out of the wagon and called the uniform over who listened to Andy's instructions before departing for Central, siren whooping and lights flashing.

Gordon pulled out his cell to alert the troops that the memory stick was on its way.

▲

Chapter 17

The three of us returned to the dirty job sifting through the ashes, concentrating around the forlorn toilet bowl. We didn't expect to find anything else but it gave us something to do while forensics had a look at the stick.

We had only time enough to get covered in soot and ash again when Mac's cruiser drew up with a squeal of rubber.

"Come back on the computer, guys," he called, as he stepped into the crime scene wagon. "Central is sending through stuff as we speak."

We didn't need telling twice. We shrugged off the filthy suits and crowded into the wagon, four large men severely tested its capacity. Andy as the most techno person took the keyboard and established the link with Central and within seconds greatly enlarged portions of the pictures of the young girls flickered up.

"The computer guys have been able to pull back some of the pics to show digital detail that didn't show on the originals we looked at," Mac said, turning to me. "Recognise anything? You're the only one of us who's been inside Withers' and Fatilofa's houses."

"It's not Withers' and you guys have been inside there, so unless you recognise anything...?"

They shook their heads. I peered closer at the screen's top right hand corner.

"I think these were taken inside what was Fatilofa's place right here. Remember, I said no expense had been spared on the interior?" I pointed at the screen. "That looks like a section of red velvet wallpaper with gold dragons embossed on it. Bet you there's some of that in the remains of the house outside."

"If you're right we have an absolute tie in that Fatilofa is operating a kiddy porn ring," said Mac. His cell buzzed and he listened for a moment. "That was the autopsy boys. As we thought, the male corpse was Withers."

"Now we know some of what we're dealing with," I said. "Maybe we'll never know exactly what Withers role was, and I reckon he was peddling and scouting for Fatilofa while he was on his plumbing gig. That's what the memory stick was for and it could have also been his insurance over Fatilofa if they had a dispute over money or whatever. Sure to have been something to do with betrayal and money; the sex we know about."

"Guys, guys," interjected Mac, "we'll sort out who exactly offed Joan and Evelyn and why, and probably some of these other poor girls, not to mention Withers and his hooker friend, when we've got Fatilofa and more importantly Vic."

"Find one and we'll find the other." I spoke with more confidence than I felt. "I'm sure Fatilofa hasn't realised she's a cop otherwise he wouldn't have been stupid enough to snatch her in the first place. Secondly, if he'd found out since, we'd have had a third body in the fire. He must still think she's got some use as a bargaining chip, with me at least."

"Not just you, pal." All three cops spoke in unison.

"I've had an idea!"

And by way of answering their enquiring looks, I pulled out my cellphone and dialled.

▲

Chapter 18

"Leo, sorry to disturb your weekend, but I don't know my own codes. Can you check my office voice mail from your home?"

I glanced at the cops, who were looking askance at me.

"Maybe the perps are so dumb they didn't search her carefully enough to find her cell. It's worth a shot. Victoria only ever called me on my landline. Don't think she's got my cell. I mean, who checks voice mail these days?"

"We all do, mate. Especially during a major," said Mac wearily.

I knew he was pissed with me because he only ever called me mate when he wished I wasn't.

In a minute Leo came back on my cell.

"Boss, there's a couple of whispered messages that I can't understand then a last one with no voice only background sounds. The machine has recorded the call at just after one a.m. day before yesterday."

"That puts it after Fatilofa's house was torched. Can you play back the call?"

"Hang on, boss."

I held up my cell so everyone could hear. After a short silence came the sound of a jet, loud enough to be possibly climbing away. Then before the jet's rumble completely died a fire truck siren spooling up then fading was followed a second later by the wail of a police siren.

Mac took charge.

"Andy, planes are prohibited to take-off over the city after 11.30 p.m. Get onto the airport manager see if any jets were authorised to take off late Thursday night around one in the morning. Gordon, check with Otahuhu and Papatoetoe fire boys and the local law to see what was happening."

He turned to Andy who had an answer already.

"Airport says an Emirates Airbus had a technical hitch that held them back and then took off to the East at 12.58 p.m. climbing out over the south-central suburbs."

"Thought so," said Mac. "That'll be Otahuhu and Papatoetoe. They're the only ones with fire stations and cop shops."

Gordon palmed his cell and said, "The law followed the fire truck to a pile-up on the Great South Road that would have put both units on Papatoetoe main street at that exact time, give or take."

"Vic probably couldn't speak," I said, "but she had the presence of mind to dial me and hope I could work out her location from the sounds at the time."

"OK, here's what we are going to do," said Mac, looking straight at me. "We are going to wait for back-up then saturate Pap main street smashing every door until we find Vic, which is the correct procedure by the book."

My heart lurched with disappointment and I saw Andy and Gordon's faces fall.

"Unless," Mac continued, "The civilian we have amongst us gets it into his head to act irresponsibly like some sort of super-hero and take matters into his own hands."

He paused. "In which case we will have to accompany him for his own safety."

I grinned. "Let's go!"

We piled into Mac's unmarked on the theory that Fatilofa knew mine, and Andy and Gordon's police cars were too obvious. We didn't know exactly where Victoria's call had come from. We were still searching for a needle in a haystack although like most crims they probably thought they were so smart they couldn't conceive we were getting close.

"Watch out for large black cars, specifically a Chev Caprice," I said. "Maybe Fati's men are confident or silly enough to park on the street."

Mac idled his cruiser along St George Street crawling with busy Saturday shopping traffic.

"Mike and I'll check parked cars," Mac directed. "You guys in the back see if you can spot anything on the upper stories. We're coming up to the intersection now with the fire station a couple of hundred metres off the main street. I'm picking we're looking anywhere in this block from here on up to the next set of lights."

"There we go, guys. Bingo." I nodded surreptitiously at a shiny black Chev hemmed in by lesser cars outside a three-story block that at street level hosted an adult video shop, an emporium selling island goods and a moneylender that doubled as a pawn shop.

"Don't look now." Gordon spoke quietly, trying not to move his lips. "I think the two dudes leaning on the second-floor balcony might be the heavies who paid you a visit, Mike."

I waited until the cruiser had moved down the street and glanced back casually.

"Yeah. The one this end is the arsehole who broke my office door. Maybe I can collect damages after all."

"OK, guys." Mac got our attention. "I'm going to park down the next side street, then we'll split up and walk back like we don't know each other. Access upstairs must be through the street level shops. We don't want to cause a panic with the public when we show our weapons so we'll go in one at a time through the adult shop seeing its window fronts are painted over.

"Maybe the shop is a front for Fati's real hardcore stuff. We can check that out later. Probably not too unusual four men going in there even if we are the wrong colour for around here.

Gordon, once we've neutralised whoever is in the shop including customers, you'll have to keep guard and make sure they stay neutral, if you know what I mean."

Mac waited for Gordon's nod before continuing. "Put the closed sign up. If there is a way out the back and up some stairs I'll lead us as quietly as we can. I'll go in first. Give me a minute to make like a customer and if I can't work it out, I'll return and we'll think again."

We strolled back up the side street to the crowded main street. The adrenaline was working hard and I knew the others must be pumping, too. Not a soul paid us the slightest attention. I browsed through the emporium's goods on trestle tables set up on the footpath. Gordon leant on a lamp-post outside the adult shop. Andy kept walking slowly and Mac went straight into the adult shop as though that was his only mission in life. I held my breath. To me, the other two were obviously cops on full alert, but again no-one gave them a second glance. The minute passed and Mac didn't come out, so we went in one at a time with a pause between us, me last.

We were the only customers, thank goodness. The Poly behind the counter barely glanced up as I entered. I marched over rapidly and socked him on the nose as hard as I could. The cops rushed over and Gordon flicked the sign closed and quietly shut the street door.

"He would have recognised me," I explained. "I had a little run in with fatso outside Fatilofa's house. Couldn't risk him raising the alarm."

The man I'd last seen spread-eagled on the tarmac like a whale moaned and sat up, holding his bloody nose. He opened his eyes and went as pale as a Polynesian can when faced with the deadly black muzzles of three Glocks and a Beretta.

Mac led off up the stairs and we cautiously checked the first floor, mostly offices deserted on a Saturday. The second floor was a different kettle of fish. We'd seen the heavies on the second floor balcony and the main corridor had apartment doors both sides.

Mac signalled me to stand by as backup blocking the far end of the corridor while he knocked softly on each door. Andy, gun at the ready, stood to his left out of line of sight and fire from whoever answered the door.

This was standard police procedure we'd done plenty of times, and I only hoped Mac and Andy weren't as strung out as I was. No doubt they were and all went well as they cleared each apartment. No one answered their knock.

The tension ramped up as they neared the middle apartments, those probably with access to the balcony. Mac paused, looked at Andy then me, took a breath and knocked softly on the door we had considered the most likely.

Silence, then a gruff query. "Who the fuck is it?"

Mac looked at Andy again and shrugged. "Mac."

"Who the fuck is Mac and what the fuck do you want?"

"I have cash for Mr Fatilofa."

He stepped closer to the peephole so that the thug inside couldn't see he was holding a gun not cash.

"Mr Fatilofa ain't here right now, so fuck off." Revealing Fatilofa was known to him.

I watched, fascinated, from my end of the corridor as Mac and Andy by some means of silent communication came to a decision. Mac stepped back to the opposite side from Andy and fired two quick shots through the door a little below the peephole.

I heard a scream from the other side. This wasn't exactly procedure. Then a door between me and the far end of the corridor banged open and Fatilofa burst out with a sawn-off shotgun raised to his shoulder.

I had no doubt he was coming at me with the intention of sending me to join the Withers family. If I'd been a cop I might have said something stupid like "Freeze or I'll shoot." Fortunately, I'm not, so I dispensed with the formalities and squeezed the Beretta's trigger. A neat round hole appeared in his forehead and Fatilofa sagged to the floor like a deflating balloon.

I spun round to see that Andy had booted the door clean off its hinges the instant Mac loosed off his second shot. I rushed to the door, weapon at the ready, mightily relieved that the two of them had the situation under control. The thug Mac had shot through the door was moaning on the floor clutching his midriff and I recognised him as one of those who'd smashed my office door.

"Probably doesn't feel like coughing up for damages right now," said Mac.

Andy had three other heavies covered, shocked by Mac's ruthless shooting of their comrades into giving up without a fight. The stack of weapons Andy had kicked out of reach grew as Mac patted each down.

Gordon came up, shepherding in front of him the bloodied thug I'd punched. He said, "Looks like I missed the action. I called in the cavalry as soon as I heard the first shot."

"Good on you, Gordy," said Mac. "I can hear them now."

I stood over the thug writhing and moaning on the floor. It was clear he was going to live. I had no immediate intention of shooting him again, but his watching cohorts didn't know that.

"I've just drilled a bullet through your boss's head, so tell me quick or I'll plug this arsehole again. Where's the girl?"

▲

Chapter 19

The nurse led me to the room next to the recovery ward where Victoria lay. A saline drip was plugged into her arm under the sheets and the screen monitor flickered with the steady beat of her heart, beeping electronically as it did so. She was pale and serene.

"She's sleeping a lot," said the nurse, "and all the signs are good. The monitor will pick up any change and there's always one of us close by."

When she left, I moved to Victoria's bedside and gazed down at the face I'd feared I would never see again. I couldn't help feeling guilty and therefore angry with myself for being the cause, as I saw it, of nearly costing this woman her life. My failure to take another woman's plea for help seriously had already cost Joan and her daughter Evelyn theirs.

Sometimes being a detective struck me as lurching around like a bull in a china shop, breaking and destroying, with no clue as to what I was supposed to be doing other than upsetting people in the hope they'd get angry enough to make a mistake.

Often it worked, sometimes at a cost I was not prepared to pay. Like now.

I made a mental note to listen to Leo a little more carefully next time. If I ever had another client who was a victim of abuse I'd personally sort the bullying bastard out, free, gratis and for nothing.

Watching Victoria as she slept, I experienced a profound gratitude that she had not been required to pay the ultimate price. Her survival had let me off the hook. I'd learned to live with losing Susan. I wasn't certain I could repeat that feat and remain sane.

I wondered if the churning in my heart and the moisture in my eyes, that threatened to become tears, could be love and then realised that now wasn't the time to go there.

Surely neither Victoria, nor anyone else, would deny me placing a small kiss of gratitude on her forehead. I glanced around to make sure the door was closed and no nurses lurked nearby. I bent to kiss her, softly brushing her hair aside. As I did so Victoria's eyes flickered open and she raised her head slightly so that my kiss aimed for her forehead grazed her lips.

Her eyes held mine as recognition dawned and she pursed her lips as though savouring the taste of my kiss. A smile, wan, but a smile nevertheless, lit up her face.

"Hello, Mr P.I.," she whispered. "I knew you'd get my call."

WAR BRIDE

S.S. Tyndareus, 1945

Chapter 1. Emma.

Emma pedalled slowly prolonging her pleasure feeling the early morning spring sun warming her back. Work and boyfriend problems seemed a million miles away as she pondered the unusual peacefulness of the greening fields stretching away flat to infinity on either side of the path. It was as though she, serenaded by skylarks high above, was alone in a sea of green wheat rippling gently in the morning breeze.

Sudden and startling behind her came the whine and roar that she, like everybody, knew to be the engines of a Lancaster bomber. Awfully loud and awfully close behind her as it swept by a few feet over her head. The wind of its passing as it pulled up and banked away, waggling its wings, sent her tottering off the path into a shallow drain. She caught a fleeting image of the tail gunner waving madly as the plane passed above.

Somewhat surprised at her own temerity, she yelled and shook her fist at the aircraft as it turned away to the east towards Ely Cathedral. Ruefully she surveyed her muddy summer dress and white cotton cardigan that was white no more. What an age it had taken her to save up the clothing coupons to buy both.

Despite her ruined clothing, Emma couldn't help smiling at the thought of those fly boys having a bit of a lark. Young men who risked their lives every day dealing death and destruction so that she might cycle peacefully along a lonely path.

She decided to carry on to work rather than return home to clean up. If she went home her mother would fuss and carry on and insist that Father ring up and complain to the local airbase commanders. When she got to work Stella and Linda, her workmates in the Home Guard supply section of the Ministry of Food, fussed around her and helped her clean off the worst of the mud and grass stains.

"Dear, oh lors! What happened to you, dear? Here, come into the ladies before Mr Pettigrew sees you and sends you home. Me and Linda will sort you out."

Emma, inexplicably, was reluctant to say anything other than she'd fallen off her bike.

Linda wasn't going to let her get away with that.

"What do you mean fell off your bike? Why did you fall off?"

Perceiving Emma was holding something back, Stella piped up. "Come on, ducks, out with it. We won't say anything. What happened?"

"You know, on fine days I come along the path beside the river? Well, there I was, minding my own business when this aeroplane came up behind me. Gave me one hell of a fright, pardon my language, and made me topple off. Lucky I only went in the drain and not the river."

"I've never heard you use a swear word before. You must have been scared. Did you see its letters?"

"No, it turned away too quickly for that. Anyway, I was floundering in the mud."

"Did you see which way the cheeky sod went?"

"Towards Ely, I think. They must have thought it a big joke, the rear gunner waved fit to bust."

"Towards Ely? Then I bet they were heading for Mepal, you know, where the New Zealanders are. They fly Lancasters. Sounds more like the sort of thing Yanks would do though. Are you sure it was a Lanc?"

"Yes, it certainly was. But look, I don't want to do anything about it. I don't want to get those boys into trouble. If it hadn't taken me so long to save up my coupons to get this cardy I wouldn't mind. I was cross at first, but I don't mind now. It was all rather funny."

"I suppose it was a bit of a lark. Now let's see if we can't clean you up, then we'd better go out and get on with some work. Old Petty will be wondering what on earth we're getting up to in here. Probably itching to come and look, dirty old bugger."

The task of reconciling invoices with deliveries didn't entirely occupy Emma's attention during the slow hours before lunch. She smiled as her thoughts returned to the gunner waving madly as though he were on a fairground ride rather than at the tail end of a deadly machine. She wondered what the rest of the crew were like. After all it must have been the pilot who decided to buzz her and waggle the wings.

In the split second as she was falling Emma had seen the pilot glance down at her and give a little nod of his helmeted head as though in apology. Then in a blur he was gone and the big bomber wheeled away. There was something majestic and brave about the whole thing that made her think how inconsequential her job was at the Ministry of Food, made worse by Mr Pettigrew, their insufferable supervisor, who wouldn't even let them listen to *Music While You Work.*

No matter that she once considered office work only a stopgap until she could get into the W.A.A.F. She'd applied to join as soon as she'd turned eighteen more than a year ago and been told that her application had been accepted, but that she would have to wait until required. On hearing nothing she had applied again after D-Day, thinking they must surely now need all the volunteers they could get only to be advised that the opposite was the case and she should stay in the 'vital' job in the supply section of the Ministry of Food. She sometimes wondered if her father had pulled strings at the Air Ministry to keep her close, just as he had leaned on Pettigrew to get her a job.

Emma unsuccessfully tried to stop herself checking her watch every few minutes, willing the hands to go around faster as lunchtime neared. She joined her workmates at the Lyons on the corner for their usual tea and sandwich and a good old natter mostly about their respective boyfriends with occasional happy diversions assassinating the character of Mr Pettigrew.

"I've told you about the lovely corporal I shagged silly over the weekend. Now you tell me how you're getting on with that Jeremy of yours, Emma dear," Stella demanded.

As usual, taken aback by the older girl's earthy forthrightness, Emma spluttered, "All right. You know how men are, after one thing. But at least Jeremy isn't likely to disappear."

"We don't know what you see in him, apart from money, for the life of me we don't." Linda looked at Stella for support. "He might be always around, but he's like a rooster around hens. You know we saw him with that common as muck tart Jane Standen pushed up against a tree in the rec with her smalls around her ankles, don't you?"

"That was before I started going out with him. Anyway, I don't let him do anything like that to me and after all he is a man and men need frequent release of that kind, don't they." Emma's voice trailed off lamely, aware she was revealing her naivety.

"Cor, you don't know much about men, do you ducks?" Linda chuckled. "Look, I don't know why you bother with the likes of him and his Hooray Henry friends. Why you don't take up with a nice fly boy or some such is beyond me."

"You know why, and it's got nothing to do with his money even if his parents are the biggest landowners in the county.

I've told you before about Tim and Jack. I couldn't bear to lose another person."

"Oh yeah," protested Stella. "It was sad when your brother went missing, but that's nearly three years ago, girl. As for Jack, well, you hardly knew him, I'll bet, and he's been gone for more than a year."

"You can't stay in mourning forever, especially not these days," added Linda.

"How on earth can I move on when Father and Mother are forever on about Tim as their only son and remind me constantly how it's up to me to carry on the family name? Yes, I do miss him and Jack too, although I only knew Jack for a short while. He was a nice boy far from home and ever so lonely. I think he had only been on two or three ops when he didn't come back."

"It's up to you girl, but we can tell you you're missing out on an awful lot of fun with the chaps. This war isn't going to last much longer, you know. Surely no more of those nice boys are going to get the chop."

"I know, but I can't let Father and Mother down and they do seem to like Jeremy," Emma sighed. "Look, enough of this. Time we went back to work and harassed old Petty."

"You might not care about Jeremy's money, but I'll wager your parents do. Why otherwise would they like a coward who's hidden away from the war in a reserved occupation working for his father?" argued Linda. "Wasting time with his cronies, more like!"

"Enough, enough, leave off, ladies." Emma laughed as she gathered up her coat and headed for the door.

"Half a mo," Linda stopped Emma. "What about the dance tonight? You're on the organising committee so you must come."

Emma frowned, confused and uncertain, and paused before responding. "I don't think so. This morning's caper has upset me a bit."

Off the cuff it was the only excuse for not going that she could come up with even though she knew it wasn't the real reason. If she went it would have to be with Jeremy and she found herself not relishing the idea. She hoped Jeremy wouldn't turn up at her parent's house after dinner as he often did.

She wasn't upset, almost the opposite. Somehow her anger rather than the actual incident had made her realise she had an inner strength. She didn't know if it was her fright and fear at the sudden appearance of the monstrous bomber that had made her angry, or even if she *was* angry; or if she had a sudden insight into what it must be like for those on the receiving end.

Now that everyone was convinced Britain was going to win and despite all the evil things the Nazis had done, Emma couldn't help feeling that enough had already been done in retribution. So many thoughts clamouring for space, and this too surprised her because she had hardly given any consideration to the ferocity with which the Allies had wreaked vengeance on the Nazis.

She wanted some peace and quiet to sort things out in her mind.

Cycling home after work Emma passed the spot where she had fallen off, which set her thinking what a strange day it had been.

First her quiet ride shattered, causing her to tip into the drain. Then her good-natured argument with her workmates who seemed far more aware of the changing order of things than she or her parents.

Perhaps the girls were right; she suspected she no more loved Jeremy any more than he loved her. It was expected of them both and had been as long as she could remember.

▲

Chapter 2. Steve.

Steve's was the only crew flying from Mepal that morning. The rest of the squadron had been stood down after being tasked for strategic support. Then the day's operations were cancelled as the armies overran the target. Steve's faithful war horse, N for Nancy, had displayed a rare bit of temperament in her starboard outer engine.

The ground crew had worked most of the previous day and much of the night to replace it. Now, while the rest of the squadron relaxed, Steve's crew were required to take Nancy for a test flight.

Because operations were in one of those lulls that came frequently as Allied ground forces advanced ever more rapidly, the controller had been less specific than usual in determining a flight plan for their test flight. Steve decided to fly an extended circuit, climbing at full power towards the Wash then, if all was well, back across the Fens at about 5000 feet.

He wanted to land in time for a late breakfast and to give the ground crew time to sort out any problems. Also as luck or bad luck would have it they had lost a couple of crew, one to injury; broke his arm playing rugby and the other to an unspecified illness. Neither would be coming back for a while so they had two new boys on board. This would be a good time for them to get used to each other and see how they might cope when the heat was on.

It was one of those early spring days that held promise for the summer to come. There was scattered cumulus, but the forecast was for fine and clear. Everything went like clockwork, with Nancy purring as loud as a contented cat. The two new chums turned out to be anything but; both veterans of disbanded crews, who slotted in as though they'd been with Nancy from the beginning.

Nearing Mepal on the return, Jimmy on the radio had got clearance to fly straight in on a short circuit. Steve let Nancy down in a shallow dive with plenty of power on, giving everyone a good view of the flat countryside as they sped by. As always Steve marvelled at the neat, carefully tended pattern of the fields with the green of new crops beginning to emerge from the dark brown, almost black, peaty soil.

Steve had the aircraft descending through 2000 feet when he spotted the girl on the bike. She was easy to see, riding on a path running along the bank of a river away from them towards the church spire of March town. The girl had the path to herself and was dawdling along, seemingly oblivious to the bomber's presence.

"What do you reckon, chaps," Steve called up on the intercom. "Worth a look?"

"Go for it, skip," piped up Sandy from the bomb aimer's station. "She won't take us much out of our way, so we'll still be in time for brecky."

"Hang on then, boys. Bill, give her a good wave as we go over."

"Roger that, skip," came Bill's disembodied voice over the intercom from the rear turret.

Steve gave Nancy a little bit of rudder and pushed the stick forward to drop the nose and pick up speed in a shallow diving turn. It had been a long time since he had deviated from his hard-learned policy of avoiding unnecessary risk. But in the wink of an eye with barely a moment's hesitation he decided to do a beat up. Maybe he threw caution to the winds because the sight of the tiny figure pedalling along below in the bright spring morning reminded him of the joy of being alive. Besides, he thought, surely peace couldn't be far away.

Steve eased Nancy down to 300 feet and pushed the throttles open until she was racing along above the river like the Flying Scotsman express over the rails to Scotland. The girl didn't hear the bomber until it was almost overhead, when she looked round in fright and promptly swerved off the path and tumbled off her bike. In that split second her eyes locked with Steve's, and he registered her as a very pretty girl indeed.

"Is she all right, Bill?" Steve called, hauling Nancy back on track to Mepal knowing she couldn't have seen their recognition letters in that brief time.

"Yeah, skip. She's either shaking her fist at us or waving. Any rate, she's on her feet."

"Good-oh. Better keep this little stunt to ourselves, boys. You know what the brass thinks about this sort of carry on."

▲

Chapter 3. Emma.

Emma didn't tell her mother about her early morning encounter with the bomber knowing the fuss would culminate in her father complaining to the base commanders. Her mother noticed the stain on her cardigan, and Emma said she'd tumbled off a stool filing documents on a high shelf. No more was said.

Over dinner Emma choked off her mother's incessant prattle about the coming and goings of the 'good' families, including Jeremy's. She steered the conversation towards what was troubling her.

"What are things going to be like after the war, Father?"

"Same as they've always been, my girl. Nothing for you to worry about."

"But surely the men who've been fighting for us won't just meekly accept the crumbs rich people like us have tossed them in the past. Surely women know what it's like now to be useful and valued and earning their own money?"

"Mark my words, young lady, things will settle back to normal. Everybody will know their place just as they've always done, including you."

"We'll see."

Emma surprised herself at her own boldness. She had never openly doubted her father's words before.

As had become customary she disappeared up to her room after dinner leaving her parents to listen to the BBC war news. She tuned in to Tommy Handley's 'It's That Man Again,' guaranteed to cheer her up no matter what.

She was slightly annoyed when she heard the familiar rasp of Jeremy's MG roadster as he downshifted to get in the driveway. She heard his footsteps crunch on the gravel and then his booming voice as the maid answered the door. She wished she'd had the foresight to tell her mother she was unwell and didn't want to be disturbed.

Shortly the maid came up to announce that Master Jeremy had arrived. Emma didn't conceal her face-pull from the maid, who in the few months she had been with the Handley family had become confidant and friend to Emma. She hadn't dampened the maid's enthusiasm by telling of her less than successful attempt to join up when the maid confided her plan to be off into the W.R.A.Cs as soon as she was old enough.

Emma reluctantly tidied herself up and slowly descended the stairs. Her mother steered her into the drawing room.

"There you are, dear. Thought you'd gone missing. Jeremy's here. So good of him to pop around, don't you think?"

Before Emma could answer her mother fawned. "Can I get you another drink, Jeremy?'

"Very kind of you, Mrs Handley; don't mind if I do," replied Jeremy with a smirk, and, as an afterthought to Emma. "Hello, old girl."

His mode of address grated with her because she considered herself neither old nor a girl. Her look of annoyance was missed by both Jeremy and her mother, busy with smiling obsequiousness.

"I'll come back at nine take you to the dance, what?" stated Jeremy.

On the point of demurring Emma was forestalled by her mother.

"Emma was so looking forward to going. After all, she is on the committee and has to put on a good show, don't you, dear?"

Instead of going straight to March Town Hall Jeremy detoured through Upwell, sliding the MG to a halt in the courtyard of the Five Bells.

"Jeremy, we're already late for the dance. What are we doing here?"

"Got something to ask you, old girl."

Jeremy's wink was exaggerated.

Emma was thunderstruck as she guessed what was coming. Jeremy's friends, already in the bar and in the know, gathered round as he got down on one knee.

"How about it, old girl?"

His friends start chanting, "Yes, yes, yes."

Emma, as though in a trance, didn't protest as Jeremy slipped a ring on her finger. They all climbed into cars, seemingly impervious to fuel rationing due to the privileged status of farmer's sons in 'reserved' occupations, and roared off to the dance. The carpark was full of air force trucks and vans; theirs were the only private cars. Bicycles leaned four or five deep against every available wall. The dance was in full swing.

Jeremy immediately disappeared through the crowded fug saying, "I'm off to the bar, I'll get us a couple of tall ones. Back in a jiff."

As Emma expected, he didn't come back, though she had hoped this night of all nights might see him behave a little more thoughtfully than usual. Giving up waiting for him Emma fought her way through the crowd and saw Linda behind the bar, sweating to keep up.

"Have you seen Jeremy?" Emma shouted to Linda who nodded in the direction of the supper room. Linda poured Emma a glass of shandy, mouthing over the din, "Talk to you later."

Emma edged her way to the end of the bar where it was less crowded and happened to glance through the servery to the supper room next door. She saw Jeremy slapping the bottom of their maid then turn round and grab one of his friend's girlfriends and do a mock twirl with her. Emma had a rush of revulsion and self-pitying anger. She struggled to understand why she gave in to Jeremy's marriage proposal, or even came out with him at all this evening. It seemed to her that the boys she grew up with were boorish from the day they were born into privilege.

As though in contradiction, and even though he was older than her, she didn't recall her brother Tim as anything other than kind and considerate to his girlfriends. She did remember how devastated Susie was when his fighter crashed in the Channel in the summer of 1942. Did Susie still wear Tim's engagement ring?

Jack too, her first and only boyfriend besides Jeremy, was the opposite of boorish. He was a quiet, even shy boy only two years older than her when they met at a dance like this. She was just getting to know him when he disappeared.

When Jack didn't turn up for their date to celebrate her eighteenth birthday at the cinema in March, Emma feared the worst. He'd never said which squadron he was with and she'd never thought to ask. He wore no shoulder flashes so she assumed he wasn't with the New Zealanders at Mepal.

At the following week's dance she had overcome her reticence and went around the hall asking servicemen what had happened to him. It took ages to find someone who remembered him. A terse 'got the chop' was the only answer she got. Emma did learn that a number of Englishmen served with 75 Squadron at Mepal and Jack was one of them. The next day she requested and was granted an interview with the station commander who confirmed as gently as he could that Jack wasn't coming back. Aware of her barely controlled grief, the Squadron Leader detailed his driver to take her home.

Jack's death coming two years after her brother's didn't completely drive Emma into her shell. She did shrink from getting to know servicemen after that. She found unbearable their cavalier attitude of invincibility. She wanted to shake them to make them realise the danger they were in. The Americans were the worst with their brash confidence that they were doing the British a favour, completely ignoring the fact that the British had been fighting the fascists for two years longer than them.

She allowed Jeremy to drift into the role of her boyfriend as something of a relief, after nine months or so of rebuffing amorous advances of tipsy servicemen. Yes, she encouraged his interest if only as a convenience because he had money and a car and access to petrol. She tried not to lead him on nor make promises to him that she had no intention of keeping. So she tolerated Jeremy for the time being, but this marriage proposal had taken her by surprise; caught her off guard. She needed some time to think about what she should do next. She frowned ruefully to herself as she realised that if she had to think about it, then her question was answered.

"It's not yet the end of the world, you know."

A voice at her elbow jolted her out of her reverie. She wasn't aware she had let her disconsolation show and quickly regained her composure.

The voice belonged to a stocky chap wearing the uniform of a Flight Sergeant Gunner in the Royal Air Force with New Zealand shoulder flashes. She smiled, not at all put out by his approach, well used to it from the invariably polite chaps. Instinctively she kept her ring hand in the pocket of her jacket.

"Come and have a drink with us," he said. "You look a bit sorry for yourself all on your own. Or did you come with someone?"

"Yes, I did. He seems to have disappeared."

Emma glanced around the hall searching for Jeremy yet relieved that he still appeared to be occupied elsewhere.

"In that case, come and meet some friends. My name's Bill, by the way."

Before she had a chance to reply Bill looked at her keenly.

"By any chance were you cycling along between Doddington and March early this morning?"

Emma sputtered into her shandy and remonstrated, "Was that you in the Lanc that made me fall off my bike?"

Her anger evaporated instantly as she began to laugh with Bill as he struggled to speak.

"I'm sorry, but you looked so comical when you tipped into the drain. I was the rear gunner. I thought you were waving, not shaking your fist."

"I suppose your friends are the rest of the crew. Not sure I want to meet them now," she joked.

Bill guided her through the moving mass on the dance floor. When they got to his group she noticed straight away that not all of them had New Zealand shoulder flashes on their Royal Air Force uniforms.

Bill called to the circle shouting above the dance floor din. "Look who I found lying in a ditch!"

The uniformed men, some with girls, looked up with interest. "This is Emma. Careful what you say. She's the lass we knocked off her bike this morning."

One by one he introduced them all including the girls, who didn't seem at all standoffish like Jeremy's friend's. They were friendly and interested, not seeing her as a rival to be taken down a peg or two. Bill made the last introduction.

"And this is Steve, our skipper who caused all the trouble this morning, but who always brings us safely back."

Steve, shrugging in mock denial, held out his hand, as had all the others, to shake hers. As their hands touched Emma felt a frisson that she had never felt before. Their eyes met and in a sudden rush of mutual shyness both snatched their hands apart and looked away. Emma's heart missed a beat as though something hugely significant had happened. She couldn't have said what and any idea of what it could mean after so brief a contact was lost to her. If someone had said, 'love at first sight' she would have replied, 'what an absurd idea.'

The group's conversation gradually drew her in, while part of her mind continued to wrestle with what had just happened. She concentrated on keeping that preoccupation unnoticed, and her expression as neutral as possible. She stole glances at the pilot when she was sure he wouldn't notice while he lit one of the girl's cigarettes or was engaged in conversation. He was a tall man, nearly a head taller than Bill. Slim, but then who wasn't these days, with light brown hair.

Bill wasn't deceived. He had noticed the fleeting exchange and the slight rush of colour to his skipper's face. He had never seen Steve be anything other than laconic, immensely confident even in extremis at altitude with a night fighter on their tail. He did notice that, in contrast with the rest of his friends, Steve and Emma never exchanged another direct word.

Emma and Bill danced a couple of times, joining the throng that shrieked with the sheer joy of making a hash of the jitterbug then segueing into a slower foxtrot. When the break came Bill led Emma to Steve.

"Come on, skip. Your turn. Ask the lady to dance."

To Bill's inward amusement Steve asked Emma to dance in a formal manner, without his usual easy wit and charm. Equally formally, Emma accepted. Bill watched them circle the floor in a waltz holding each other at arm's length with distance enough between them for a heavy bomber to fly through. He wondered if anyone else had noticed the ring on her finger, or if she was a widow even though she couldn't have been more than nineteen or twenty. Being a widow wasn't uncommon these days.

She hadn't said anything and everyone was too polite to ask. Most of the group, including the girls, had been together for long enough to learn not to pry or get too close in case a tragic story lay behind the façade, as it usually did. All in good time. If she lasted in the group one of the girls would find out her story and tell one of the boys and so it would gradually become known.

Emma was in total confusion inside, belying her cool exterior. A thousand things to say to open the conversation passed through her mind to be instantly dismissed as facile, obvious, puerile. So she did nothing but smile. She had an overwhelming urge to bury herself in this man's arms instead of being held in such a stiffly formal way.

That stage of the evening saw every other couple on the floor locked together with their partners as though to never let go.

As the waltz ended Steve was ushering her back to their group when Emma heard Jeremy's boorish voice above the hubbub. With a start she realised she hadn't given him a thought from the moment Bill had introduced her to his crew. This on her engagement night! Jeremy staggered across the dance floor, elbowing couples aside.

"There you are, old girl," he slurred. "Been looking everywhere for you."

He grabbed her arm and for a moment it seemed Emma would be the subject of a tug of war as Steve still held her other one. Jeremy didn't notice Steve who slowly relaxed his grip and let his hand slide down Emma's arm until their hands touched and she felt his fingers tighten on hers.

She couldn't help herself responding by grasping his hand as though offered to a drowning person. She felt his fingers lock on to the engagement ring on her wedding finger. Their eyes met for the third time that day, this time for slightly more than a fleeting moment.

She knew her face betrayed her emotion. Then she was gone.

▲

Chapter 4. Steve.

Steve and all but the two Scotsmen of his crew were coming to the end of their tour. This made the crew of Nancy one of the more experienced in the squadron. They all realised it was wishful thinking that the European war would end before that day, but it was going to be a close-run thing.

Common wisdom had it that crews nearing the end of their tour might well be experienced, but they also became stale and started taking shortcuts that flirted with danger in their rush to reach the end. Taking on board two new crew, no matter how experienced, was unusual and somewhat unwelcome in a tight-knit, well-practised crew such as theirs. On the other hand Steve was aware that new crew on board made the old hands, including himself, buck up their ideas.

Steve was a thoughtful pilot who generally took no risks. That morning's beat up on the poor girl on the bike was a rare unbending for him, partly triggered by relief that the two new crew knew their stuff and were clearly going to fit in.

The crew respected Steve rather than liked him. He maintained a distance from them, although he was courteous and friendly enough. He probably spoke more freely to the ground crew than anyone because at least they were not likely to be killed and disappear from his life. He had learned painfully, from the loss of friends he had served with, that survival was a chancy thing.

Anything that could divert him from concentrating on survival, and that included the distraction of friendship with crew or members of the fair sex, that could affect his judgment in the slightest was to be avoided. Sometimes at the mess party after the loss of a comrade he struggled to remember anything about whoever had got the chop.

Not only did he want to protect himself from the agony and distraction of loss, he had seen what it had done to the girlfriends of those left behind and certainly didn't want to visit that on anyone. Wives and mothers and family got official notification from the station commander.

Girlfriends usually found out waiting in the local pub or dance for their date who never turned up. Eventually someone who had seen them together would take her aside, but there was no gentle way of telling that their lover would never be coming back. He had seen too many times a poor grief-stricken girl being ushered away by her friends.

Steve had dismissed the morning's encounter with the girl on the bicycle as an amusing incident. He wasn't above giving in to the urging of his crew, especially when there was little risk. If they were reported he wouldn't mind shouldering the blame.

He had long given up worrying about discipline from the brass. He got on well with Mac Baigent, the CO. They held each other in mutual respect. He knew Mac would never ask the impossible and was strictly fair in the allocation of tasks. In turn, Mac acknowledged Steve as one of his most experienced pilots and a steadying influence on the squadron. Especially since they had gone onto daylight raids and therefore how the leaders behaved in the air was open for all to see.

In the week before they had flown ops on three consecutive days; all daylight raids on railway yards and viaducts ahead of the advancing armies. In some ways those were more demanding than the night raids on the cities because precision was vital. No-one wanted to be responsible for dropping seven tons of high explosive on their own troops, or for that matter civilians in occupied France.

As though annoyed at the heavy workload Nancy had protested 'enough' and spat all the oil out of the starboard outer. Now after their flight test on this clear spring Friday morning they had been stood down. The reasons were not passed on from on high but they were grateful nevertheless.

After the flight test tiredness overcame Steve and he declined, as he generally did, to accompany his crew to the coming evening's March Town Hall dance. Bill and the others, used to their skipper being a bit of a loner, had long given up trying to make him change his mind so left him in peace as they trudged off to their quarters for a kip before lunch. Then came the serious business of preparing for the dance.

Before he dozed off Steve's thoughts strayed to his crew. He was glad the two new boys, Archie the engineer and Sandy the bomb aimer, fitted in well. Both Scotties, although apparently they'd never met before.

He privately marvelled at how his multi-national crew got on together. Although 75 Squadron was supposed to be the New Zealand bomber squadron there were only three Kiwis in his crew. Steve realised this wasn't that unusual in the squadron, and that most of the other aircraft captains, unlike himself, were New Zealanders.

It didn't seem to make any difference though; he still thought of Nancy as a Kiwi crew. The New Zealanders, Jimmy the wireless operator, Dan the mid-upper gunner and Bill the rear gunner had been with him straight from Lancaster finishing school to join 75 Squadron in September 1944. Paul, the other Englishman, had been a schoolteacher and copped occasional ribbing for his pedantic approach to navigation and everything else. Steve always backed him up. "Now, chaps, he hasn't got us lost yet. I'll pull his other leg if he ever does."

Steve puzzled about Bill. If he was close to any of them Bill was the only one he let himself consider a friend. Maybe it was the coincidence of their birthdays being within a day or so of each other's in April. The fact Bill wasn't an officer didn't make much difference in a squadron well known for its informality between ranks.

He knew little of Bill's pre-war life in New Zealand except that he had English relatives and seemed to have connections handy to the airfield. Steve was intrigued by Bill's stories of growing up in the far north of the North Island. The 'Bay of Islands' sounded idyllic compared to the drabness of Peterborough.

Besides, Steve was grateful that, for whatever reason, they had an empathy because Bill's quick calls for evasive action had saved them from fighters more than once.

Steve woke refreshed and, after a leisurely lunch, went for a walk in the direction of Mepal village. He got to the Three Pickerels to find it closed for the afternoon. The poster for the dance on the notice board next to the pub door caught his eye. He imagined himself solitarily drinking with the rustic locals while everyone else was having a good time at the dance in March and had a premonition he might miss out on something.

He resolved to hitch a lift with Bill who had a van that he kept at his aunt's place in Sutton village bordering the southern perimeter of the airfield. The van was big enough to take them all and girlfriends. Seeing him as something of a colonial hero returned to the old country in its hour of need, Bill's relatives had given him the use of the van. Turned out that the family had bakeries in every large town in the East of England.

The van was fairly well clapped out and petrol rationing had made it redundant as a delivery van. It still had the firm's bakery logo writ large on the side, which made Nancy's crew the butt of every possible joke concerning buns in the oven and urgent deliveries. They'd heard them all. For all that, the crew were grateful to Bill as none of them fancied the alternatives of cycling or crowding into the back of a lorry to run the risk of being spewed on during the return trip.

The dance was in full swing when they drew up outside March Town Hall. Bill with his catering connections hurried off to make sure arrangements were in hand for the supper. Archie and Sandy as the newbies volunteered to get the first round in. The others sorted out a table and got the girls seated.

Steve felt a momentary pang of envy at their easy camaraderie and ease with their girlfriends. But his crew were used to his reserve and didn't appear to notice and in the din of the dance it soon melted away. Steve even enjoyed a foxtrot with a pleasant girl who said she worked in a shop in Wisbech High Street. He was about to ask her for another when a tall Canadian cut in and foiled that plan.

Bill eventually emerged from the throng, his grin wider than usual. He had a girl in tow. She looked vaguely familiar and when Bill introduced her as the girl on the bicycle the penny dropped. Steve's glimpse of her had been from the rear and above as he had concentrated on keeping Nancy straight and level at illegal altitude at near 200mph. He hadn't had time for a good look and had laughed with the rest when Bill reported she had fallen arse over kite into the ditch. Now face to face it didn't seem so funny. But the girl was smiling as Bill and the others chortled over the incident.

Steve studied her as Bill introduced her to the group and, with a shock he'd never felt before when confronted with a pretty girl, realised she was beautiful. Already tall her high heels made her taller than Bill. She was pale in that special English way. Her hair, fair rather than blonde, hung down her back in a glossy sheen, not at all like the permed coiffures favoured by most of the girls. She was wearing a dark blue corduroy jacket over a light blue pleated skirt that matched her clear blue eyes.

When she locked eyes with him, Steve felt his reserve pierced as though without a word spoken she knew exactly who he was and everything about him. Momentarily taken aback he hastily released her hand which he realised he had been gripping too firmly and longer than was polite at a first meeting.

Bill swept her off for the jitterbug, something Steve hadn't yet mastered. Emma, Emma...He repeated her name to himself as he watched them laughing on the dance floor. He was aware that Bill had some sort of finder's keeper's rights to her and, in deference to his crew, Steve had on every similar occasion backed away.

Bill brought her back flushed and panting after the exhilaration of their exertions and more or less pushed Emma towards him.

Steve couldn't help himself. He had no idea what made him ask in such a formal manner if she wanted to dance. He felt a fool as soon as the words came out of his mouth. She immediately took the embarrassment out of it by accepting equally formally. He waltzed holding her stiffly, their awkwardness made obvious by the couples gliding around them glued together as though nothing could pry them apart.

Steve and Emma glanced quickly away if their eyes should meet, as though they were gauche teenagers. Beyond facile pleasantries they said little after they had both decided, 'Yes, it was a nice evening' and 'Yes, the band was good.'

When the set ended Steve was guiding her back to their table when a civilian, somewhat tipsy, intercepted them and grabbed Emma's hand. The man seemed unaware or uncaring that Steve was holding her other arm. As the man dragged her away Steve let his hand slide down her arm until their fingers locked. Much to his surprise she held firm, as she had when shaking hands on introduction. He was sure she returned the pressure of his grip. He felt a ring on her finger that he hadn't noticed before.

As the man tugged her way she met Steve's eyes openly and directly and an expression passed fleetingly over her pale and beautiful face. Anguish or joy Steve couldn't tell but, despite that he knew almost nothing yet everything of her, he fervently hoped it was the latter.

▲

Chapter 5. Emma.

Emma let herself be dragged away while every instinct fought against the good manners of her upbringing and told her to stay. Yet it was beyond reason to feel something for somebody after such a fleeting moment. Jeremy hustled her into the MG chortling they were off to Sidney's party.

Emma up to then had tolerated Jeremy's friends hiding out from the war in protected occupations. Yet sitting in that car as it rushed along lanes like black tunnels she wished she could have been back at the dance, secure in the midst of a circle of friends, so unlike Jeremy's. Bill and the pilot's friends clearly felt a lot for each other.

She wished she was back in the Town Hall preferably encircled by the arms of that tall, cool, calm pilot whose obvious inexperience with girls made him all the more charming.

Monday morning Emma again cycled along the tow path. This time rather than getting lost in private thoughts she scanned the sky. There was the drone of aircraft, but this time flying high and purposeful as though the war had resumed after the weekend, even though the concept of weekends had long been forgotten.

She realised the irrationality of her expectation of a repeat visit from a low flying bomber when she arrived at the office without anything more than the sun's reflected flash from an aircraft high above. She and Linda pushed through the staff door together.

"You're looking a bit sorry for yourself, love. Didn't fall off your bike again, did you?"

"No, nothing like that."

"Well, what then? Come on, tell Linda. You know I won't say anything to no one."

Emma couldn't contain herself.

"You know you saw me with that group of air force boys at the dance, New Zealanders mostly, some of them anyway, based at Mepal. They were nice in an old fashioned way, sort of shy like boys. Well, I know they are boys really; they're only about my age. There was one, a flying officer I think, who did something to me."

"What do you mean? Did he grab you, like interfere with you?"

"No, nothing like that. He looked at me, that's all."

"Blimey girl, you might have caught something," laughed Linda.

The morning passed in the usual tedium of shuffling supply requisitions and ration details and untangling the various snafus. Sometimes Emma wondered how, with their bumbling bureaucracy, they could ever have expected to win the war in the face of the well-known German efficiency.

At lunchtime in the Lyons, Linda and Emma were joined as usual by Stella. Despite promising she wouldn't say a thing Linda couldn't help herself.

"Our girl has gone and got herself smitten."

Emma blushed, not willing, yet, to admit even to herself that such a thing could happen. "What about Jeremy then? We are engaged."

"Oh, that tosser. You'll be well shot of him. A leopard doesn't change its spots you know. Slipping a ring on your finger won't make him change the habits of a lifetime."

"I know you're right. It's just that I don't want to hurt anybody, including Jeremy."

That evening her mother observed her moping around, and at the dinner table pressed her why.

"I hope you haven't had another set-to with your young man now you're engaged? Jeremy is such a nice fellow."

"No, no argument, I just don't want to go out with him anymore. He didn't give me a chance to say whether or not I wanted to be engaged to him. I've decided I don't!"

"Oh, that's such a shame and the Southgates such a nice, well-respected family. I suppose there's another man involved. I certainly hope he's suitable?"

"Mother! Why does there have to be a man. I'm perfectly happy on my own. Jeremy hasn't been much of a boyfriend, you know. I'm dead certain he wouldn't be much of a husband either."

Even as she protested Emma inwardly admitted the truth of her mother's intuitive assertion that there must be another man. She couldn't stop thinking about the pilot and how he had gripped her hand for an instant.

The thrill that ran like an electric shock through the connection of their hands had, in that second before Jeremy pulled her away, forcing their hands apart, transported her being incandescently to a higher level of awareness.

Every morning, in all but the worst weather she cycled along the same path hoping for a repeat, but no aircraft came close. Then one bright morning when she had almost given up and was back to enjoying the ride to work for its own sake she became aware that someone was pedalling along behind her, puffing to catch up.

When she glanced to see who was making such heavy weather of pedalling she nearly tipped off her bike, again, to see it was the flying officer.

"Steve, isn't it?"

She knew full well it was, but Emma was unwilling to admit her knowledge and the hurt she had felt at his absence.

"What on earth are you doing here?"

"Thought I'd come out early for a bike ride."

Steve assumed an air of innocence, neglecting to add that he'd borrowed Bill's van, thrown his bicycle in the back and waited where the path crossed a road.

"If you've come from Mepal you must have started early to get here."

"I only know your Christian name, Emma. You haven't been back to any of the dances and I couldn't think of any other way to see you again."

They pedalled on together exchanging banter to find out more about each other. Steve noticed Emma no longer wore a ring and decided on the blunt approach from the start.

"Are you engaged or married or widowed or what?"

"None of those," Emma replied tersely. "All in the past now. End of story."

"Then, if it's all right with you I would like to take you out. When I can. May I ring you when I next know I'm not flying?"

"Of course you can. Watch out for low flying planes while you cycle along this path, you don't want to fall in the river."

With that Emma smiled sweetly at Steve as she disappeared through the Ministry of Food's door, leaving him to pedal back to the van.

They went out usually to quiet little river-side pubs as often as they could. Emma became accepted by the crew and their girlfriends. She saw Jeremy still surrounded by his cronies and with a tarty blond in tow and they carefully ignored each other.

Emma rushed home from work every afternoon to see if Steve had left a message with the maid.

Operational duties took him away often for two or three days at a time. Emma would listen for the aircraft departing and returning though it was uncertain which squadron was flying overhead at any one time from the nearby bases. She became reconciled to his absences and her fears for his safety diminished as she learned of his own and his crew's long experience.

▲

Chapter 6. Steve.

With some surprise Steve found himself back at the van with no recollection of cycling there. All he could think of was that she'd said yes, yes, she'd said yes.

Bill was at his aunt's house when Steve dropped the van back.

"Thanks, pal. She thought I'd ridden all the way from Mepal. Must have felt sorry for me because she said yes, she would come out with me."

Bill kept the envy out of his voice and spoke lightly.

"Good on you, skipper. That girl could be something of a catch, as if you didn't know."

Over the next few weeks Steve saw Emma as often as he could. His previous determination to keep at arm's length all but the job in hand was abandoned and justified by the rationale that the war must nearly be over.

They were still going on raids, in the last few days of March to bomb the viaduct at Munster and the oil plant at Lanendreer. Flak had been heavy, but no enemy fighters were seen. Flak he couldn't do anything about and he found his concentration slipping as he thought about Emma.

He was relieved that opposition from enemy fighters appeared to be a thing of the past because he had a feeling he'd lost the vital empathy with Bill when it came to escaping the attentions of the Luftwaffe.

One evening when they met at the George in Chatteris, Emma broached the subject of her parents.

"They know I'm going out with you. I'm pretty sure they don't approve, mainly because you're not landed gentry from around here. Peterborough might as well be the black industrial north as far as they're concerned. I think it's time you met them and charmed them into submission."

"Crikey, we must be getting serious if it's time to meet the parents," Steve joked. "'OK, you say when and I'll turn up in my best uniform and put all my ribbons up. That should impress them."

"I wouldn't bank on it. They'd be impressed if you were from a wealthy farming family or royalty or, even better, both. Are you?"

"Afraid not, sweetheart. Pretty sure I'm not related to the king. Dad keeps an allotment so you could say he is a man of the land, though I don't think that qualifies him as a wealthy farmer. In other words, what you see and love is what you get."

"Oh well, never mind. Back to plan B with the charm and the medals then."

The following week Steve was in the van as Bill drove the crew to the Friday dance in March.

"Drop me off at the gate, thanks, Bill."

Steve pointed to an imposing entrance with a well-proportioned house visible at the end of a gravel drive.

"Not coming to the dance tonight then, eh, skipper?" said Sandy.

"Must be serious if you're meeting the parents," Bill commented. "Better look out, skipper, you might be signing up for life if you're not careful."

There was slightly more edge in his voice than he intended, that drew a sharp glance from Steve. The other crew members noted the awkward silence that followed.

"Yeah, well, thanks for the lift. Don't wait up."

Steve watched them drive off, weak red tail lights disappearing in the dusk, and wondered if Bill had feelings for

Emma. He recalled the easy way he had with Emma right from their first meeting at the dance that seemed much longer ago than the four or five weeks it really was. And Bill seemed able to make Emma laugh in a way he never could. The burden of command, he thought ruefully.

Steve strode up the drive and couldn't help admiring the house, half-timbered and brick and all leadlight windows. More like a mansion than a house. Another rueful smile as he compared this with his parents two up and two down terrace end.

Emma answered the door as soon as he pressed the bell. She flew into his arms and gave him a quick kiss.

"About time, my flying hero. Come on, let's get this over with. We're having a sherry in the drawing room."

She took his hand and led him forward.

"Mother, Father, this is Flying Officer Steve Mathews."

"Sir, Mrs Handley, thanks for having me. I hope I haven't put you to any trouble."

Mrs Handley spoke dismissively. "It was Emma's idea. Rationing is even worse now than it was two or three years ago, as you know I'm sure."

"Oh, come on, Mother. You have never had any trouble getting the food and treats you want," Emma interjected. "Rationing or no rationing."

"Now, now, young lady. No need to speak to your mother like that. Let's go into dinner."

Emma hung back to whisper to Steve.

"Ignore them. I do. They're so old fashioned."

The dinner progressed awkwardly. Emma's bright chatter could not mitigate the elder Handleys' disapproving manner.

Afterwards Mr Handley harrumphed. "I suppose we'd better leave the ladies and adjourn for a port."

He held up his hand to forestall Emma's objection.

Steve thought how ridiculous. Here he was a decorated officer in the RAF and yet he couldn't help feeling a little intimidated. When they were seated Mr Handley began.

"You know, Mrs Handley and I don't approve of Emma gallivanting about with your sort."

"What sort would that be, Mr Handley?"

Steve resented the man's blinkered view that had pigeon-holed him by his accent. His rank and decorations seemed to count for nothing.

"Don't get me wrong, young man, I realise you and your pals are doing a fine job saving us from that fool Hitler." This was said with something of an ironic sneer. "But I'm damned sure when this is all over, and it will be soon, you'll be off like a shot to God knows where. Emma has no idea what it would be like to live in a dingy, working class hovel. Mrs Handley couldn't stand that. We have already lost Tim to this ghastly war. Emma is all Mrs Handley and I have left in the world."

"Sir, Emma and I have only known each other for a few weeks, but that's enough to know that we have something special. In my situation I cannot offer her anything until this war, including in the Far East, is over. So I cannot make any promises to her or you until then. If it is any consolation to you Emma understands that, and I hope you and Mrs Handley will too."

After flying daylight raids to Wesel, the unfortunate city located on the Rhine that blocked the Allied advance, and the railway marshalling yards at Hamm, Nancy and her crew were reprieved from flying for the first few days of April.

With a weekend at their disposal Steve, his interest piqued by Bill's tales of New Zealand, decided to take the train to Whitby on the Yorkshire coast where Captain Cook had served his apprenticeship.

Steve wanted to see the statue of the man who had claimed that faraway place for the Empire and given it the values that led to Bill and all the other New Zealanders coming to England's aid. Besides, he and Emma had never been to Whitby and the idea of the seaside appealed to them both.

Out of season and after nearly six years of war, Whitby was almost deserted. They found a hotel on the Esplanade facing out to sea not far from Cook's monument on the cliff above the harbour. They were welcomed by the proprietor, an elderly lady who puffed up the stairs to show them their room. She had a twinkle in her eye and a kindly smile when she handed them the key.

"There you are, Mr and Mrs Mathews, I'm sure you'll be very comfortable."

Steve was amused to see Emma blush.

The instant the door shut they were in each other's arms. Their pent-up passion rendered the world outside their room irrelevant. Eventually satiated and pausing for a breather, Steve checked the time.

"'We've missed dinner, darling. I hope the old lady won't be upset with us."

"Oh, I doubt it. I have a feeling she's seen right through us and doesn't mind at all."

As though on cue there was a soft knocking on the door.

"Sorry to disturb. I've left a tray here. Thought you might need supper."

Emma buried her face in the pillow to quieten her giggles, while Steve stifled his laughter to reply.

"Thanks so much, Mrs Weatherly. Sorry we missed dinner, we, um, lost track of time."

The weekend passed in a flash. Steve told Emma much of what intrigued him about things mechanical. She was more interested in his life growing up in Peterborough, which seemed to her a world away from Doddington even though it was only twenty miles as the crow flies. She had occasionally been there although never to the industrial or working class areas.

Steve told how he'd just been taken on by the giant Perkins engine factory in Peterborough as a design engineer before volunteering for aircrew. He'd come from a working class family and was an only child. He had won a scholarship to Loughborough and graduated with honours. His father worked on the shop floor at Perkins.

They wandered through the old town around the harbour. Some of the barbed wire on the beach had been dragged back enough so they could dip their toes in the cold water of the North Sea.

They said little on the journey back, the train this time crowded with service personnel heading south as though back to the serious business of war.

The following week proved hectic for Steve and the crew of Nancy. They went twice to Kiel bombing the port while others laid mines in the bay. In the evening after the second raid Steve had a drink in the mess with his CO and confided in him.

"Mac, we all know this war in Europe can't go on much longer. We're smashing to smithereens targets that have already been smashed before. As soon as it's over I intend to ask Emma to marry me. Do I need your permission?"

"Naturally you've got my permission. What about her family, what do they think about it?"

"Not too keen, I'm sorry to say. But it's not really up to them these days is the truth of the matter."

Mac held a match over the bowl of his pipe until he was satisfied it was drawing.

"This thing isn't over yet; there could be more heavy ops still to come. I think you're wise to wait it out before you ask her. Besides, we may have to go out to the Pacific and see off the Japs. There may be dispensation for married crew, but I wouldn't bank on it."

Mac was right. On the overcast day of April 14th 1945 the battle order was posted with Nancy listed to take part in the coming night's raid. After weeks of daylight raids the change back to night operations came as a disappointment to Steve because it signalled a halt to tactical ops and the return to heavily defended targets. Sure enough the CO drew back the curtain at briefing to reveal the target for the night was Potsdam on the outskirts of Berlin. The Reich had drawn what defences it had left around itself, like circling the wagons against marauders.

Take-off was scheduled for 2300 hours and about an hour before that Nancy's and other crews climbed into the back of the lorry as it headed for dispersal. The WAAF driver pulled up in front of the looming dark aircraft then called out. "N, Nancy. Good luck, boys," as she always did before gunning the lorry to the next aircraft in dispersal.

When they had got down to five ops to go to complete their tour the ground crew had made a point of congregating at the hatch and shaking them each by the hand and wishing them luck as they clambered in. The NCOs felt as proud of Nancy, if not more so, than the aircrew. Now with only three ops to tour's end tension mounted.

Steve called up each of the crew in turn confirming checks complete and when satisfied waved the chocks away and swung Nancy onto the perimeter track. Like all cautious skippers, Steve normally tarried until nearly the last aircraft rolled by on its way to the control caravan. This time he felt he'd rather get on with it and taxied Nancy to lead the mass of

Lancasters snaking their way towards the head of the main runway. He held her on the brakes and with four Merlins singing as loud as they could waited for the Aldis to flash green from the caravan.

"'Let's go, boys," Steve called as he had each time from the beginning, and let the brakes off. Archie locked the throttles wide open as, heavily laden, Nancy gathered way on her headlong rush down the runway. Steve felt her going light as the tail came up with plenty of runway to spare and lifted her off at 110 knots indicated airspeed. By the time they crossed the airfield boundary Archie had the wheels fully up and locked.

Steve held Nancy in a wide climbing turn through the overcast to emerge in a clear blackness barely illuminated by starlight. Their turn brought them back over the unseen airfield and Paul called a course for Steve to steer over an invisible East Anglia south east towards Germany.

He visualised Emma in the blackness below listening perhaps wondering if it was him as the mass of aircraft passed overhead. He brought himself back to the task in hand and, as though to re-establish his concentration called on the intercom, "Keep a sharp eye out for friends, boys. We can't see 'em, but they're out there."

Occasionally they did see the vague shape of a Lancaster silhouetted against the starlight or the red glow from a Merlin's exhaust. Now and again they felt the buffeting from the slipstream as another aircraft crossed close ahead of them. Mostly they flew on in complete isolation as though there were not hundreds of aircraft around them, all intent on the same grim task. One thing in the dark at twenty thousand feet even radar-directed flak was inaccurate. Radar-equipped night fighters were a different proposition, although again height and darkness made it difficult for them.

Sandy came on the intercom confirming he had a good H2S radar fix on Cromer unseen in the blackness as they passed over the coast. Steve, no doubt like all the others, felt his usual rise in tension as they left the safety of the land far below. He held the bomber at their bombing height of 19,000 feet as they crossed the Dutch coast. Thankfully the flak ships were a thing of the past. Steve instructed Sandy to leave the radar to Paul secure in his navigator's cubicle. Until he assumed his bomb aimer's position on the run in to the target Sandy would feed bundles of window into the slipstream in an effort to confuse German ground and airborne radar.

Steve on Paul's instructions brought Nancy around in a slow turn to starboard, lining her up on Potsdam already visible as a fiery glow in the distance. As they crept closer Steve saw searchlights weaving across the sky. The movement of the ominous bluish central radar-predicted light was mimicked moments later by at least half a dozen more.

He watched with a mixture of horror and relief that it wasn't Nancy as another kite below and to port was suddenly illuminated by the master light. Within seconds the aircraft was coned by others. Even as the heavily-laden Lancaster turned away in a spiralling turn in an effort to break free of its unwelcome attention, flak began to burst around it.

He didn't see the outcome of that desperate struggle. Sandy's disembodied voice over the intercom dragged his attention back to the job in hand. Steve plainly saw the green target indicators dropped by the master bomber. Sandy confirmed he had them securely in his bomb-sights as he called for Steve to hold Nancy steady as they were now well into the run-in.

Sandy, broad Scottish accent devoid of expression, was completely professional in his moment of supreme concentration.

"Steady, steady, right, steady," he droned on, sometimes with a reproachful inflexion as Steve countered the effects of another aircraft's slipstream or the shock wave of close flak. The crew waited for what seemed an eternity for Sandy's "Bombs gone, no hang ups." Steve felt the aircraft give a little bounce and come light before Sandy had even got the words out.

Steve held the aircraft straight and level, sweating every one of the 28 seconds that it took for the camera flash to record their expertise. As soon as Sandy called, "Clear, skipper," Steve hauled Nancy around into the blessed black away from the cauldron and rippling flashes of the cookies going off and the still searching lights.

Steve exhaled in a long sigh unaware that he had been holding his breath. The crew also let out a collective sigh and Steve let them chatter over the intercom for a moment, knowing it relieved the tension. He called each in turn making sure they were OK.

Chatter was rudely interrupted when Bill yelled, 'Skip, fighter coming in from starboard, corkscrew NOW!'

Steve hesitated a second, decided to corkscrew port and kicked the rudder and put the stick forward hurling Nancy into as tight a downward turn as she could stand.

Dan in the mid-upper and Bill in the tail blazed away, making the aircraft judder with the recoil. It didn't deter the enemy pilot. Steve ducked involuntarily as tracer streamed above his canopy. He could feel Nancy had been hit. All his concentration was on controlling the aircraft in their mad dive for safety. A black shape streaked across, disappearing as Sandy, now in the nose gunner's position, took a last shot.

Steve eased the kite back onto level flight. Paul, as efficient as ever, called through a course before Steve had asked for it. The Havel River dissecting Potsdam was clearly visible and

Steve was aware that evading the fighter had cost them height and kept them too long in the congested target area. He called the crew up again in turn. This time, chastened and quiet, they answered in the affirmative. Except there was nothing from the two gunners.

When things settled down Steve asked Jimmy, his radios quiet for the moment, to go back and check on Bill and Dan in case it was only the intercom malfunctioning. No need to take the portable oxygen as they were climbing back through 9000 feet. Jimmy had just eased himself out of the r/op station when Archie, Scottish accent as broad as Sandy's, came up on the intercom.

"Skipper, starboard outer's losing oil pressure."

Steve glanced out to his right to see nothing except the glow of exhaust as normal.

"Brand new engine, eh, should get us home?"

"Not a chance, skip, pressures gone. Better feather the prop now."

Before Steve could order the start of the fuel cut-off and feathering sequence he was horrified by a tongue of flame spurting from the engine cowl. Within seconds the tongue became many, licking back over the wing. The slipstream at 200mph carried the flames, shooting like a blowtorch, back into the night. If it had been an inner engine the tailplane would have surely caught fire.

Steve pressed home the Graviner switch even though instinct told him the fire was already too fierce to be controlled by the in-built extinguisher. He was right. The flames spread inexorably along the wing towards the inner engine.

While he desperately considered what he should do next a part of his brain was screaming EMMA, EMMA and he couldn't be sure he hadn't shouted her name out loud over the intercom. How unfair to get so close to the end of their tour, the end of the war, for this nightmare to happen. He glanced at Archie who gave no sign he was aware of Mike's anguish. The engineer was fully engaged cutting fuel to the starboard inner engine as the fire crept closer.

Steve felt the burning wing beginning to lose lift and realising that there was nothing left for him to do called, "Parachutes on. Take up abandon aircraft stations."

He realised as he did so that Jimmy wouldn't be plugged into the intercom and the two gunners, if they were alive, couldn't hear him.

He knew that Nancy had only seconds to live as the fire came closer to the starboard inner wing tank. He could feel from the attitude of the aircraft that he might not be able to hold her level much longer to give the crew time to get out. He felt a deep sadness for Bill, Dan and Jimmy who would surely perish for lack of instruction to bail out. Then a slight shift in trim indicated the rear turret was traversing through its complete arc and with a rush of relief he knew Bill at least was going to get out. He could only hope the other two went with him.

Sandy had the forward hatch ready to release and was looking expectantly up at Steve. Archie and Paul, pedantic Paul, were also 'chuted up and standing by. Steve had a last rapid look around at the fire still burning. It had not progressed much more, but was still as fierce.

"Jump, jump, jump," he yelled.

Holding the Lancaster steady required all his strength. With a tap on his shoulder and a sorrowful salute, Paul, the last of his crew to bail out, slid into the black void.

Steve tried letting the controls go to see if she would stay level enough for him to go out of the hatch above his head. He wasn't surprised to find Nancy's burning wing dropped viciously and again he applied all his strength to keep her in some semblance of flight.

He had lost all sense of where he was in relation to Potsdam so was surprised to see a large body of water ahead reflecting the burning city. With no chance of being able to get out against the centrifugal force the thought that he could put her down into what must be one of the lakes of the Havel River flashed through his mind as his only chance. At least the water might put the fire out.

He was only a passenger now. Nancy, beyond control, staggered through the air. Steve thankful and surprised the altimeter and airspeed indicator were still working saw that he was only 150 feet above the water and not far off stalling speed. If he could keep the starboard wing up he might have a chance of ditching her.

He had no such luck. The crippled wing struck the water first. At 100 knots the impact of the water ripped the wing off. The aircraft broke up cartwheeling in a massive eruption of spray and flying debris.

His last conscious thought before he slipped away was again, 'Emma, oh my darling Emma.' By the time what remained of the cockpit came to rest in the shallows of the Havel River near the Glienicker Bridge, ironically their bomb aiming point, mercifully Steve was beyond sensation.

▲

Chapter 7. Emma.

Emma knew asking Steve to meet her parents was a risk. With all he had to endure flying on operations he might consider this was a bit too much. She was overjoyed, therefore, when the doorbell rang to find him standing there, dashing and wonderfully heroic in his RAF uniform.

She'd tried to dissuade her father from taking Steve off after dinner for, she supposed, the traditional man to man. Her father would have none of it and she had to remain in the drawing room listening to her mother go on about Jeremy, of all people, to whom she hadn't given a moment's thought for weeks. Eventually Emma's patience snapped.

"For goodness sake, mother. You marry him if you think he's so wonderful."

Thereafter stony silence reigned until Mr Handley, as unamenable as before dinner, asked the ladies to join them. Emma caught Steve's eye and got a small non-committal shrug in reply. The conversation jerked along awkwardly until Emma put them all out of their misery. "You're flying early tomorrow aren't you, Steve? You need to get back, don't you? I'll see you out."

Steve thanked Mr and Mrs Handley for their hospitality and followed Emma out.

"Was it too awful, darling?"

"About what I expected. I can understand their fears. Their whole world has been turned upside down. That must be hard at their age to comprehend."

"You're probably right, but the war has affected everybody, not just my parents. Sure, they've lost Tim and that's terribly sad, but it's not my fault and I can't turn back the clock"

"I know, dear Emma, but you are a link to some sort of normality as far as they're concerned, that things might carry on as before the war."

"None of us yet know what is going to happen for certain. The only thing that *is* certain is that you and I have to make the most of every minute."

The following week brought perfect spring skies, cloudless and blue, that to Emma's chagrin also made it perfect for flying. She didn't expect to hear from Steve so was pleased when the telephone operator at the Ministry of Food placed a telegram from him on her desk.

Stella and Linda were agog even though the operator had already whispered its contents. "What's it say?"

"He wants me to go away with him this weekend."

"You're going, aren't you, girl?"

"Oh dear, what will Mother and Father say if I do?"

"Never mind them. Steve might be dead soon; you love him so you have to live for today. Anyway, tell them you're going on a course or something."

"No, what Steve and I have is special. I don't want to spoil it by lying to my parents. I'll have to tell them even though they'll disapprove. They'll get over it."

The train journey north through York and Scarborough to Whitby was heavenly as two nights and almost two whole days stretched to infinity before them. North bound trains were far from crowded and were running near to timetable.

Emma hardly noticed that Whitby was almost deserted and only this small hotel open for guests. Even in this coastal town the black-out had been relaxed to the dim-out which lent a cheery air to the hotel. She did notice that Steve discreetly signed the register with just his surname.

When the landlady addressed them as Mr and Mrs Mathews she couldn't help blushing when she realised the old lady knew perfectly well they were not married. She thrilled at hearing the sobriquet Mr and Mrs for the first time as something she joyfully wanted.

Following their blissful weekend in Whitby Emma had only the briefest contact with Steve. He didn't say much about what he was doing except it was mostly daylight raids in support of the advancing armies. She heard on the radio and read the next day's paper's account of activity so she knew more or less what 75 Squadron had been up to. Although losses were not as horrific as they once were there were still unelaborated references to aircraft that failed to return.

Emma was relieved when she got home from work the second Friday after their Whitby weekend to find Steve had left a message taken by the maid. He had been digging sandcastles at the seaside in Kiel, which Emma knew was their private code for mine-laying, and would meet her in The George in Chatteris the following evening.

Steve had again phoned the house and this time the message was taken by Emma's mother as it was the maid's day off. He asked Mrs Handley to let Emma know he couldn't meet her that evening as they were being held on the base for reasons as yet unknown. Emma rushed home from work on Saturday excited at the prospect of the coming evening. By the time Emma got home her mother had gone out to a meeting and hadn't written anything down on the message pad.

The George was strangely empty for a Saturday night. When Steve hadn't arrived by 8.30, an hour and a half after he had said he would, Emma approached one of the few air force officers propping up the bar.

"Big one, back to night raids, Berlin apparently," was the terse reply. Emma made her solitary way home disappointed.

She wasn't too worried as this had happened before and she knew Steve would tell her all about it the next day or when he could.

Emma still had not heard from Steve by Tuesday of the following week. The Ministry of Food rumour mill had it that a large raid had gone to Berlin or, more accurately, to nearby Potsdam. Nobody knew why when that city had already been flattened. Perhaps something to do with the bridge or railway yards.

She rang the base commander at Mepal and got put through to Mac who didn't beat about the bush.

"Terribly sorry, but one 75 Squadron aircraft failed to return and it was Flying Officer Steve Mathew's 'N' Nancy."

"Did anyone see what happened?" asked Emma with hope in her voice.

"Again, I'm sorry. Aircraft from other squadrons also failed to return. In the dark it is impossible to say if the only aircraft visibly in trouble because of a fire was 'N' Nancy."

"Is there any hope they might have landed somewhere?"

"Regretfully, unlikely. Even if they had managed to land on one of our forward airbases in France we would have heard by now. If the crew has been taken prisoner we should find out soon from the German authorities."

Emma, distraught and distracted, went about her work and home routines. In the absence of any information she clung to the hope that the crew had survived and been taken prisoner.

She rang the base every morning and Mac directed her calls be put straight through to him when he told her as gently as he could the same as he had the day before.

At the end of the week Mac was able to tell Emma that German radio had announced 'little damage to Potsdam from the raid,' as they always did, and the 'downing of many bombers.' This last was clearly not true because 3 Group only lost three aircraft, one of which was from 75 Squadron. The German report said that 'one of the identification letters of a downed aircraft was 'N' Nancy, with all crew perished.'

Less than a full month after Nancy and her crew failed to return from Potsdam, which turned out to be 75 Squadron's last night operation of the war, Victory in Europe Day was declared on Tuesday 8th May 1945.

By then Emma knew she was pregnant, though she hadn't had it confirmed.

She had assumed that war's end would mean the end of her job at the Ministry of Food. But as Mr Pettigrew explained, food rationing was likely to get worse and besides, there was still Japan to defeat. Stella and Linda were keenly aware of the part they had played in urging Emma to forget the past losses of Tim and Jack and to follow her heart with Steve. They were well aware that with Steve's loss Emma had for the third time suffered a grievous blow.

"Please come out with us this afternoon, Emma dear. Try and forget what's happened at least for today. V.E. day will go down in history and you wouldn't want to miss the P.M.'s or the King's speeches, would you?" pleaded Stella. "The party will go on all night."

"I'm pregnant," whispered Emma. "I can't come out."

Stella and Linda exchanged glances. "How do you know? You'd only been with Steve a short time."

"I just know. Anyway it's more than a month since we went to Whitby."

"Ah, the famous Whitby weekend. We didn't think you took any precautions and we were pretty sure it was your first time.

Emma, dear, what's done is done. The question is; what are you going to do now?"

"Why, I'm going to keep him of course. He's Steve's as much as mine. He will live on through this little one."

"It's a 'he' then, is it, although how you can tell I just don't know?"

"I don't really know, he just feels like a boy. Steve and I talked about having a boy. We hadn't thought about a girl."

Emma's mother was appalled at her news.

"How could you bring shame on our name?"

"Mother, I loved him. I still love him. He promised he would come back. Please don't make things worse."

"You cannot have a bastard in this house. You must marry Jeremy as I said in the beginning."

"I'm not marrying Jeremy or anyone else for that matter. Besides who would want me carrying another man's baby?"

"I intend to contact Jeremy whether you like it or not. There is no need to tell him of your condition."

Emma's father kept silent during those exchanges. He seemed diminished by the war's end in Europe and the changes occurring in the district. Emma was grateful for his neutrality at least.

"Mother, you are wasting your breath. Jeremy won't want anything to do with this family now and even if he did I don't want to have anything to do with him."

"Well, then, what are you going to do to get out of the mess you've got yourself into?"

"I don't know, but what I do know is I will be all right. Furthermore this baby is all I've got of the man I loved with all my heart and I'm going to give him or her the love I would have given Steve. If you're worried about me being around home embarrassing you I've got friends, you know."

The subject of Emma leaving home faded as she and her mother maintained an uneasy truce. The excitement and sense of achievement at winning the war in Europe quickly subsided into the dreary routine that had existed before.

Efforts now turned to beating the Japanese. The newspapers said prospects for a quick finish did not look good in light of their fanaticism.

On a thundery, stormy Sunday morning in June Emma was moping around the house, declining to accompany her parents to Matins. Her friend the maid had already left their employ and it was proving difficult for Mrs Handley to find a replacement so Emma answered the knock on the door herself.

Although she knew him fairly well by then she was surprised to find him on her doorstep.

'Mac, please come in. I'm sorry, but my parents are at church.'

'That's all right. I hoped they'd be out. It's you I've come to see. How are you, Emma?'

Emma blushed and glanced at him askance fearful that somehow he knew she was pregnant. She relaxed when she sensed from his demeanour that his inquiry was his usual kindly concern.

"I'm fine, although I do miss him dreadfully."

Mac handed her a letter.

"We found this amongst his kit. Nearly all the crews left something like this to pass on in the event something happened, never expecting it to. I don't know what Steve wrote, and please bear in mind that whatever he wrote cannot be binding on you. You must get on with your life, as must we all."

Emma took the envelope and clasped it to her breast and could only nod agreement.

"Also it might interest you to know that 75 is leaving Mepal next month, not going far, only to Spilsby. After that it seems probable that we will be sent out to join our forces heading for Japan."

"Oh Mac, you will all be so missed when you go. It doesn't seem fair that after all you and your men have been through that you should have to do it all again on the other side of the world."

"That's as maybe, my dear, but that's war and it isn't over yet. Ah, one other thing; Bill Allen, you remember Steve's rear gunner? Seems he was the only one to survive and has been located as a prisoner of war. As soon as this thunderstorm passes we will be sending aircraft over to bring another lot of PoWs back. Bill is sure to be among them."

"That's good news at least. Mac. Thanks ever so much for coming and telling me all this."

Emma had mixed feelings of sadness at the imminent departure of the people in the squadron that she had come to know and joy of a sort at the reappearance of Bill, though she couldn't help wishing that it had been Steve.

After Mac left Emma opened the letter. It was only one handwritten page.

Dearest Emma,

I know it is a dreadful cliché in all the movies, but if you are reading this it means I haven't come back, 'failed to return' as the brass so delicately put it as if it's my fault. But don't worry, I'm sure to turn up like a bad penny. Those Germans haven't made a cage that can keep me in for long. I will be holding you in my arms again soon.

In the extremely unlikelihood that I don't turn up please don't be sad. We have had a wonderful time. Good enough for most people's lifetime. If good old Bill makes it, try and be nice to him. I know he has a soft spot for you. Nothing like mine, of course.
Chin up.
Your ever- loving Steve.'

Tears spilled down Emma's cheeks as she sobbed in mute grief. She recalled the contentment and joy of being with Steve, which only made her sadness more profound as each thought of a happy time was immediately followed by the crushing realisation that she would never know another.

A few days later as Mac promised Bill telephoned asking if he could visit Emma. She found herself eager to see him and next day, after a cursory greeting from her parents when he arrived, she took him out onto the lawn. She settled him in the shade of the old flowering cherry tree and poured some lemonade.

"Dear Bill, I'm so glad to see you. Sorry Mother and Father are a bit off-putting, but you know how they are."

"That's all right. After what I've been through coping with grumpy parents is a cinch."

"Was it terrible?"

"At the time, it all happened so quickly I couldn't think beyond getting out. Self-preservation, I suppose. We didn't have Monica switched on. Should have, it might have given Steve early warning of the fighter coming up on our tail. He chucked it around all over the sky, but we copped a burst. Looked like we'd got away with it at first, but the intercom had gone dead or mine anyway because I heard nothing after Steve levelled Nancy out again.

"After a while I noticed we were on fire and getting very low. When it became obvious he was having trouble holding the aircraft steady I was pretty sure it was time to get out. When I saw someone hurtling past in the slipstream I knew the order to go had been given so I did.

"I'm awfully sorry, but apart from that first 'chute I didn't see any others. I don't know what happened to whoever was first out, but anyone surviving would have been found by now even if they'd ended up in a German hospital. Steve was terribly brave to stay with the aircraft to give us a chance to bail out. I wouldn't be here talking to you if he hadn't."

"Did you see Nancy... again?" Emma couldn't bring herself to say 'crash.'"

"I saw her cartwheel into the water. It was light from the city burning on each side of the river. From the way it went in I'd say Steve was trying for a ditching. I'm so sorry, Emma, the crash could not have been survivable."

"Dear Bill, at least one of you is safe. You are safe aren't you? Mac and a few of the others have kept in touch and he said you might be going to the Far East."

"Probably. We've been issued with tropical kit and it looks like we might be getting new kites. But I'm not going to worry about that now. It may be months before we go. Can I see you again?"

"Of course you may, Bill. I'd like that as a friend. I can't imagine I'll ever want to be with a man again other than as a friend. I almost feel as though it is the kiss of death for a man to have anything to do with me after my brother Tim, then Jack and Steve."

Bill was a little taken aback.

"If that's what you want, Emma, then that's how it shall be. Perhaps in the future you might change your mind. You know how I've always felt about you. Steve was one lucky guy, especially as it was me who found you first looking lost and lonely propping up a bar."

Emma laughed.

"I'm not exactly a treasure to be found, Bill. Anyway, strictly speaking, Steve found me first from a thousand feet up, you might remember."

"Maybe, but you'll always be a treasure to me."

"Perhaps you'll change your mind when I tell you something you should know." She paused before plunging on. "I'm going to have Steve's baby, and look, I'll understand if you don't want to have anything more to do with me, even as a friend."

Bill recoiled, shocked and dismayed. He remained silent.

"Come on, Bill, it's not the end of the world, you know. You said those exact words to me ages ago if I'm not mistaken."

Bill found his voice.

"No, no, you're right; it isn't. It, it's just a bit to take in that's all. Look, it's getting late I must get back."

Emma wasn't surprised she didn't hear from Bill for a week or so. Perhaps a little disappointed, especially as she had made clear to him she couldn't entertain any romantic thoughts. But to see him as a friend, a link with the past, would have been nice. Then again, perhaps it was too much to expect a young man of twenty-two, a boy really, to be seen out with a scarlet woman.

Then early one evening Bill phoned to say he would be in the Three Tuns in Doddington and would she meet him there that evening. She was grateful he had chosen a meeting place unfrequented by her and Steve. She couldn't have borne seeing familiar places that reminded her of happier times. She found Bill in the snug nursing a pint. He rose to his feet.

"Good of you to come. Shandy right?"

Emma nodded thanks and sat down when Bill returned with her drink. Bill raised his glass to her.

"Chin up."

Emma wondered at him using the exact words that Steve had in his letter, but replied in kind.

Bill hesitantly began to speak.

"Emma, you must know how I feel about you. I've thought a lot about you, us, the baby, over the last few days. I realise I'll be a poor substitute for Steve, but I'll love you and your baby just as much as he would have, if you'll let me."

"Dear, dear Bill. That's awfully sweet of you and I know you think that now. When the baby arrives, might it not be a different story?"

"No, no, definitely not. That child will need a father. I thought Steve a good mate, a cobber or as you poms say, a 'wizard chap' and I love you. You'll need a man, me, even if you can't love me the same way you did him."

"Oh Bill, you are so kind and sweet. Let's just see how we go for the next little while. You may change your mind when 75 gets posted and takes you away from dreary England. What will happen to me then?"

"Why, you'll become a war bride, my war bride."

Over the weeks that followed Bill saw Emma on every opportunity he could. By unspoken agreement they avoided the watering holes and dances that had been familiar in what seemed a past life to them both.

The squadron's training for the Far East tapered off to almost nothing as the Allies leap-frogged ever closer to the Japanese mainland. It became evident that 75 Squadron would not be posted and so remained in a state of limbo.

Emma began to enjoy Bill's cheery company of old. They both managed to put some of the tragic past to one side. Emma occasionally had pangs of guilt and bouts of thinking what might have been. She usually dismissed these doubts while gradually accepting that Bill's proposal was right for her and, more importantly, the baby making his or her presence felt more every day. New Zealand was so far away surely the stigma wouldn't follow them there.

On the 15th August 1945 Bill phoned full of excitement. "They've surrendered. The Yanks dropped another bomb. It's really all over this time."

Emma could hear the church bells pealing and car and truck horns belting out V for victory in Morse. She joined Bill and a bunch of his air force friends celebrating madly in and out of the pubs in Ely, and dancing with the happy throng in the town square.

Bill had to shout above the yells and cheers of the crowd. "We're going to be disbanded. Seventy-five isn't going to the Far East. We're going home, home at last to New Zealand!"

For a moment Emma thought Bill had forgotten his offer now that the prospect of going home had become a reality. Her spirits, sky-high one minute sank low the next and tears welled. Bill noticed and twigged what she must think.

"Chin up, Emma, this means we can get married. March Registry office will be open again the day after tomorrow. Will you be my war bride?"

Emma hesitated only a moment before flinging her arms around Bill's strong neck.

"Of course, I will, dear, dear Bill."

On an unusually cold, blustery, wet day in the last week of August 1945 in Ely, the Registry Office buzzed with excitement as they completed the formalities. Emma's father begrudgingly lent them his car and a handful of petrol coupons so they could have a brief honeymoon in Southwold. Emma forbade herself to recall any thoughts of her seaside Whitby weekend.

Married men were among the first to be repatriated to New Zealand. For reasons known only to the brass, brides were to travel later. Barely three weeks after their marriage and with the hectic schedule occasioned by embarkation arrangements the newlyweds hardly had time to be alone together.

Bill sailed from Southampton aboard the Royal Mail Line Andes on the 25th of September 1945. He wasn't sure whether the lump in his throat was from waving madly goodbye to Emma or from the RAF aircraft overflying the vessel honouring and saluting the over 1500 New Zealand air force personnel on board.

With the war over and the squadrons departing with almost unseemly haste as though they couldn't get out fast enough, East Anglia rapidly become empty and morose.

Where only a few weeks previously the sky and fields had reverberated to the sound of Merlins and American Cyclones, now the only sound of engines was the lonely chugging of tractors as farmers ploughed the fields ready for winter wheat after the last of the potatoes were lifted.

Emma patiently waited for her travel documentation. She resigned from the Ministry and her departure went largely unnoticed except for a sad little afternoon tea put on by Linda and Stella.

Mr Pettigrew had been promoted elsewhere and the new manager wasn't interested. The two girls maintained a polite interest in Emma's journey and new life across the sea, but mostly they bubbled over with excitement at new boyfriends and their own prospects for imminent marriage.

Emma rather surprised herself as well as her mother and father by reaching a quiet truce. They had accepted her pregnancy and decision to go with Bill as a fait accompli. Her father in particular had softened his attitude as Emma's departure became inevitable.

Emma in turn realised that they did love her in their own way and all they wanted was the best for her as they saw it.

It was a glum little family group that waited on the March Station platform of the up line to Peterborough. Emma had insisted on travelling to Liverpool by train even though her father had wanted to drive her. She knew the journey as winter neared would be too much for him as well as her mother. Eventually the train huffed its way into the station. With tears streaming and last embraces Emma boarded an empty first class compartment. She lowered the window and waved and waved until her parents were lost to view in the steam and smoke as the train drew away.

Emma was crushed by the melancholy of saying goodbye to her parents and the unspoken possibility that she would never see them again. The long cross-country train journey left her weary as the disconnection from all that was familiar added to her sadness. She tried not to entertain the possibility that Bill would not be waiting for her, that she was leaving a sanctuary for a vague promise of a life so very far away.

Her mood lifted to something a little cheerier as she joined hundreds of other war brides, some showing far more progress in their pregnancy than she, waiting dockside to board. Most of them chattered brightly, filled with excitement at the adventure they were embarking on. Emma wished she could share their optimism but, while going through the motions with a couple of girls who had noticed her reticence, she wondered how many of them were carrying the child of a man other than their husband's.

Her spirits plummeted again when it became clear that the ancient, rust-streaked vessel tied up alongside was to be the ship she would be cooped up in for the next six weeks. The Blue Funnel Line coal-burning Tyndareus hardly fitted the picture of the luxury liner she'd imagined would be whisking her off to a new life in the South Pacific.

There was a fair bit of ribaldry exchanged with the dock workers.

"Not good enough for you, eh?"

"Watch out them Maori cannibals don't eat ya."

"What you want to leave this luverly climate for then, ducks?"

The rain swept down, driven by November's cold nor'wester.

In preparation for casting off the old ship belched into life, pouring thick black smoke from its long straight funnel. There were no speeches, no fanfare nor bands playing. The ship, with only a little roll on, slowly nosed into the Irish Sea. Many of the ladies became queasy, or sobbed, wishing they'd never left, all romantic notions forgotten.

Emma felt none of that. All she could think of was the child growing within her, Bill and the likely strange new life that awaited her in New Zealand.

▲　▲

WAR BRIDE
Postscript– Sixty-Five Years Later

Sarah wasn't familiar with the rental car or used to the heavy traffic. Nor was she accustomed to the rain and gloom of a wet autumnal English afternoon. The headlights streaming towards her added to her distraction. But she was determined not to let any of this faze her.

She was on her second circuit of the roundabout before she spotted the exit to Mepal village. She silently thanked English drivers for their patience, reflecting that had she similarly dithered at home she would have been blasted by horns and given the finger.

After the bustle of the A142, the road to the village was a blessed relief. She drew up next to a picket-fenced enclosure on the edge of what might have served as the village green. Old trees, dense and wide-spreading – oaks, she thought – ringed the green. The rain had reduced to a drizzle although the trees still shed drops as though weeping.

No-one emerged from the white-washed cottages that bordered the green. The only shop appeared closed. She opened the gate to the enclosure and went to the stone memorial in the centre. And there it was. Proof now that once long ago this was where her grandfather and hundreds of men like him had lifted off.

She looked out past the trees and through the gaps between the cottages at the flat land stretching seemingly to infinity. There was nothing to give any sign this had once been an airfield: no runways, no hangers. Nothing but fields of wheat and in the distance a cluster of low farm buildings.

A wave of immense sadness came over her as she realised the passing decades had obliterated from the earth all signs of what had once been the wartime base of the New Zealand heavy bomber squadron. Past deeds of valour and heroism in the name of freedom and honour were marked only by a simple stone memorial.

She had neither spoken to nor seen anyone. She drove back to the troublesome roundabout and took the exit to an industrial area that had a sign advertising a RAF museum. The rain started up again and, harried by traffic, it was some time before she located the museum's entrance tucked behind a steel and glass office block.

The curator welcomed Sarah in, the only visitor. He pointed out some of the exhibits, mostly fragments from aircraft and pictures on the walls of smiling aircrew standing self-consciously heroic in front of their giant machines.

After she had slowly circled the single room studying the exhibits she felt let down, as though she'd missed something significant. Sighing, she approached the curator to thank him. He was busy in his office tapping away at a computer, and appeared surprised she was still there.

"That would be a Kiwi accent, would it?" he said, not unkindly, as though aware of her disappointment. "We get quite a few Kiwis in here. Not surprising, I suppose, but not so many now and fewer every year. Had a father stationed at Mepal with 75 Squadron, did you?"

"Grandfather. Two ."

"Two?" the curator exclaimed.

"Yes, my step-grandfather and my birth grandfather. My real grandfather was killed. My step-grandfather was in his

294

crew. But it's my birth grandfather, my real grandfather, I'd like to know more about."

"Well, you know we have lists of all the crews here, don't you? Would you like to look up your grandfather's?"

"If it's no trouble," she said, "His name was Steven Mathews and my step-grandfather was his rear gunner, Bill Allen. He was the only survivor from the crash that killed my grandfather in 1945."

"Let's have a look."

The curator got down a large cloth-bound book, the end one on a shelf containing some ten or eleven identical journals.

"We do have it all on computer too now. Still, visitors like to see these original journals written at the time. Here we are, N-Nancy and the details of the crew at the time she was lost or 'failed to return' as the brass liked to term it. Follow each crew member's name across and you can see that their discharge date is entered in the last column or, I'm sorry, miss, the date they were killed. Here's your step-grand-father, Flight Sergeant William Allen discharged October 1945 and 'killed in action 15th of April 1945' against the names of each of the other six crew."

Sarah studied the names again, tears blurring her vision. The curator had seen this many times before and it never failed to move him.

"There, there, miss, it was all a long time ago."

He passed her a box of tissues.

Sarah wiped her eyes, feeling a little foolish at how her emotions had caught her unawares for the second time in as many hours. She laid a finger on her grandfather Steve's name. She stared at the entries against his name and noticed that the killed in action date had been neatly ruled through and overwritten with pencilled tiny, faded letters with a repatriated date in 1948 and discharged date in 1950.

She asked the curator what that meant. He fetched his glasses and peered closely at the entry.

"Ah," he said, "That means that the original entry was incorrect. That happened a lot. Like 'risen from the dead,' so to speak."

"What do you mean?"

"Well, Flying Officer Mathews might have been a prisoner of war and repatriated during 1948. Seems rather too long for that to be the case because most PoWs were back in Blighty by the end of 1945, or early '46 at the latest."

"But he was killed, not taken prisoner," said Sarah.

"Or someone has come in here and mucked about with this journal without me noticing. At any rate, these hand-written journals were discontinued in May 1946 when the last of those detained were repatriated. So someone has changed the details after that. Records held at the Ministry of Defence will clear the matter up. I can make an official request online if you like."

"Would you? I'd be so grateful. Are you sure you've got time?"

The curator smiled and gestured to the room empty of visitors.

"Don't get many in here on wet days like this, or any days as a matter of fact," he finished forlornly.

Shortly he handed her a printout which showed that after continuous service F.O Steven Mathews was discharged from the RAF on 13th March 1950. The computer printed another couple of pages.

"Here are notes taken from his medical records made during his convalescence in England 1948 through 1950." The curator began reading aloud the summary.

"From this account it was a miracle F.O. Mathews survived being shot down over Germany. He was badly injured and burned, especially around his face. The Russians overran the

German military hospital shortly afterwards. They assumed he was a German. F.O. Mathews was so severely injured he knew little of this at the time. He couldn't see or speak although he could hear a little. Eventually, the Russians got around to patching him up; enough of a good job to make it known to the British government they should come and collect one of their own."

The curator handed the page to Sarah and pointed to an entry concerning disability payments and a last known address dating from 1953 to where the payments should be sent.

Sarah sat in her car studying the Peterborough address the curator had handed her. Aware that her time in England was running out, she wondered at the worth of following up an address last current more than sixty years ago.

Perhaps it would be too cruel for her father to know, after all this time, his birth father was alive, if he was. It would make no difference now to her recently passed away Grandma Emma. On the other hand, Sarah knew it was the inheritance from her grandmother she was spending on her overseas trip. Maybe she owed it to her memory to find out what had become of Flying Officer Steve Mathews.

By the time she arrived back at the roundabout on the main road Sarah still hadn't decided whether to turn left to Peterborough or right, south towards London for the last few days of her travels and the long journey home.

As a break in the traffic presented itself she let impulse make her decision. She flicked the indicator left.

▲   ▲   ▲

Dedication

Dedicated to the memory of my Mother who came to New Zealand in 1946 as the war bride of the man to whom she remained happily, blissfully married until they both passed peacefully away within a few months of each other in 2011.

**Murdoch and Ida,
March, Cambridgeshire, 13th September 1945**

About the Author

John Mack is the author of *Closing the Gap and Other Stories* published in 2014.

He has been writing and editing for trade and club publications for many years. Since 2008 he has been Bay of Plenty correspondent for *New Zealand Classic Car* magazine. He has been Editor of two regional magazines for commercial fruit growers since April 2011

He is a graduate of Whitireia (Wellington) Polytechnic's Creative Writing Course and has had stories published by Rural Women New Zealand in their *Ragwort and Thistles* collection of short stories and by the New Zealand Society of Authors (Bay of Plenty) in their Tauranga Memories collection.

www.johnmack.co.nz

www.ingramcontent.com/pod-product-compliance
Lightning Source LLC
Chambersburg PA
CBHW060406260626
47160CB00006B/2458